SHOWBIZ,
AND MORE

SHOWBIZ, AND MORE

ALLAN WARGON

PIED PIPER
BOOKS

Copyright © 2011 Allan Wargon

Excerpts from this publication may be reproduced under licence
from Access Copyright, or with the express written permission of
Pied Piper Books, or as permitted by law. A reviewer may quote brief
passages in a review. Otherwise all rights are reserved and no part
or all of this publication may be reproduced, stored in a retrieval
system, or transmitted in any form or by any means, electronic,
mechanical, photocopying, scanning, recording or
otherwise, except as specifically authorized.

Copyright is registered with the Library of Congress
and the Canadian Intellectual Property Office

Library and Archives Canada Cataloguing in Publication

Wargon, Allan
Showbiz, and More / Allan Wargon.

ISBN 978-0-9865671-2-4

I. Title.

PS8595.A7734S56   2011   C818'.54   C2010-904814-8

Typeset by Gordon Robertson Design, Toronto, Canada.
Printed and bound in Canada by Friesens

10 9 8 7 6 5 4 3 2 1

Published by Pied Piper Books
825941 Mel-Nott TL, R R 2, Shelburne, ON LON 1S6 Canada

This work is dedicated to all readers.
May they long prevail.

Contents

SHOWBIZ
1

AFFAIRS
173

THREE STORIES
251

SHOWBIZ

1

For the first time with Chip I felt afraid. His anger was so unexpected. I stared at him from the doorway, down the long mahogany slab. As his desk it was kept at coffee-table height, then raised by a hidden hoist for Board meetings. He had *The Bulletin* open before him; other dailies lay spread on the polished wood. Having those reporters in for a drink had been my doing. Had been, I had thought, my success. And it had seemed to have gone smoothly, until this thunder had descended. The normally bright blue eyes, cupid-pink skin, silver hair were all scowling dark.

It says I was drinking!

It says, I replied as evenly as I could *that you had a glass in your hand as you talked. What's wrong with that?*

My mother might see it.

*

Dusk settled like a noose. It was a Lilly night, but I had to stay. I had just finished my urgent tasks when Chip and Terry looked in, as they often did when they worked late. And asked if I'd like to go to dinner. I had already cancelled Lil, so I willingly accepted.

We crossed Broadway and walked the few bleak blocks up-town. The buildings, now virtually deserted, loomed in the damp fog. The pavement was dank, cold. Terry's heels made even clicks on the concrete. She clung to Chip's arm, and tucked in the silk scarf at her throat. It was good to see the lights of Laurent's.

Inside all was warm, burnished, bustling.

Ah, monsieur Hope! sang the delighted maître d', as if he hadn't seen Chip for weeks. Terry had told me they'd been there two nights before. Their no-reservation regrets were smilingly waived, and the majordomo scurried to get us seated and served.

Terry sniffed hungrily at a luscious word painting of duck in aspic, boned, stuffed and pressed, but mock-heroically bit her lip and settled for *sole à la normande*. Chip ordered *filet mignon*, medium rare. And his usual *hearts of lettuce* salad, which was the Laurent's fancy name for half a small iceberg sprinkled with lemon and placed cut side up in a silver .dish. I, ever the non-pay-ing guest, asked for a mushroom omelet.

Behind the waiter came the grizzled wine steward. Chip said *Let's have a bottle of your best red, unless* — he turned to Terry — *you'd rather have white with your fish . . .*

She raised a nay-saying chin, displaying her smooth neck. Around the low scoop of her purple frock an orange edge vamped her auburn hair. No one in the office said Terry's outfits might be a bit sensual for a secretary. Everyone liked her. Or pretended to — no one wanted to incur Chip's displeasure. Terry was not only the dressiest of the women but also, at first glance, the most feminine.

The steward said *We have a very good Margaux, or* — he made a kissing gesture with his fingers — *a Lafite-Rothschild. But it's a bit more expensive.*

Yeah, Chip said nodding with a grin *it would be.*

4

I knew he was only being funny. Our employees, particularly the production staff in New Jersey, were a United Nations. At other times, when he'd said things like *they wouldn't Jew us,* or *he's hymie,* I silently understood it was just the prevailing culture talking. But this time that snide reference to Jewishness riled me. I could feel myself reddening. Maybe it was the build-up of such remarks, or delayed reaction from that earlier bizarre scolding. After the steward had turned away I burst out with *Do you realize what you just said?*

Terry looked up sharply. *Iz, Chip didn't mean . . .*

I know. But stereotypes hurt. And lead to the gas chambers.

Chip raised an eyebrow. And looking at his handsome face and figure, in the flawless pin-striped suit, he was so perfect . . . I regretted my assault. *It's okay. You're not alone* I said. *The world simply doesn't like Jews. They've never forgiven us for inventing God.*

Oh, come on! Terry said. *There were gods before Jews.*

Of course I replied, becoming even more heated. *But the imaginative leap from that to a single, invisible, omnipotent, universal God was new. Besides, Jews have always been disturbing. A handful of people in population terms, yet we've shaken the world over and over again: Moses, Jesus, Marx, Freud, Einstein . . .*

But not you Terry said. *You weren't there. You didn't do those things.*

No. You're right. I'm only a hack journalist. Or I was. Now I don't know what I am.

Chip continued to gaze at me. *You're my friend* he said.

*

Abruptly, without knocking, Sandy swept in, wafting ahead a breeze of perfumed air. I lifted a paper fallen from my desk. His

5

eyes were glinting. In his thick Hungarian accent he said *Ve got to raise the share price!*

Done I said, wondering what this was about. *We have that liquid waste thing. But it still needs state approval —*

Never mind. Dis can't wait. You'll do it? And he was off, his scent trailing. Sandy was always improving his image, with small success. Clothes never sat well on him. Shirts at odds with jackets. Ties too loud or dull. But his round moist face was totally vigilant.

Sandy was clever, very clever. Chip had found him working as a bookkeeper on a dam project in Idaho, and had brought him along. Now Sandy was the chief financial officer.

*

We held the new press conference in the top-floor auditorium. It had rows of red padded seats, and a projection booth at the back. On the front screen was an artist's rendering of the liquid waste plant, dominating the room. Along the auditorium's inside wall were tables that our girls had spread with white cloths and an inviting array of cups, spoons, carafes, colored napkins and plates of food.

There was a good turnout of environmental and financial columnists, and general reporters. Some flocked to the coffee and goodies. Others spurned the snacks and sat waiting with their notebooks and recorders. I introduced Chip. He recognized a few of the news people and greeted them charmingly. Then he spoke about our joint venture with the Alabama firm. It would supply its know-how for cleaning liquid industrial waste. We would build the plant and operate the facility. *Filth in and drinkable water out.*

The story was well featured in all the major papers. Height was a public company, and our stock rose more than two dollars.

The following Sunday I finally found out what was going on. The sky over the Park was brilliant with promise. Morning clouds were in full retreat. Chip had invited me to his swank apartment. It was supposed to be Terry's, but he paid the rent. For appearances he had a smaller one on the floor above, for which the company paid. Officially it was for any out-of-town executive, like Chip. But he hardly ever used it, nor did anyone else.

*

We have a chance, Chip said *to change the basis on which we work. Big as we are, we've always had to wait hat in hand on the client. Now we intend to take over Favorable Finance. They have a big pile of cash and twenty-one branches across the country.*

The background to this, Chip explained, was that the idle grandson of Favorable's founder, having spent all his inherited funds, was ready to sell the 40 percent of the shares he still held. And other major shareholders were willing to part with another 19 percent. All, of course, for the right price. Sandy was negotiating that now. Helped by Peter Noel, the president of a small company of planners that Height had bought a year ago. Peter, pretty much a playboy, had heard of the Favorable possibility on the cocktail circuit.

But isn't that . . . I began.

Out of our line? Well, Chip said *when I was selling peaches back in the Pittsburgh Saturday market, the women would pinch them and tell me they're not ripe, or too ripe, or this and that. I had to learn just to smile and take the money. Essentially, we still do that at Height. But think, if we had our own money — think of all the great things we could do!*

Chip's smile was boyish, eager. He meant what he said, which was thrilling. It opened a whole new world. Yet I was momentarily arrested by the peaches. Peaches? I hadn't heard of that before. It reinforced the feeling I'd always had about Chip: that he'd never been motivated solely by money. He'd bought Height with rare daring from an indifferent California conglomerate by persuading six of his fellow staff engineers to mortgage their homes and borrow whatever they could. Those six became the vice-presidents. Together with Chip they made up the Board. Now everyone called them *The Silver Seven*.

We have to keep this very quiet Chip said. *The bargaining is delicate. It could backfire on the Street. You'll write the press releases. They'll have to be exactly timed.*

I said I'd be honored. It was the biggest thing that had happened since I'd joined Height. Which, formally, had been only a few weeks before. For the first three months I'd insisted on just trying the job, with only my expenses paid. No regrets on either side if it didn't work out. Chip had laughed and shrugged when I put those terms to him. But at the end of the time Sandy had asked for a bill.

No . . .

Don't be a fool!

When I raised it with Chip, he said *Iz, in a few months no one will remember whether you were paid or not. And you need it, don't you?*

*

It was true. My little savings were almost gone. And then there was Lil. The first time I'd come to Height to interview Chip for a series of business profiles my paper was running, the receptionist had led me into the court off which the vice-presidents had their offices. Three on each side. And each with his own secretary's desk outside his door. That left a center corridor one had to negotiate past all these attractive women to get to Terry's office, and through it, Chip's. A bit bewildered, I dropped my eyes. That's when I saw Lil's legs. Her back was to me. She was bent over the desk of another girl, pointing out something. In passing I glimpsed, between the gray hem and low heels, those lovely legs. When I came out after the interview, which, surprisingly, had become a brought-in lunch, I looked for that gray dress. And saw her pleasant face, and the blonde hair held back in a classic bun. It was as stirring as Chip's apparent taking to me.

*

The next meeting about Favorable was not until the following Saturday. At Sandy's home, in Bayshore. I took the train. Great drops of rain were drumming down, streaking the dusty windows. But as I got off the sky broke, spilling sunshine. I had no umbrella, but feeling lucky, I walked the rest of the way.

Sandy's elaborate house looked like a developer's model home. Boxed barberry hedges on both sides of a spotless driveway, leading to the false stone front and a wide double garage. Pulled up to the closed, white paneled doors was a shining MG roadster, flaming red. I supposed this was the opulence Sandy craved, but that he couldn't afford in Manhattan.

Peter Noel was sitting on the brocaded couch, sipping coffee. His scuffed moccasins had been heeled off. Above bare feet he had on blue corduroy trousers, a flowered orange shirt, and a long brown vest of some kind of fur. *Camel* he said when I asked. Sandy poured me a cup from the gilt-rimmed urn. Gilded figurines held up lampshades, the candy dish, a huge mirror over the mantel. The thick beige broadloom was threaded with metallic gold. There was no fourth cup.

Isn't Chip coming? I said.

Peter replied *We don't need him to plan the press campaign.*

Who is it to be aimed at?

Our lenders, the Favorable people, the market.

The market Sandy put in *is jumpy.* He pronounced it *jzhumpy. Ve got to be very careful.*

I saw myself writing releases with subtle emphasis and precise timing. *All right. I'll need your input ahead. On time. I intend to run this like a military operation.*

Screw you! Peter cried, leaping up. *Nobody's climbing my back!*

Eh, eh, easy! Sandy said, flushing with alarm. *Ve got to be together. Isaac—*

Sorry I said. I realized I'd impinged on Peter's celebrity status. Self-claimed, mostly. But I wondered what else he had to be edgy about. He'd been paid nearly a million for a company whose assets were little more than salesmanship. And he had a gorgeous mulatto assistant he was obviously living with. *I only meant,* I added *that I don't want to let down the schedule.*

Peter, somewhat mollified, sat again. And took from his inside pocket a small slim cigar. Sticking out from his teeth, it spoiled, I thought, his leading-man looks. But Sandy was now talking to me, soothing things. I liked his *Isaac.* Chip, perhaps unconsciously, because of its Jewish sound, had from the start called me *Iz.* And now, except for Sandy, everyone in the company did.

*

We talked strategy. None of it was strange. At Columbia I'd taken a year and a half of business law. But, while still a freshman, I had landed a small job on the *Law Journal*. Then, after mixing with journalism students, and writing a few freelance pieces for the big dailies, I realized I liked reporting more than law.

Peter offered me a lift back to Manhattan. The MG was his. He dropped me right at my door.

*

You mean Mummy dearest, don't you? Lil said. She had stretched across me to take the bedside phone. I cherished her bare breasts pressed against my chest, her long, loose golden hair nestled against them. She was a gift, immaculate and utterly precious. *Yes,* she said *you may. If your homework is really done and you're in your p.j.'s by nine. That's in —* she gestured for my watch — *less than an hour. Well, it has to be! And Kris must know where you are, and have the phone number. Okay? Okay, sweetie. Good night.*

We'd gone to bed before dinner. Lil came to me overnight each Wednesday and Saturday, unless something unusual interfered. Midweek she'd first go home, give her three girls their supper, make their school lunches, and see to what they needed for the morning. Then, and on Saturday afternoons, she'd take a cab to my place. We'd have wine while she broiled the chicken and tossed the salad. The menu, our routine, rarely varied. But this time I'd been in Boston with Chip for two days. And too hungry for her to wait for food.

It was a joy, watching her undress. Always it was with grace, and gave me the sense that she was preparing herself as an offering. When she took the pins out of her hair, smiling as it cascaded down, and slid into bed, she made it seem it was our home, our nest.

2

The takeover caused a brief storm on the Street. But my press releases had prepared the market. After some nervous trading the prices of both our stock and Favorable's rose slightly. Peter reminded everyone it had been his idea. To prove it he had a seventy-five-thousand-dollar bonus. But Sandy's was a hundred thousand, and an immediate seat on Favorable's Board. For a week the little treasurer was beaming. Despite being denied what he wanted most: to be made a vice-president of Height.

*

The media rioted. "Minnow Swallows Whale!" Chip, now chairman and president of both Height and Favorable, got the largest play. Suddenly he was a star. Stories and pictures popped up everywhere, under headlines like "Hope of Height" and "Jet-Propelled President." For years he had been quietly using the company plane. Now there were shots of him standing beside it, taken at a heroic low angle with the Height logo on the fuselage showing over his shoulder. Invitations to speak began coming in from business groups and universities. He had me write speeches for every one. He said *Then we'll have support for the things we want to do.*

*

No one had yet suggested what we might want to do. But in that heady mood I wrote an upbeat bit of blank verse:

> *The wheel will not grow square,*
> *And the computer*
> *Won't declare itself*
> *In favor of the abacus.*
>
> *Technology will shape the future*
> *And we, at Height,*
> *Intend to shape technology.*
>
> *We grow . . .*

It went on in that way, suggesting, not quite promising. And ended with:

> *So our activities,*
> *In all their forms,*
> *Will aim at expressing*
> *An abounding love of life.*

The press did a double take. We got pieces headed "Who's Kidding?" and "President Goes in for Poetry." But it was mostly good natured. And two columnists wrote thoughtful essays about capitalism and social conscience. Excitement stayed high around the office.

*

We were renting two floors connected by an inner staircase. And the penthouse auditorium on a per-time basis. Sandy and the other senior executives were upstairs, on the 18th floor. My room was on the 17th, left of the foyer one stepped into from the elevators. The court with the vice-presidents was on the other side of the foyer, to the right.

During my first weeks, going to and fro from Chip, I'd seen that Lilly wore no rings. And that all of her, above those astonishing hosiery-ad legs, seemed pleasing. One night, noticing her leave, I'd caught up just outside the building. I supposed she was aware of my interest, so I asked straight out if she'd have a drink with me. She said yes, but only for a few minutes, because she had to get home to her children.

So we skipped booze and looked for a coffee spot. Lilly said she wanted to stay close to the subway. The Street was a dark ditch churning with impatient people and smothering exhaust fumes. But we rounded the corner and went into the shop by the Exchange. The day's mess was being cleared. A skinny boy was mopping the floor, but he paused long enough to let us pass. Behind the counter a radio was giving news of the death, in Paris, of Maria Callas. Over stale coffee Lil gave me her home number and address.

*

I went there on Sunday. It was on 111th, west of 5th. A ratty, rent-controlled building. Scattered trash lay in the entrance. Poverty stalked the stairs. There were orange peels, gum wrappers, peanut shells on the landings.

But Lil's apartment was bright. The walls were pale yellow, covered with colorful kids' paintings. Her three clear-eyed daughters regarded me with suspicion. But they became more cheerful when I gave them the chocolates I'd brought. We left them munching, and walked down to the Park.

I said *You don't look old enough for three children.* I guessed she was a year or two younger than I.

I had Kristen at sixteen.

You married at — fifteen?

No, seventeen. When he came back from tour. It was the one time he was sent to sea. He was a signalman, normally land-based.

She told me she was a navy brat, born in Pensacola and raised in Honolulu, except for six years in a convent school in Connecticut.

You were taught by nuns? What did you learn there?

She laughed. *Sex, sex, sex! That's all we girls talked about.*

She had also learnt English, perfectly. In the office she was a general dictionary, of whom the other girls, instead of looking it up, asked about spelling, grammar, words and phrases. More than that, Lil had a flair for the language. If it wasn't for having to provide for the three daughters, which kept her at jobs like being a secretary at Height, she could have been teaching it.

Don't you get support?

Not from him, my ex. I've been divorced for eight years. Separated longer than that. Ever since I was pregnant with my youngest, Ginny. I almost lost her from his punching me. He said she wasn't his child. Worst luck, she was. Almost anyone would have made a better father.

What brought you to New York?

He did. After he got out of the service he tried for a job in radio. But he couldn't keep one here. Though I think he's still in radio, on the technical side. Somewhere in the Midwest.

Sun now smote our feet, and then our faces. A breeze rustled the maple and oak leaves. We were passing the upper pond. Rippling water drove the toy boats. The children and their parents were all absorbed. We were virtually alone. I looked at Lil. Some of her fair hair was blowing. She seemed fresh and clean.

You don't mind where you live?

Among the blacks? Not at all. And anyway that apartment is all I can afford. I was lucky to get it. Before Height I worked at City Hall.

Oh. Schlep.

She nodded. *Luckily.*

I really wanted this woman. I said *I'm not much of a prospect.*

As a husband? I've had one, thank you.

I don't have any money.

Alas.

And I'm not much to look at —

Don't be cute she said. *It doesn't become you.*

Well — We stopped moving. *What is it you want?*

She looked up at me, then down. *I'd like to be your — lover.* Her sideways glance was mischievous, amused. *I hope you're not shocked.*

I was, a bit. I wasn't a virgin, but my encounters had been few, and more-or-less honorable. It wasn't that I hadn't always been looking. I could easily become aroused. But I had always steadfastly drawn the line at prostitutes, and I'd never had anything remotely like a mistress. Lil's words had elated me. We walked on. I reached for her fingers and she slipped them into mine.

*

Late Monday morning Chip came to my office. He confided that Height had just bought part of a Pittsburgh baseball team.

16

It's good business he said, smiling at my surprise. *Do you know of another that gets constant free advertising?*

He was right, of course. To my annoyance, every ordinary radio and TV newscast ended with sports gossip and scores. Let alone what was in the newspapers and magazines. But I wasn't pleased. It wasn't my idea of how we should be spending the Favorable money.

Chip was staring at my straight chair, scarred deal desk and bare walls. The room had been used for storage before they'd cleared and managed to furnish it for me. *Iz,* he said *you should fix this place up.*

*

I went out and bought a round teak table. And a console that combined files and a liquor cabinet. And two comfortable armchairs and a desk chair with leather seat and back. Why not? I thought. If we're buying toys, I might as well have some. I added blue-purple drapes to cover one wall, lamps, and a long walnut planter of live philodendron. Then some framed Japanese prints. And for whimsy, a few perky Chinese paper-and-feather birds.

Chip was charmed. *This den,* he said *could also serve as a kind of clubroom for any of our people from out of town.*

So I stocked scotch, brandy, sherry. All the bills went to Sandy. About them nothing was said.

*

Chip then decided I ought to decorate the entrance foyer. And have it tell the story of Height.

Terry gave me material about the last few years. But in New Jersey I discovered solid stacks of records and photos. Piled as the work had been done, they went back to the firm's beginnings. In Pittsburgh.

Russel J. Height had hung out his shingle there the very day the nation's first subway had opened in New York. Pittsburgh was surging; the young engineer was soon busy. He did hydroelectric works, flood control projects, docks. Then extensions to steel mills. And, unusual for its time, a round tunnel. The firm expanded. It had five engineers and eighty-three other workers, when, in 1917, R.J. went off to France, a captain in the corps of engineers. He came back a decorated major. And was promoted to full colonel in the national guard. But he was carrying some nasty shrapnel; his health went steadily downhill. When he died his widow sold the firm to the California company. From which, three decades later, Chip redeemed it.

3

What isn't clear I said to Lil *is who owns what.* I was picking off pieces of chicory, adding them to the lettuce. Lil was checking the hot chicken, shielded from splatter by the striped gray apron she left with me. We were also having sliced tomatoes, sprinkled with basil, olive oil and salt. Under the candlelight the red slabs gleamed on their white platter, setting off the green salad, our wine glasses, the sparkle of stainless steel cutlery, Lil's blonde hair as she bent to the oven.

Your boss got shares, like all the Silver Seven. But I think Chip must have the most. Maybe he bought them from the others. When they were having problems meeting payments, or whatever. But if so, what did he use for money?

His salary?

Then what did his family live on?

Peaches?

She was kidding, but also being careful. It made her uneasy to talk about the company. All the inner-sanctum ladies were confidential secretaries. And to Lil, that responsibility was serious. Also, she didn't know, and neither did I, just what my job was. It seemed to be whatever Chip wanted. It wasn't clear what, if any, status that conferred on me. But my virtual unlimited access to Chip impressed others. Twice, quite senior engineers, unable to see him, had talked to me. I told both I had no special influence. But the first replied that I was a good *interface*. And about a week later the other said *Well, aren't you his assistant, or something?*

*

For the foyer I didn't need the whole history of Height. But I was curious. Under cover of research I dug it out from the stacks, and from chatting with long-time employees. And it was plain Chip was the force that drove it. The other directors, I guessed, were good engineers, but none had Chip's imagination. It was Chip, right from the precarious buy-back, who had brought in the jobs, picked the right people, and moved Height into dams, bridges, long underwater tunnels, big industrial buildings, airfields and military bases. The latter we ran under contract, supplying all personnel and supplies that weren't strictly service. And it had been Chip's idea to open a second office in Philly, and then, ten years later, another in New York, on Wall Street. Masked by his quiet air, Chip had a flair for drama.

*

Sandy frowned at the big photos in the lobby. I'd chosen black-and-white blowups of major works, with captions in color. Engineering glamour. *We're now a financial firm too* Sandy said. Which was true, but the display was what Chip had wanted. Sandy shook his head. *This is misleading. Before long* he added, leaving *it'll be meaningless.*

*

Chip hadn't intended to become president of Favorable. He'd meant to keep the previous president in place, but the man proved resentful, and for retirement had negotiated a very healthy severance package. This had to be approved by the people who'd supplied money to buy the Favorable shares. These lenders, mainly two smaller merchant banks, now became very prominent. Each had a seat on the Favorable board, and were consulted about every important move. Except for that past president, and some of the board members, the rest of Favorable's executives and staff remained intact. Because no one in Height, not even Sandy, completely understood their complex mix of loans and investments.

Beyond this, I knew nothing. I'd made a courtesy call on Favorable's head of PR, and he, worried about his job, had pledged total cooperation. But in truth our working together was just talk. Whenever Chip and Sandy, plus the two new Street types Sandy had hired, went off to a Favorable meeting, they stepped out of my world. I didn't mind. For me those were times of less pressure.

4

Her daughters, Lil told me, were drawing wedding dresses. It made me realize that we were being unfair. I proposed a picnic. The next Saturday Lil prepared sandwiches. I rented a car and arrived midmorning. Staring men loitered on the building stoops. Kids were playing stickball in the street. Parked amid rusting wrecks, the shiny rental looked too tempting. I paid the biggest boy there three dollars, with an offer of later giving him as much more, to guard it.

*

The girls hushed at my announcement that I had something to say. They sat in a row on the sagging couch. Pretty girls, prettier in looks than Lil, though none promised her perfect legs. Kristen, almost thirteen, and Ginny, eight, were blonde like their mother. But Dawn, the middle one, at eleven, had thick dark hair and a somewhat fuller figure. If the father had suspected any of them of not being his child, I would have thought it would be her. But I suppose by the time of Ginny he was anyway abusing his wife.

Look, I said, as the upturned faces were fixed on me, *you children come first. Your mother never puts anything ahead of your basic needs. And I agree absolutely with that. But there's more to her than being a mother. You girls know that, don't you?*

They nodded uncertainly, solemn faced.

Well, in that other part she's sometimes lonely. And I get lonely too. We like being together two evenings a week. Yet that doesn't leave you out. You always know where she is when she's with me —— you have my phone number and address, right?

Kristen said *Yep.*

And any one, or all of you, are welcome to come too. Though if you all come we might be a bit crowded at night.

Every man's dream Lil said. *To be in bed with four females.*

The girls giggled.

Now, I went on *neither your mother nor I want to get married.*

They were silent.

We think things are better as they are, at least for the time being. But that doesn't mean we can't be a little like a family. Starting now . . .

*

I drove them to The Cloisters. We got out and walked the grounds, then to the edge of the cliff. Through the trees and bushes we could see, below us, the broad Hudson basking like a contented giant. Small ships were crawling over its middle. We crossed it quickly, pushed by traffic. Until now the driving had been manageable, but going over the river became nightmarish. The steel panels clanked and clattered, adding to my anxiety. I'd had a license since nineteen, but had driven little. I was both concentrating and confused. The girders swept by in a blur. We emerged from the bridge as from the belly of a dragon.

With relief I steered on to Teterboro, where the company aircraft was kept. Then slowly back around to the County Park. We ate lunch beside the creek. Lil said it made her long for the sea.

5

Chip's full name, I'd soon learnt, was George Adams Hope. As a boy he was always working with his father. Hence, the neighbors said *A chip off the old block.* Despite its triteness, or because of it, the name stuck.

I had this tidbit from Terry. She'd feed me a few whenever I was being set up for some tough assignment. This time Chip wanted speeches for events just a day apart. And in the second one, he said when I later saw him, it might be a good time to announce his employee investment plan.

Is it final?

We'll pass it when the board meets.

But that's not until — unless you're going to hold a special meeting.

He looked at me with annoyance, knowing I was right.

*

The plan was omitted from the speech. But it made me wonder about his impatience. Because it should have first been explained to the staff, and press-released before it leaked out.

Chip's idea was that all employees — we had about twelve hundred of them — even from their initial day on the job, would be eligible to invest in a plan that would purchase for them shares of Height at market price, but with the company matching each person's investment to the extent of 20 percent in the first year, 35 in the second, and 50 in the third and from then on. So that after three years everyone participating would be buying shares at half their actual cost. The company would be paying the other half. There would be sensible minimum and maximum limits. And the plan would be administered by a committee of five voting members: three of them employees and the other two from the bank that would handle the transactions. In addition, Chip intended, there would be two non-voting members, himself and Sandy, but with veto powers to be used only in the spirit of the idea. Once the plan was working well at Height, he meant to extend it to Favorable.

Combined, that would mean roughly four thousand persons could benefit. It wasn't what I thought he might do with the new money. But I had to admit it was fair-minded. And sweepingly generous.

I was with Chip, and he told me to stay, when Sandy came in to object. Especially to the non-voting positions. He said that the veto power was practically purposeless, if it could be used only to further the plan. As if constrained by a constitution.

Chip got up to adjust the blinds on his big windows. The sunlight was cut back to a soft infusion. I noticed he seldom asked others to serve him in such ways. It was partly a sense of self-sufficiency, and partly, I thought, his innate modesty.

I don't want them, the employees, to feel Chip said, sitting again *that we're controlling it. If you and I can't convince them of what's best, we shouldn't have a vote anyway.*

Sandy pointed out that the plan was bound to be popular. If it went on long enough the company would become employee controlled.

I hope so said Chip.

To Sandy that smacked of socialism. He'd fled Hungary in '57, with nothing, and wasn't about to write off twenty years of worming into the innards of capital. The little Treasurer — his head barely came above Chip's chin — was wearing a smart dark suit, a pale blue shirt, and a rich, subtly-colored red tie. He'd used some of his bonus to have himself completely outfitted by the Avenue's most-fashionable business clothier.

Vell then, he said *vy not have a voting trust?*

Chip answered slowly that he would think about it.

*

When I got off the bus and looked over the Park, and above it, I could dimly see, despite the street lights, a crescent moon veiled by moving clouds. But as I approached Chip and Terry's building the passersby, sounds of traffic and distant sirens dispelled all but the immediate reality. I had no idea why I had been invited. Yet I was always too flattered and curious to refuse.

There were just the three of us. We were sitting at the low round table, picking what we wanted from the cartons of a delivered Chinese dinner. Chip and Terry were using forks; I struggled with chopsticks. The paper sleeve they had come in I had crumpled and put in my jacket pocket, being too uncertain to put it on the table or ask for a wastebasket. I couldn't yet share the other's ease. Chip was open necked, in shirtsleeves, the cuffs folded on his forearms. Terry had taken off her office clothes and was loosely wrapped in a green silk robe. When she bent forward I could see the top of her bra. With bare feet she looked less sexy. More like a tired housewife enjoying a meal she hadn't had to prepare.

Behind her the wall was hung with large framed photos of her son. From age two, she said, to one about a year ago, just before he was sent to boarding school. The way she referred to the photos made me think that my privileged visit had something to do with him. He was twelve, Terry informed me. He was bright and literature interested him. Chip was paying for the boy's education because, he said, he didn't want him deprived. But, so far as I knew, neither of Chip's own children had gone to a private school. He almost never mentioned them, or his wife and house near Pittsburgh.

Three bottles of Chinese beer had come with the dinner order. However, none of us liked it, and Chip had opened a chilled white wine. Terry drank little, except before her first sip, to toast *being together.* They were both congenial. No business was discussed. It seemed I was being treated as a family friend.

I warmed to this, while slightly feeling that I didn't yet justify it. I didn't want to transgress by speaking of anything personal. So I brought up the recent report of the national Harris Survey showing that the President's approval rating had fallen below 50 percent. But Chip appeared uninterested in politics. Maybe that's why I asked about the voting trust. *Has there been a decision?*

Chip frowned. *I guess we'll have to have it.*

Oh I said. I sensed that it wasn't prudent to push what I didn't understand.

Sandy's very keen on it. He argues that our lenders would like it. What's it got to do with —

Iz, Terry said *it's an internal issue. Chip has turned Sandy down on several other things and doesn't want to squash him yet again. He wants to keep Sandy happy.*

Okay... Anyway, what wrong with a voting trust?

Chip sighed. *It'll be controlled by engineers.*

My surprise was complete.

It's because Terry said *of the shares they already hold.* She explained that in the past, before Height went public, when its shares had only nominal value, they were used to sweeten certain jobs. If an engineer had to be sent to Timbuktu, or to any difficult job, he was given some to make the assignment more attractive.

Not only that Chip said. *Engineers are the highest paid. They'll probably take most advantage of the plan.*

Oh I see I said. But I didn't really.

*

Yet it started me thinking about my own small stake. One day, soon after I began work officially, Sandy said flatly that I shouldn't be speaking for a company in which I owned no shares. So I got my bank to buy me a single one. Now I could afford more.

My wages, after I'd refused the first three months' payment, had been set on a par with those of mid-level engineers. The amount was billed monthly, on a freelance basis, made up of fee plus expenses. The latter covered cabs, meals with anyone involved with Height's business, even the liquor I kept in my cabinet. All invoices were sent to Sandy. Probably they were checked by his assistant, Lyall Bishop. Nothing was ever challenged. For the first time in my life I had money to spare.

*

That's when I took Lil for a two-day trip up the coast. Kristen had been invited by a school friend for a weekend pajama party. That girl's mother, who knew Lil from parent-teacher meetings, had generously included Dawn and Ginny too.

It was mid November, but warm. In a rented car we drove straight through to Maine. Then we began stopping along the shore. It was almost all privately owned, but we went directly to each person's door, said Lil loved the sea, and that we'd merely look and leave no litter. Only once were we refused. The woman claimed her husband was sick and she didn't want him worried about us.

*

Sun and spray were a benign bath. Salt smells quickened and then soothed our senses. The surf repeated its endlessly enticing promise. Gulls circled and transfused us with their cries, making us feel freer. Sometimes we'd throw them bits to eat. And we'd search in tidal pools for the tiny animals that got trapped, or stayed there. Occasionally we felt we and they, the wind and water, the birds and all creatures around were in a separate world.

Lil visibly softened. Even her expression became languid, as if all tension and trouble had drained away. We sat on a flat rock and looked out at the vast ocean.

When I was little, Lil said *I thought the sea was God. I prayed to the waves for what I wanted. I did that even as a teenager. It's funny, because despite the convent and the nuns I never believed in pie in the sky. But, if my father — he commanded a destroyer in the Pacific war — hadn't come back, if he'd been killed or drowned, I would have felt that God, that is, the sea, had him in tow. And I would have felt that somehow it was all right.*

Fortunately she added *he survived.*

After a moment, while I absorbed this, I said *If he ranked that high, why didn't he, or doesn't now, help you?*

He does. Every Christmas, a check. Well, a small one. He's on a pension. Not a bad one, actually, considering that when he retired he was given a fourth stripe to pad it out. Also there's always something personal from my mother. And they're good about gifts for the girls.

Do you see them often?

28

No. They live in Hawaii.

Still — wouldn't they want you better off?

They have their own life. My first pregnancy was pretty embarrassing for them. And they never approved of my marriage. Or worse, my persisting in it, for as long as I did. By the time Ginny came, and the beating . . . they tried to rescue me, but I was stubborn, and they finally felt my life was such a mess that they'd best steer clear of it.

What about theirs?

Oh, it's wonderful! They're crazy about each other. My father thinks my mother's the most glamorous thing around.

Why, what's she like?

Lil laughed. *She has great legs!*

6

Isaac . . . Sandy said, beckoning me into his office. He didn't ask me to shut the door. Gone was most of his former anxiety. Along with his smart suits, he now wore an air of assurance. *Listen, we're forming a little syndicate.*

To do what?

An investment syndicate, to buy shares.

Height's?

No. Well, not necessarily. Anything that looks good. Want to join?

Who's in it?

Me, Lyall, Ivor Williams, Ron Squirrel, some others.

Williams and Squirrel — Sandy pronounced them *Villiams* and *Skvirrel* — were the financial types he had hired from the Street. The concept of buying stocks, of becoming a serious investor, had never been part of my thinking. The idea rather confused me. *Chip too?* I said.

No.

Well . . . thanks I said. *I don't really have the money.*

Sandy's look of amused disdain plainly, permanently, stamped me a loser.

*

I did have some money. Several thousands had piled up in the bank. Expansively, I thought of buying a car. Rentals weren't cheap; I'd been surprised at the cost of the trip to Maine. But with visions of more trips to the country, I began pining for a go-anywhere Jeep. The problem was where to put it. My apartment building, like almost all others, had no space for cars, and the cost of parking in Manhattan was prohibitive.

However, the impulse began to propel me. I hurried from the office at noon and went by cab, frustratingly, in slow starts and stops, to the dealership. The showroom models were dazzling. The army version tempted me, stirring notions of combat and adventure. But the back seat was too small for both luggage and Lil's daughters. I wrote a deposit check on a station wagon.

The salesman said it would take a week or more to bring in the black one I wanted. That gave me time to research parking. I was almost resigned to finding a place in one of the outer boroughs when suddenly, inspiration! Before Height, during the year I had been writing the *Roving Reporter* column, I'd done a piece on a riding stable in the west Nineties, where they boarded horses for the rich who rode in the Park. They also rented out some rides, but boarding was their main concern. The Greek owner had begun as an immigrant stable boy who eventually, after many years, bought the business from his retiring boss. He'd put on pounds and played the jolly Zorba, but I knew his personal life was unhappy. He had a wife crippled with MS, and a surly son.

I went to the equestrian place on Saturday morning. Sun and cloud caused a shifting streetscape. Some riders were just coming out. The sleek horses made hard and then softer sounds as they clattered across the sidewalk and onto the asphalt. I walked into the archway's gloom, struck by the stable smells. There was manure, the dry scent of straw and the sweetness of hay. Behind a wall of bales, just as I recalled it, there were two cars parked, still with room for a third.

My newspaper story, already yellowing, was framed under glass on the office wall. *Ah, it's you!* the owner said. *You write-a me again?* I explained that I couldn't, and about the car. He seemed very dubious, until I told him that I wouldn't be using it every day, just once in a while.

He screwed down his face, thought, frowned, pouted, and came up smiling with a price less than half the commercial rate. *And where you now?* he said.

In PR. Embarrassed, I added *on Wall Street.*

Ah. Like-a most of my customers.

*

They're snakes Lil said that night. The table was set for three. Ginny was lying belly down on the living-room couch, propped up on her elbows. We had made up the couch with sheets, a pillow

31

and a couple of blankets. Whether needy or bored, she had decided to come with her mother. Of course I had welcomed her. And elated by my earlier success at the stable, I'd bought books for the girls. Ginny was reading one. But I wondered how she would feel when Lil and I shut the bedroom door.

How do you know that? I said to Lil.

I had lunch yesterday with Philip Marcoux.

Marcoux's column was widely read. He could write about whatever interested him, and almost everything did. Especially gossip, which came from his many sources, mostly in the professional and upper layers of society. And he was known for lunching with attractive women. But privately he preferred men.

I didn't know you knew him.

I have since City Hall. Put out the plates please.

She gave Ginny the wings and a bit of breast. Then took off her apron and sat down with the bearing of a duchess. On her dress was the little silver and platinum pin, in the shape of a destroyer, which her father had given her. He'd had it made for her mother, and a second one for Lil. Her air of self-possession, even dignity, in defiance of poverty never failed to impress me. By comparison, the financial wizards were gross.

Squirrel, she said *was caught insider trading and for the sake of his firm's reputation, had to be kicked out. That's why he was available. Williams, though* — she paused and put a napkin to her lips, which were never painted for our get-togethers — *is a whole other story. He'd been loans manager at First Commercial. Then for two or more years, president. That was a reward for marrying the chairman's long-time mistress. Whom the old man had tired of. Then he tired of Williams too.*

Mom, Ginny said *are they still married? That man and the —* what's a mistress?

Girlfriend. Yes, they are. Have some of your salad.

So Lil didn't mind talking about Sandy's new associates. Because they weren't connected to the inner court. Indeed, since they'd come a rift had developed between the engineering and financial sides of the business. Bridged only by Chip.

*

He's gone to a Favorable meeting Terry said.

How long, I said *can he go on running both companies?* We were in her office. Not knowing Chip was out, I'd brought the draft of a new speech. Chip read my drafts carefully. But he seldom changed anything, unless he thought I had gone too far, or, occasionally, not far enough. Usually he delivered them word for word, with the intended cadence and inflection. He could do that while seeming casual and relaxed.

Terry shrugged. Then took a phone call, but motioned me to stay. After it, she said *Stick around, Iz. Chip needs you.*

To write speeches —

He's finding finance difficult. He needs someone close to him — other than me. A male friend.

Oh, I said. *Well I'm here. I'm not going anywhere.* Flippancy aside, things were finally beginning to make sense. *I won't let him down.*

Slight derision rose in Terry's stare. *You're not the first, you know. Before you, in my time, there was Ian Ross. And before him, someone else. There's always been someone.*

Suitably deflated, I said *Did Ross work for Height?*

33

Still does. He's in Canada, in Ottawa, smoothing our govern-ment projects.

I wondered where I'd be sent. Israel? More likely, Lapland.

7

Christmas approached and the office emptied. Chip had been invited by the governor of Texas for talks about still another dam on the Colorado. The vice-presidents took the week to be with their families. Two, like Chip, had homes in Pennsylvania. One of them ran the company's business in Pittsburgh, which was still the original office, though now in a much larger building. The other, Lil's boss, did the same for Philadelphia. They came to Wall Street for a day or two every week, and of course for directors' meetings. When they were away, their inner court secretaries covered for them. This meant those girls had to be knowledgeable and effective. Lil certainly was. Their jobs carried a lot of responsibility.

The sole bigwig around was Bruce Hardwick, the executive vice-president. His office was separated from Chip's only by Terry's. Bruce was a big handsome man, fit and sober. He some-times said that if Chip was the heart and soul of Height, he was the rest of its body and mind. But for his steady hold, he liked to believe, it would all fly into whim and fancy.

*

For Christmas dinner I went to Lil's, bringing wine and presents. The stairways were as usual strewn with litter. But some tenants had risked hanging wreaths on their doors. Lil's displayed a big red bow. We had baked potatoes, turnip, stuffing, cranberry sauce, and two piping hot, split broiled chickens. Lil was no cook, but through practice with me she had perfected broiling. We also had fruitcake, and the girls were each allowed a glass of port. They got quite giddy on it.

*

When Terry asked me to drop in for a drink I assumed Chip was back. But she was alone with her son. In school he had been given an A for a short story. The boy writhed while Terry told me that he was now working on another. It would be a thrill for him to meet a real writer. Now I understood why she had made a point of his photos.

I could honestly have demurred, but that would have spoilt her scenario. So I sat down and talked with Tim about writing. About how difficult it is to convey an idea clearly. And to stick to plain language. In short, to write simply. *Not easy* I said.

He nodded and sighed. That, and his eagerness, somewhat surprised me. He was evidently a talented boy who would be attractive one day. But with braces on both rows of teeth, a shock of unruly reddish hair, and a face freckled like a field of dandelions, he meanwhile bore burdens. On his mother too, when I'd looked closely, I'd seen faint freckles. She was on the phone in the kitchen, giving us time to talk alone. Tim told me he was ragged at school for not joining sports teams.

Does Chip encourage you to play?

He shook his head.

To write?

No.

What do the two of you talk about?

We don't he said.

Tim had the good grace not to ask me to read what he'd written. But I requested a copy, and said I would get back to him later. Touched by his predicament and his pain, I wished him well as he went off to bed.

Terry brought in two mugs of mulled wine. She leaned back in the lemon armchair. Dressed now in mauve slacks and loose green silk blouse, she looked different from when I'd arrived. While Tim and I were talking, she must have changed. She looked good, and we both knew it. Her pretty feet, neatly pedicured, the nails painted a light shade of burnt pink, were propped against the low table. She held the drink under her nose, breathing its heady fumes.

I said some nice things about her son, then asked if he saw his father.

We were divorced when Tim was two Terry said. *We're not in touch.* She took a long sip, then went on. *Tim's father soon remarried. Some woman with children. They live in Nebraska. Near Omaha, I think.*

You weren't married long. What went wrong?

It didn't. It got me to America.

I hadn't, until then, heeded the occasional odd cadence in her speech. Her pronunciation and phrasing always seemed faultless. But sometimes there'd been a slight rhythm that wasn't quite English. I'd taken it as another of her singularities.

From where? I said.

Latvia. Riga.

Really! And was your husband Latvian?

That wouldn't have helped. He was an American, selling med-ical equipment.

But wasn't that still cold-war time? I didn't think there was any trade with the West.

Not officially. But we had a good health system, especially if you were upper class, and they wanted the latest instruments and supplies.

How did you meet?

She smiled. *I had a part in a semi-amateur play, and one night someone brought him to it, then backstage.*

And you overwhelmed him.

Shrugging, she said *I wanted out of the Soviet system.*

Well, congratulations.

I paid a price. The first year was horrible. He took me to his bachelor pad in Minnesota. The building wasn't bad but we had what must have been the smallest apartment in it — one room and a tiny kitchen and bath. And then he wanted to save money for a house, so we moved in with his parents — pig farmers. Oy . . . even under the Russians there'd been theatre and literature and music. I'd come here for more life, not less. Then I got pregnant.

And you had the baby.

With those people I had to. I was trapped. No money, and I knew too little English. But I could leave Tim with his grandmother, so I took lessons — language, typing, business, and studied hard. Very hard. As soon as I could I got out.

I was silent, wavering between sympathy and skepticism. I doubted that culture of any kind had ever meant much to her. Yet she'd made herself into a person of poise, who spoke, and seemed to mean, well. With her natural attractiveness it was easy to see how she got ahead. And it wasn't just looks. At least two of the inner-court girls were prettier. One was decidedly better built. Hardwick's secretary, who wasn't at all bad, also had an M.A. Nor did this woman have anything like Lil's legs. But all of her exuded a subtle sexuality. Which, I felt, she could direct at any man.

*

It was soon after the holidays when early one morning the phone rang.

Bring an overnight bag Terry said. *We're going to Washington.*

We left that afternoon from the office. A taxi took us to Teterboro. Chip didn't believe in the company having chauffeured cars. He maintained that the cost of salaries, pensions and upkeep amounted to more than cabs. He directed the driver to the Height hangar, on which there was a white skim of snow. The copilot took us across the cold tarmac. He helped Terry and stood by as Chip and I went up the steps into the plane. Inside it was warm. The captain was already at the controls. Minutes later we were in the air.

Towering clouds tore past. Gray piled darkly on gray, in heaped-up masses, with whitish breaks between. Then light spilled, flitted, flooded through the cabin. And again grayness embraced us. The plane shuddered. The white-shirted pilots nodded and conversed softly. We could see their backs, hear murmurs, but no more. Seven seats were for passengers. I sat across from Chip and Terry. The captain turned and calmly said *Please fasten your seatbelts.* Chip leaned over and did Terry's. There was now an unusual roar. The cabin rocked once more. We seemed to be climbing. Anxiety rose too. Terry had shut her eyes. But suddenly there was sun, and an even blueness. The engines settled into a steady drone.

Terry unfolded the bar and made drinks of orange juice and vodka. Then Chip quietly told me we had a morning meeting with the President's Chief of Staff.

*

On landing we were met by an elderly man in a dark suit. And with very shiny shoes, making me conscious of the scuffs on mine.

He rode with us to a hotel. It was nice enough, but not near any of the well-known places. Then said he'd be in the bar while we freshened. My room was a few doors from Chip and Terry's suite. They joined me as I was waiting for the elevator. On the way down I asked who the other gentleman was. Terry said *Our lobbyist.*

At dinner, speaking low, he summed up for Chip the current state of federal politics. They spoke about a Height project slowly making its way through Committee. A woman stopped and greeted the lobbyist. He was gracious but didn't introduce us. She took the hint and soon left. *It's all right* he said. *She works in the Executive Building.* I gathered we were in this hotel just so we wouldn't be likely to encounter political people. Terry seemed disappointed. She kept glancing around the dining hall, as if hoping to recognize someone famous.

*

At breakfast there was only Chip and me. He said Terry was having a bite in their suite, then going sightseeing.

Why are we here? I said.

39

Because we were asked. Cole will tell us what it's about.

Are we going to the White House?

He shook his head. *He's coming here. We've a separate room for the meeting.*

*

We waited until well after the appointed time. I reflected that we could have flown here this morning and saved the hotel costs. Except, maybe, for this room. And as Terry wasn't taking notes, she needn't have been on the trip. But I supposed it was to compensate for Chip's absence at Christmas.

Finally the door opened and Harry Cole came in. He'd been made Chief of Staff after the last election and I knew his face from pictures. But he was shorter, broader and colder than I expected.

After introductions, when we were seated, he said *Mr. Hope, you've been getting a lot of good press lately. We could use some. Since Watergate the media have been as watchful as buzzards. They pounce on any wound or weakness. Well, that's the game. But you're outside it. We'd like you, in your talks, to support our programs.*

Chip's face showed a slight cast of concern. But he was silent.

Mr. Hope isn't a political person I said.

We don't want political speeches. Nothing obvious. But while talking in a general, even philosophical way, you could include the President's objectives. Relate them to business if you like. But I think you've now got a platform from which you can move beyond that. You know, become a statesman.

If he agrees with what you want I said.

Cole's look could crush. *Make it agree. You can twist anything if it's done cunningly enough. Didn't they teach you that in journalism school?*

I felt myself flushing. I glanced at Chip.

How will we know what the objectives are? he said.

I'll send you a list, and keep it updated. All right? Cole stood up and held out his hand. Chip rose and took it. *And,* Cole added *this is absolutely, totally on the q.t. I haven't been here. This meeting hasn't happened. Can I count on that?*

Chip nodded. Cole looked at me. *I'll speak for him* Chip said.

Okay. Just before opening the door Cole turned and said curtly *Thanks for coming.* Then he was gone. The whole thing had taken less than ten minutes.

*

On the return flight, out of the pilots' hearing, I said *Do you want to do this?*

Of course Chip said. *The contact is invaluable.*

Terry was listening. But there was no reason not to include her. She'd anyway know it all from Chip. *Do you support the administration?*

We support both parties. Contributions are a cost of business.

Well, I said, after letting it all settle *I suppose it's a little like a summons from the Commander in Chief.*

*

At college I'd been briefly in the Officers' Training Corps. And hated it. The shouted commands, the idiotic marching up and down. Luckily the Draft Board had dropped me because of my left eye. An ophthalmologist said the condition was starting to become a cataract. I'd been putting off doing anything about it, but from then on I'd been wearing glasses. Now, absurdly, this convoluted call to the colors rather made me feel like saluting.

8

Inwardly I did celebrate when Lil came into the bedroom, took off my robe, which she had taken to the bathroom, and was wearing only the tiny amethyst earrings. I'd impulsively bought them at the last minute in Washington. Chip and Terry had waited in the cab while I ran back to the lobby shop.

I supposed they knew about us, but it was never mentioned. In the office Lil and I were careful to avoid anything personal. Yet occasional glances, the coincidence of dates, must have given us away. Or, for all I knew, the women talked freely.

She was a treasure, my Lil. Altogether agreeable in bed, and as company. But she had quirks. Some subjects we had to skirt around. She said she felt safer living among Negroes because they were stronger; she believed they had harder bones. She couldn't see that this was a sort of inverted snobbery. In the same way she thought Jewish doctors were superior. She always took her children, or went herself, to Mount Sinai. Her tube tying, after Ginny's birth, had been done there.

*

Not long afterwards Sandy asked me to write a newsletter about leasing.

Leasing? What?

Planes. Ships. Railroad rolling stock. Whatever! Sandy, when enthused, used to be eager to explain. Now, with me, he was merely impatient. The newsletter, he said, could be sent to potential clients. Then condensed into a press release.

It was a good idea, I thought, but a bizarre addition. Sandy cut my thinking short by saying that the leasing was to be a new division, headed by Williams.

Chip confirmed it. That meant things were happening in the financial area that I wasn't being told about. True, it wasn't particularly my affair. But now, as never since I'd become an intimate, or close to one, I felt excluded from part of Chip's concerns.

*

That extended into almost everything to do with Favorable. Chip would go there for meetings, along with Sandy and usually Squirrel and Williams. If I chanced to see him afterwards he always looked tired and a bit down. It took a lot to diminish Chip's attractiveness and typical brightness. I suppose the financial stuff bored him, but he didn't speak of it. And neither did I.

*

Cole is coming he told me. *He'll meet with us after the President addresses the United Nations.*

Where? I said.

My place. Six-thirty. Can you make it?

I had to make it. I wondered why Chip was treating me with such uncalled-for courtesy. But I said only *Of course.*

*

Chip's own apartment was small, sparsely furnished, lifeless. Stagnant as a tomb. The closets were mostly vacant, except one in which there was a row of business suits hung in plastic bags. And another with some detergents and a vacuum cleaner. But some cleaning woman kept it spotless.

Terry brought up a tray of appetizers, and bottles of scotch and bourbon. And then left. And from a kitchen cabinet, which also looked totally clean, Chip took three sparkling glasses, a silver spoon, a bowl and water pitcher. He filled the pitcher after letting the tap run cold for a few minutes. Into the bowl he put ice cubes from the fridge, which was otherwise empty.

Cole arrived only twenty minutes late, saying affably that he never allowed enough time for New York traffic. He took a small amount of scotch, with a few drops of water, but no ice.

Here's what I'd like you to think about he said, unfolding a sheet of paper that he'd taken from his inside breast pocket. He handed it to Chip, who held it angled, so I could see too. It listed: patent to General Electric for gene-altered bacteria; visit of Tito to the U.S.; improving relations with former communist countries, and several other topics. *These are all forthcoming* Cole said.

And this would really help? I said.

Cole smiled slightly. *The media copy each other. Most newspapers, radio, TV, repeat what the others say. Yes. It will help.*

Good Chip said. *We're glad to do it.*

9

The weather turned cold. A blizzard blasted the Mid-west. Manhattan had snow on and off for about ten days. The Street was a slushy river; people waded, stomped, cursed. Then a whopper hit New England, piling up record-breaking snowfalls — Providence, Rhode Island, reporting thirty-eight inches. We had an important speech in Frisco in a week's time, but I hoped by then there'd be no problem. When I took the draft to Chip he was on the phone, but beckoned me in.

All right, Frank he said, frowning. *I've never questioned your judgment.* He was talking to the captain of the plane. I wondered where Chip wanted to go. It wasn't anything I knew about. Again I had that slightly alarming feeling of being left out. Chip put down the phone and sighed. *Frank says it's just not flying weather.* I suppose my silence became a question. *It's my daughter's birthday* Chip said. *I promised I'd be there.*

Oh I said. *When is it?*

Tomorrow. She'll be sixteen. There's a party, and everything.

I can get you there! I said with sudden excitement. *I have four-wheel drive!*

*

By the time I picked Chip up at his place, with the large boxed present he was bringing, it was beginning to get dark. And snowing heavily. And to complicate matters, it was Friday afternoon. The snarled traffic was a savage shambles. The six-o'clock news came on as we reached the first stretch of highway.

The radio said the state police, in both New York and Pennsylvania, were asking people to stay off the roads. The forecast was for strong winds and blowing snow, then a cold night. I had on a wool-lined windbreaker, a toque and warm boots. But Chip had only his dark tailored overcoat and galoshes. Except for his head. Before this I'd only ever seen him hatless. But now he was wearing an old gray felt cap with furred earflaps. From his maroon muffler up he looked like a farmer. And the tilt of his chin had changed. He seemed out for adventure.

We could see ahead about two car lengths. Sometimes in blasts of wind I had to stop, running the risk of someone, equally blinded, hitting us from the rear. Then all at once the road became smoother, with less snow. Our speed improved. But abruptly I had to pull up — just ahead towered a big dark shape. With a blinking blue light.

Following behind it was slow, but safe. We traveled that way nearly another twenty miles. Then at a crossroads, where there was a lit motel with a flashing sign, the snowplow turned around. From then on we were bucking deep snow, which was blowing all around us. And the drifts were getting deeper. Our headlights were often just clearing the ridges. I began to get frantic. If we got stuck we'd be helpless. We had no shovel, no rope, not even an emergency light. Fuel was down to nearly a quarter tank. Before, whenever we had passed abandoned cars, I had felt smug. Like a fool I had gloried in going on. In bravely taking Chip through.

He had intently watched our progress, mostly without comment. I was relieved when he finally said *Maybe we should return to that motel.*

But turning back, where we were, was another ordeal. We were in a total whiteout. There was no visibility. From our own track

I could turn only a few feet at a time. Ahead a bit, then reverse, then ahead again, and reverse. While sideways, we could be struck from either direction.

But, slowly, we made it. At the motel other struggling drivers had stopped earlier. All that was left was a last room with two single beds. Chip signed for it. And for the supper of pancakes and sausages in the small coffee shop. Tension had left us too tired to talk. Neither of us cared to phone; describing our plight would only cause worry.

Our room was warm. We fell asleep to the dulled roar of the storm.

*

In the morning we had eggs with our pancakes. And tanked up on coffee and gas. I firmly refused to let Chip pay for any auto expenses. He shrugged but didn't insist. We turned west again.

The wind had dropped. And plows had been out overnight. Snow still blew across the road but was seldom higher than the hood. We drove easily through some low drifts. For just one I had to back up and charge through. Conditions improved as we continued. There were service stations and food. By mid-afternoon we were moving smoothly.

*

The worst was over. There was no longer any unease about our physical welfare. Yet I was disappointed. Chip had been companionable, and there had been a sense of shared daring. But I had hoped that, closely confined as we'd been, there would have been more intimacy. I was aware, acutely, of almost everything about him — his good-looking face, his hands, the way he sat, the drying

47

wetness on his galoshes — everything except what he was feeling.

Chip, I said, breaking the silence *when is Height going to do those good things?* I immediately regretted that. It sounded childish.

But he said *I'm working on it. There's a lot that has to be done before I can get to it.* I had assumed that, so I waited for him to go on. *I mean to* he said after a moment. *I mean to do things that will really help people. Improve their lives.* He sighed, then added *And maybe justify mine.*

*

The afternoon was sinking when we neared Pittsburgh. Snow had stopped falling. Pale blue sky, flushed with rosy purple, was spreading over the low, receding bank of angry dark cloud. Traffic had much increased.

Chip told me to continue north. We had passed the city proper when he directed me onto a secondary road. Then off it to a graveled side road. We passed several farms with orchards, and then came to his home.

The house, lit up in the early dusk, looked large. But so utterly plain. White clapboard, a black roof, and dormers above two wide bay windows flanking a small porch. The front looked something like a face with very large bulging eyes and heavy peaked eyebrows, suggested by the dormers, and overtopped by a kind of low dunce cap. Even by country standards, what I had seen of them, it lacked style.

*

Susan, smiling pertly, came down the worn wooden steps like a fairy princess. She was blonde, as Chip must have been. A long silver necklace set off her snug white bodice, which gave way to

48

a white flared skirt frilled with silver and touches of pink. She raised the hem, pausing on the last step but one, displaying, with the flourish of a foot, low white pumps. Then with a cry of *Thank you!* flung herself into her father's arms. I wondered how he had known her sizes.

*

We adults were cloistered in the kitchen. The dining and living rooms had been given to the young for food and dancing. The music was loud; no one said to keep the noise down. In our group, mostly of parents, people had to lean forward to be heard. We had wine and sandwiches. Some men drank beer from the bottle. Anne, Chip's wife, also served a plate heaped with large chocolate cookies. They were good, and had been home baked by her, like the birthday cake that an hour ago had won great acclaim.

The talk turned from local politics to Roman Polanski, the movie director who had just fled to escape a morals charge. A fat woman asked Anne if she didn't think California was evil incarnate, plagued with sex. Anne pursed her lips. *Aren't you worried* the woman pressed on *about Scott at Stanford?*

No Anne said. *It's not that contagious.*

Chip smiled. By their manner, all the guests acknowledged his status. Some who had known him earlier were more forward. But all stayed clear of the silent gulf separating him from his wife.

*

I was given their absent son's room. There were sports trophies, pennants, a large poster of a scantily clad Marilyn Monroe. On the bureau, between cast-iron bookends, a dictionary and a few novels. Dickens. Thackeray. Dreiser. *Collected Poems* of Robert

49

Burns. Old bindings. Possibly family heirlooms, long unread.

On the same upper floor was Susan's bedroom and the guest room, in which a school friend of hers was staying for the weekend, a bathroom, and the master bedroom.

Out of curiosity I took a quick look in there. The party was going strong and I had a moment alone. Under the front dormer window there was a low chest of drawers. On it a tinted picture of young Chip and Anne. And a snapshot of a gangling boy, I guessed Scott, with an arm around his pretty sister. The entire facing wall was of closed clothes closets. Then a small en suite with a shower. And between night tables, each with a wood-based lamp, was a double bed, now piled high with visitors' coats. There was no sign of, nor room for, any sofa or cot. I didn't suppose Chip would sleep on the floor.

*

I woke at dawn, and was the first downstairs. Off the kitchen, where it had been dark when we arrived, I saw a large sunroom, full of color and light. Couches and chairs were covered with bright chintzes; there were woven cotton rugs on the wide plank floor. An old upright piano had been painted white. Anne came in, and told me that was a self-contained wing, added about ten years ago. And at the same time they'd had the front windows enlarged and bayed out. During the cold weather she kept the sunroom sealed off. Its plants were now crowded onto the bay window sills, the red, pink and purplish flowers of geraniums, cyclamen and late Christmas cactus soaring above the tangled greens. I looked closer and saw that the blooming rows must have liked that spot and her care; there were many cyclamen shoots with folded blossoms getting ready to open.

The girls won't be up till noon Anne said. She set the table for three. I asked if, like many Annes, she had been named for the heroine of Green Gables.

She smiled slightly. *My parents would have thought that too frivolous. I'm afraid it was Saint Anne. But I suspect that was an excuse. I think it was just a name my mother liked.*

Chip came down in a dark suit and tie, which surprised me. I had on my knockabout pants and shirt, which I'd worn on the coastal ramble with Lil. They were clean, but for a moment I felt I'd committed a faux pas. However, Anne too was dressed casually.

We breakfasted on oatmeal porridge, scrambled eggs, thick whole wheat toast, coffee, fruit. I felt back on solid earth, even becoming rooted in a friendly home. Because there seemed less distance now between Chip and Anne. In a familiar, almost affectionate manner, he looked at the things around him, and at her.

I was already fond of Anne. She seemed intelligent and self possessed. Good features, with no evident attempt to enhance them. Brown hair, gray streaked, and a figure shapely in a way comfortable for a woman of . . . perhaps fifty.

When we put down our cups Chip said to me *Can I borrow your car? I don't want to leave Anne without one.*

Uh . . . sure I said. *Of course.*

I'm going to a meeting.

Wondering, I said *Business?*

No. Religious. I'm going to church.

To cover my confusion I said *Oh.* But instantly I didn't want to be left out of this. *Give me a minute to change* I said hurriedly. *I'll go along. If I may.*

He cocked an eyebrow. And shrugged.

By daylight I could see that his basic house had been modest, prior to the enlarged windows and the built-on sunroom. Apart from the house stood a wooden single-car garage, elongated at the back into what looked like a tool shed.

There used to be a small barn there Chip said. *It's where I kept my truck and tractor. Also some cold storage.*

All around, on rolling knolls, evenly spaced, like ragged soldiers frozen in the snow, were fruit trees. Their twisted limbs cast sharp shadows on the fresh white mounds.

*

In the city I was told where to go by Chip. Over his suit he was wearing a clean gray mackinaw that matched the fur-flapped cap. But now he was bareheaded again. The sun was brilliant. Squinting, he said *Stop here.*

We were staring down into a wide ravine. Into it ran train tracks; there was a factory, houses, a school, some children playing. Scattered staircases crept up the sides. Even snow covered it looked squalid.

On Saturdays, after market, Chip said *I used to come here and give the kids any peaches that wouldn't keep.* He paused, watching the movement far below. *They got to know my truck, and would come running up.* After a long soft moment, he said *Well, we'd better get on.*

*

On a downtown street I followed Chip up concrete steps into a big brick house. In the square vestibule announcements were pinned up and there were low piles of printed matter. He opened one of a set of curtained French doors and we entered what had probably been a long living room. Across it, on the varnished hardwood floor, were rows of folding chairs. The four farthest rows were filled by silent people. Unacknowledged, we sat behind them. Over their shoulders I could see, where the wall had been removed, into another room. It was a step down. There, many rows of chairs, all occupied by adults, were arranged in a semicircle around a small dais. On it were three seated men, as mute as everyone else. But the atmosphere wasn't strained; rather there was a feeling of friendly togetherness.

A middle-aged woman got up. *It's been three years,* she said in a quiet voice *since my cervix operation. I resented, terribly, what it had done to me. Bitterness had filled my heart, leaving no room for God or anyone else. All that time, my dear husband was patient.* She glanced at him. The poor fellow, sitting beside her, had reddened to the ears. *Then one morning — it wasn't physical healing, that had happened many months before — I felt God come back into my heart. I was at peace. I turned to Donald.* Her speech, which had been firm, now faltered. She blushed slightly. *I hadn't meant to share this with the meeting, but I was moved to.*

She sat down. Touchingly, her husband took her hand. The silence resumed. And I realized this must be a Quaker service.

After a few minutes another person got up and spoke. Then one more. Finally the silence became prolonged. The men on the dais shook hands. People began to get up.

Chip made his way into the other room. He bent over a small white-haired woman, still sitting, and kissed her cheek.

A coffee urn, cups and plates of cookies were brought in. The congregation became convivial. And included me without question. I was feeling fairly comfortable, sipping coffee, when

Chip came over. He said *For lunch we're going to my mother's.*

Is she coming with us?

No. She'll go with the people who brought her.

*

The route ran north, beside a broad river. It flowed swiftly, sending back gleams of light. *The Ohio* Chip said.

We crossed a metal bridge of spidery girders. Beyond it lay a clean, tidy town. In a tranquil side street we stopped before a small green house. Essentially one story, with a plain front window trimmed in blue. There was a round window above, which might be for a little room or an attic. Snow had been swept from the red brick walk. Chip's mother opened the blue-painted door.

Watch those loose tiles she said. We were taking off our coats and boots in the small front hall. *I meant to set them yesterday, but the ladies on the Aging Friends committee chose to phone me. If they'd talk less we might get more done.*

Chip picked up one of the terracotta squares. *I'll do this, mother.*

No, you're not dressed for it. I'll get to it tomorrow. I have some mortar. It'll only take a few minutes.

She led us into the living room. Beams were exposed as if to support the ceiling. Pictures and framed embroidered mottos decorated the off-white walls. The fireplace was laid with sticks and split birch logs. The mantelpiece held some pewter plates and a long curved ladle. Hooked rugs softened the dark hardwood floor. On a side table stood photos of Chip and Anne, Scott and Susan, and a posed portrait of an older man. Chip picked it up. *My father* he said.

A low buzzer sounded. Walking briskly away, his mother called back *Food's ready. Come and eat.*

May I wash my hands? I said.

Under the stairs.

I found the tiny washroom, which contained a toilet and a little sink. A slit window looked out on an evergreen bush and the side of the next house. Above the sink was a small mirror, reflecting a sampler on the door behind me. Like all the others, it was framed and under glass. Turning to leave, I read *Do good, For Good is Good to Do.*

The table was in an alcove between the living room and the kitchen. The blue wallpaper was delicately patterned with white stars and pink flowers. *I like your house, Mrs. Hope* I said. *It's so early American.*

Not my doing she said. *I bought it with most of the furnishings. But it suits. It's small enough for me to manage.*

Don't be fooled Chip said. *She loves early American. I'd get her some fine pieces, if she'd let me.*

His mother looked amused. *I have all I need* she said.

I could see their resemblance. The wide brow and blue eyes. The short, curly hair. Chip's was uniformly gray, while his mother's, though white, still showed a trace of pale yellow at the nape of her neck. The same good-looking face, with its firm chin. Mrs. Hope's chin was slightly raised, as if to assert her independence. Both had trim figures. And their hands, no strangers to physical work, showed equally clean and cared-for fingernails.

The meal was of hot scones, cream of corn soup, chicken pot pie, and peach halves stewed with prunes and apricots. Chip seemed never to have enjoyed anything so much.

Thank you I said. *That was delicious.*

I didn't make it Mrs. Hope retorted. *It's all from cans and pack-ages. I don't cook much anymore.* She looked to Chip. *The peaches were dry, under ripe.*

I know. To me he said *When you bit into one of ours, the juice would run down your chin.*

We'll take tea in there his mother said. *Chip, light the fire.*

She sat beside it in a chair with rounded walnut arms. On the wall over her head was one of the framed embroideries. It said *For One Who Believes, No Proof Is Necessary. For One Who Doesn't, No Proof Is Adequate.* She noticed my reading it. She was quick to notice everything.

Isaac, she said *I understand you're of the Jewish faith.*

I'm a Jew I said. *Without, I'm afraid, much faith.*

Of the people from whom our Lord came. The people of the Book. Do you know it? The Old Testament, I mean.

Old and New are Christian terms I replied. *Jews call the Bible the Holy Scriptures. Christians named it the Old Testament to emphasize their contention that God had cancelled His covenant with the Jews and started a new one with them.*

Really! she said. *I didn't know that. Did you, Chip?* He shook his head. *Well,* she went on *it was a family quarrel, wasn't it? They were all Jews to begin with. Anyway, what does it matter.*

It matters, I thought, to the millions of people murdered because of it. But I didn't say that.

9

On his first day back in New York, Chip was particularly pleased to receive an invitation to speak to engineering students. He wanted me to write something relevant to their age and status. On Cole's list was an item about the Peace Corps. I wrote about how problem solving — a favorite engineering maxim — could be applied to help developing countries.

When Chip came back from the Midwestern university he was somber. The speech had gone well, he said. But he was appalled by the question-and-answer session. The students attacked government, business, the country's culture. *God!* he said. *It made me feel I stood for platitudes they'd no longer put up with. Is that widespread? Is that how young people really feel?*

I don't know I said. *Maybe. How does your son feel?*

I'll have to ask. Next time I see him.

Emboldened by having met the others of his family, I said *Why is he at Stanford?*

A girl. She got him interested in biology.

If that made Chip unhappy, I couldn't detect it. But I could see it was something he didn't want to pursue.

*

The next day he called me in. There was a spread of newspapers. He had marked certain stories. *I've been sampling the press* he said. *There's a lot of student discontent.*

There always has been I said. *If you don't question when you're young . . .*

Yes, yes, I know. But this is different. They seem to be questioning power per se. As if we who have some aren't doing anything right.

He seemed to have cottoned on to that notion. I could tell from the look on his face that he wasn't going to be easily dissuaded. Wondering where this was going, I waited.

Well, I have an idea he said. *Why don't we get them to tell us what to do.*

He wanted to choose a group of young people, most likely, but not necessarily, students, and give each what was needed for them to be without money problems for a year. Then they could tell us what to do.

He was quite taken with this. He wants to be liked, I thought. Even by students. But I recalled the *Do Good* sampler. His motives, I'd come to realize, were many and mixed. My qualms, of course, I kept to myself.

*

We placed an ad in several student publications. And I chatted up a couple of columnists. The response was rapid and prodigious. Stories appearing in school papers soon spread. The general media, probably because it was a slow week, made of it more "Hope-Of-Height" hoopla. I feared it might become a farce.

What saved it was Chip's sincerity. Interviewers inclined to laugh were actually won over. The young, some came to feel, were being given a chance they'd never had. There were compliments from other business leaders. And the applications, a spate of them, were positively starry eyed.

In his insightful way, Chip set up a committee of youngish secretaries to sort and choose the candidates. Those secretaries were all from outside the inner court. Terry, at least nominally, was to supervise them. They were both flattered and not overly skeptical. The only thing Chip asked of me was to explain to our personnel people. I told them they'd been bypassed because he didn't want them burdened, especially with any responsibility for the outcome. They were, I learned, glad to keep their distance. As was I.

*

Before lunch that Wednesday I was stopped by Sandy. In his hand he had a news story about the think tank. He could hardly contain his anger. *I suppose you weren't stupid enough to suggest this?* he said.

I stared at him, shocked by the implicit scorn for Chip. *Why*, I said *can't we afford it?*

That's not the point. It's how it plays on the Street. We'll need lots of good releases to offset this.

*

That evening the candlelight was lovely. Lil had just taken off her apron and sat down. We'd been sipping wine. Yet I hadn't slipped into our usual sensual languor. The morning's run-in still rankled. *Sandy thinks a lot of himself these days* I said.

Preening like a bantam cock.

Lil fell asleep right after lovemaking. I lay awake, mulling earlier thoughts. For the Annual Report I'd prepared brief biographies of our top people. Sandy had been entirely forthcoming. His name was Sándor Soldos. One of his grandmothers, he told me, had been Jewish. I'd asked which one.

Why? he said. As usual, he pronounced it *Vy?* Although he had learnt to speak English quite well, pronunciation had never been one of his priorities.

59

If it was your mother's mother, then technically you're Jewish.

No, he said flushing slightly *it was my father's*.

I wasn't sure whether he was lying or just feeling uncomfortable about the Jewish connection. However he'd gone on to tell me, with great enthusiasm, that his wife's maiden name had been Kolesey. And that she was distantly related to the early nineteenth-century Hungarian poet and politician. That was meant to impress, and it did. But I'd briefly met Klara, when I was at their house for the strategy meeting. She'd seemed to me an over-dressed peasant.

*

Chip too could claim those kinds of pretensions. When we were leaving his home near Pittsburgh I'd noticed in the hall two reproductions of artist's sketches. Both were of huge, imaginatively reconstructed, old-country houses, one crenellated, the other Georgian. Hope Castle, Derbyshire, and Hope Castle, Castle-Blayney, Monaghan. English and Irish. I asked if they were his ancestors. *Oh, somewhere way back* he said.

I drove him to the nearest airport, where the company plane had come to pick him up. He offered me a lift and would have someone from the local office bring the Jeep back. But I considered that too complicated. And I didn't want a stranger driving my still-new car.

Alone on the return to Manhattan, my mind went back to those two pictured castles. I thought about people who could identify with some particular part of the world. My forebears, part of a large Jewish population, had lived in the same Polish town for almost a thousand years. The family had survived pogroms, rapes, pillage. But under the Germans every one of my parents' aunts,

60

uncles, cousins, to the last relative, had been murdered in the cattle cars and gas ovens. The town, I'd heard, now had no Jews.

I had no feeling, none, of affiliation with it. For me it was a heap of ashes. Nor did I feel I was a native New Yorker, despite having been born in Brooklyn. My father and mother had come to America as children; they had met and married in Manhattan. But when I was growing up they still spoke to each other, and to me, in Yiddish. Although I soon answered in English, I knew I wasn't the same as other kids. Even children from families as poor as we were. Even black and Puerto Rican kids fooled around as if they felt they had rights to the ground under their feet. I never did.

10

Nonetheless my bank account was growing. By bounds. The monthly Height checks were building what seemed to me a small fortune. Except for the Jeep, and a bit of weekly cost because of Lil, my expenses were basically the same as when I'd been struggling. The rent for my apartment, in the upper west side, had comparatively gone up very little. The dozen or so blocks surrounding it were still rather slummy.

Perhaps it was the Pittsburgh trip that planted the idea of a place outside the city. A spot by the sea would thrill Lil. But a few calls to real estate brokers soon squashed that idea. The cost of coastal properties was somewhere in outer space.

*

On Sundays I began to explore to the north. Sometimes with Lil and one or more of the girls. Everything was unsuitable or too expensive. Then one day, when I was alone, I saw an ad in a local upstate paper. It led me high on a wooded hill to a striking little house. Board and batten, gray from paint and age. A steep rusting steel roof, out of which stuck a low brick chimney. Under the front peak a single square small window. Below it, up three steps from the ground, was a weathered front door, its peeling varnish faded to a yellow brown. The door too had some glass. And flanking it, on either side, was a tall upright window. Whoever had built this, long ago, modest as it must have been even then, had a feeling for formality. A sense of shape and space. Architecturally it was pure, and pleasing.

An old couple came around the corner. *Sorry,* the man said *didn't hear you.*

The woman was carrying a digging fork and a bunch of parsnips. *He doesn't hear me either* she said.

They showed me through the side door into a back room. Full of boots, ragged odds and ends, it crossed the building's breadth. At the rear of it, behind a wire barrier, chickens had once roosted. Past that room, toward the front of the house, separated by a closet that enclosed the back of a staircase, were a kitchen and bedroom. To one side, before entering the kitchen, a rough board partition separated a tiny bathroom. It held a scarred toilet, a half-sized sink, and a hip bath with a shower head attached to a hanging hose. Above the bath was a circling green curtain supported by a metal ring.

The entire floor plan could be seen at a glance. If a man lay on his back, feet to the front door, his head would be the back room, the staircase would be his body, and his outstretched right arm would enfold the bathroom and kitchen, while his left arm would hold the bedroom. That was it, except for a short hall leading from the front door, open to both the kitchen and bedroom, and ending at the steps, steep as a ladder, that rose to the second floor. *Nothing up there* the man said. *You can't even stand.*

We sat in the kitchen and drank tea. They told me they had previously used the house as a cottage, then full time for the past five years. But he was now over eighty, she seventy-eight. They were tired. The winters had become hard. Their car was breaking down. And their son had already bought them a bungalow close to where he lived, near Albany. For this old place, they didn't expect much.

It was within what I could afford.

The age of the house, they thought, was about a hundred years. Maybe a hundred and fifty. It went back to when the left over, worst land, was cleared for farming. Such small holdings invariably failed. The property was now five acres, mostly covered in second-growth forest. The original lot had been severed, leaving an adjoining large estate. Between its big house, and here, the quarter mile was thickly wooded. The estate's rich, usually absent, owner could be expected to keep it that way.

It didn't occur to me to ask about the quality of the well water. Or the condition of anything else. It was all old, cluttered, ancient smelling. But I was charmed. More, stirred. In my mind I could clean, refresh, rebuild. I had no doubts and gave a check for the deposit. For the rest the elderly couple agreed to take a mortgage with low interest and monthly payments.

*

Driving home, my head spun with heated thoughts. For one thing I could hardly wait to tell Lil. In describing it, I'd give her the analogy of the man on his back. And she, in her sharp way, would likely ask where his head would lie. Involuntarily, I grinned. Because I'd have to say *In chicken shit.* Anyway, all that could be changed. We'd be re-homesteading the place. I experienced a surge of strength. After all, I wasn't yet thirty-three, and already felt ten years younger.

*

I saw the flashing light in the rear-view mirror. The cars ahead were moving evenly; I wondered whom the cop was chasing. The cruiser came alongside and to my horror he motioned me over.

His hair was gray at the temples. The gray eyes stared steadily down at me. *Papers please. Have you been drinking?*

No . . .

When was the last time you had a drink?

Shocked, I had to think. *I suppose last night, at dinner. Some wine.*

He returned my driver's license, car ownership and insurance. *Sir, you were weaving all over the road.*

Oh I cried. *I just bought a place. Maybe twenty miles back. I'm sorry. I guess I was excited about it.*

Then settle yourself. So you can live to enjoy it.

I sat for a time at the side of the road, relieved and grateful. That policeman now seemed one of the kindest persons I had ever met.

11

The ten chosen think tankers were all in their twenties. The youngest was barely twenty-one. The oldest twenty-eight. He was the ne'er-do-well nephew of a kept-on Director of Favorable. But that hadn't had much to do with his being chosen. He'd been to Yale, and had some credentials as a hippie seer. He'd submitted some fantastic sketches, and had already been profiled in a student paper. The others made it solely on merit, both personal and academic.

The group met for the first time in an upstairs office. Immediately afterwards the cleaners had to be called, and the smell of marijuana drifted throughout the afternoon.

*

The young people, I had heard, had agreed to focus on specific subjects. But couldn't agree on what they should be.

Their next meeting was with Chip, in his office. I sat in, a little to one side, to get info for a formal press release announcing the start of the experiment. The young thinkers were gathered around the long table, some drinking fruit juice from the glasses and pitchers that had been set out for them. There were no ash trays, and no one smoked.

Chip told them they were completely free to form their own judgments. We'd merely help wherever possible. All Height's facilities would be made available. They had only to register their requests with Terry.

Chip had earlier decided it would be too complicated, and petty, to try to calculate their individual living expenses. He told them that each would be given the same amount, monthly. And for their meetings a large furnished room had been rented in a building a few blocks up Broadway.

The same company we leased the Wall Street floors from owned that location. Chip had sent me to check it out. It was a low rise, a former warehouse converted to offices. A place invested in for its future value, when it would be demolished to make space for still another skyscraper. However, the temporary makeover had rendered it quite respectable looking, even attractive.

Our room was at the back of the third floor. It looked out on the sides of other buildings, but was otherwise adequate. About fifteen persons could be accommodated at the small tables, and on the sofas and chairs. They had been left in lieu of rent by a defunct club of stamp collectors.

*

Lil didn't exactly love the little house. She was dubious about the whole structure. To her it looked rough, and would need a lot of work to make it livable. *It's really old* she said. *And so tiny.* But the girls were ecstatic. They raced up the stairs and at once claimed the loft as their own.

Come down Lil said. *It's probably full of creepies.*

Not even one! Dawn called.

We'll clean it up Ginny cried.

But there's no room for beds Lil said.

Oh, mother Kris replied. *Sleeping bags —*

*

So it was. I bought three sleeping bags. And a Coleman lantern they could read by. But they said it was too bright, and carried up candles instead. Lil kept telling them to be careful, that a fallen candle could start a fire.

Mother dearest, Dawn spoke down *we're not children.*

By then I'd done several weekends' work. The junk left by the old couple was in the back room, waiting to be dumped. In the front rooms the walls had been stripped of countless layers of paper, and the floors scrubbed. There was no longer a stale smell. A store in the nearest village had delivered a decent new double bed and a chest of drawers. A painted kitchen table with folding wings, and chairs to match, on sale at a furniture shop in my West Side neighborhood, had come up in the Jeep. The potbellied stove, which burned wood or coal, I'd kept as it was. It had a hob that swung out, so that a kettle could be kept warm without the water boiling away. And I also kept the old frig, after going over it completely with baking soda. I'd brought in a new set of dishes, cutlery, and some boxes of canned food. Lil rallied, and our first celebratory meal was a great success.

*

A day later, when I went into Terry's office, her face was aglow. She put a finger to her lips and motioned me to follow. Chip's door she shut behind us. He was at a Favorable meeting. Terry put on the table a large white cardboard box. Its blue ribbon had been loosened before. From the rustling tissue paper she lifted and held up a magnificent mink coat. Dark and full length. Pressed against her bosom, it was lustrous below her brilliant wide smile.

Wow! I said. *From Chip?*

She nodded *For my birthday.*

Oh — I didn't know. Are you having a do?

The girls are taking me out for a drink.

It was an office tradition. Whenever one of them had a birthday, the inner-court secretaries did a bit of imbibing. But these outings, I knew, always tugged at Lil's time; she alone had young children at home.

And then Chip and I are going to the Met, to hear Placido Domingo in Pagliacci.

Good I said, and made a mental note of the date, so as to remember it for next year. But I couldn't help also thinking of Anne. Whatever else she had, it didn't include accompanying her husband to the opera.

*

Our Wall Street building, the Broadway location, and a hotel, at which Height's out-of-towners usually stayed — because Chip's apartment was ostensibly occupied — were owned by the same corporate landlord. Its general manager was very friendly to us; we had been considered a flawless tenant. But he had been obliged to phone Terry, with apologies. He asked her, respectfully, if something couldn't be done about the young crowd. Apparently they were very noisy, and had been partying all night. Other occupants of the building had been complaining.

Chip promptly called the young people into his office. *If you don't settle down,* he told them *we'll cancel the whole program.*

You can't do that the Favorable nephew said. *You gave us a year.*

Not for high jinks Chip said. *You have a job to do, and because it's to think doesn't make it different from other work.*

But we rearranged our lives for this one girl said.

Then do it Chip said. *I want to see some result.*

You must give us a chance the Favorable nephew retorted. *Besides, if you cancel it won't look good for Height.* He glanced at me, knowing I was present because of the publicity aspect. I looked to Chip.

Our reputation's well established Chip said. *You people are just starting out. Consider yours.*

*

The water at the *wee house* came from a natural spring. Under a wooden lid it rose in a hooped barrel sunk into the ground. From there it was pulled through a pipe to a pump and pressure tank in the back room. Before electricity, it must have been carried in buckets. Near the spring grew many lily of the valley, escaped from some long-ago garden. Lil gathered a small fragrant bouquet for the table.

My weekends of cleaning and fixing had cut into our Saturday evenings. Lil's girls, though they *loved!* the country house, now had lives of their own. Increasingly that kept them, and her, from coming north for the entire two days. It made our midweek nights more precious. Whereas formerly Lil had been brisk in the morning, eager to get to work by nine, she began clinging to our goodbyes. I wasn't obliged to keep strict office hours, but I tried to be ready on time so as to ride down with her. We'd hold hands in the cab until, prudently, I got out a few blocks short. For those rides she'd let me pay. Otherwise fares came from her purse. I reflected that our relations were costing her money, much more than she could afford. But she refused to take cash.

*

Height held monthly directors' meetings. The faces around the raised slab in Chip's office had mostly been free of concern. But these days, Sandy, who always sat in with them, was delivering more and more detailed reports. It was stretching the under-standing of these otherwise-experienced engineers. Favorable had complicated the entire financial structure. Yet their own net worth, Sandy assured them, was way up. This did much to erase furrows and frowns.

I wanted a picture of them in session for the new Annual Report. I hired Johnny Chappelle, a freelance news photographer, to come in and take candid shots. In the best one, Chip, in shirt-sleeves, was expressively talking with his hands. The others were bent in, intently listening. It suggested a dynamic, determined Board. Its only flaw, too minor I felt, was that you could only see Sandy's back.

*

It was a Saturday, and for a rare weekend I had the full crew of females up in the country. Pale pink blossom petals were falling like confetti. The air was perfumed. *It's like Lord & Taylor's,* Kris said *only real.* An old apple orchard had remained while the for-est had crept up on it.

Sunlit, fair Ginny, a dandelion princess, was pleating a neck-lace of the golden heads. Behind her bloomed our lone purple lilac. Lil and I, along with Dawn and Kris, were cleaning the back room. We had carried out its loose contents and set them on the grass. When the floor was dry we placed back two stuffed arm-chairs and a threadbare carpet. They were part of the old-couple's legacy, but after brushing and airing them we'd agreed they would do. Also a scratched bridge table, which went behind the chicken wire, the space decided on for storage. Everything else we'd drop off at the Salvation Army store.

As the evening cooled I lit a wood fire in the stove. The girls were already up above, snuggled into their sleeping bags with books. Candlelight flickered across the roof boards. Lil said *Kris —*

Yes, we know, came her reply, scornfully joined in chorus by the others *be careful!*

Lil, by the stove, had her bare legs up on another straight-backed chair. From a bag at her side she brought out a ball of white wool, along with two knitting needles. And, not heeding my astonishment, began skillfully to ply them. Nor was she sly or smug about it. It made me aware of a matter-of-fact life I didn't share. And that this was her compromise with the little house. She'd come to accept my rustic foray as *early male menopause.* But joking aside, to her the setting was alien. It wasn't the sea.

*

For my part, I was elated. When alone there I missed Lil in bed, and even the girls to enliven the place, but I was too busy to mope. I was hammering, digging, planting. Tools and gardening were new to me, but I managed easily. When there was a speech to write, it went speedily; too many other tasks waiting. My only mild trauma was in having to return to business attire and Wall Street.

*

When Sandy saw the Annual Report mock-up he was stung.
Why did you pick that picture?
I'm sorry it shows only your back I said. *But of all the shots it was the best image.*

Glowering, Sandy said *On the Street I'm the image.*

71

12

The young people made their first formal request. They wanted the company jet to fly them over all Height's offices and continental projects, to give them, they contended, an overall view of corporate capitalism. Chip said no. Terry told them the plane couldn't be tied up in that way. Then Chip had a closed-door talk with three of them who Terry thought were the most serious. After it, he sent for me.

Iz, this experiment's going nowhere. They lack direction. They lack leadership. It could end up a laughingstock. Somebody has to take them in hand.

I felt a net coming down. But I nodded.

Will you?

Me — isn't there someone more suitable?

I can't think of anyone.

*

Our first session was stormy, and loud. Neil, the Favorable nephew, threatened to call his lawyer. *Go ahead* I said. *And while you're at it, speak to your uncle.* He was silent. *This can't go on* I said. *Time is passing and nothing is happening.*

That's not so said one of the girls who had been in the private talk with Chip. *But it doesn't show, because nobody is keeping track.*

That set off a series of accusations. Each blamed the other. Factions already formed traded recriminations.

Look, I said *like it or not, I'm in charge of you. I won't impose any ideas of my own. That would be self-defeating. But I want you all to report your thinking to me at a joint meeting once a week.*

Wouldn't it be better said the other girl *to report individually. You can see what happens when we're all together.*

No, I said *we're not going to have single confessionals. We're going to learn to be civil. And to write records. And no more partying. At least not in this building.*

Three of these people had lived in the city prior to being chosen. Two still roomed with their parents. That left them a large part of their stipend. It was they who had paid for the parties.

I'm not ruling out drinks I said. *There's no reason why you can't sip a beer, or whatever, while we're taking. But no rowdiness.*

They grumbled but gave in. We fixed on Thursday afternoons. They would have preferred Fridays, but without saying so I was afraid that would interfere with my getting to the country.

*

As it was I didn't leave until the following Saturday afternoon.

Only Dawn came along. When we arrived shafts of golden sunlight were slanting through the trees. Backlit, the old orchard was enchanting.

Far out! Dawn said.

Of all the girls she was the sturdiest. Both in build and boldness. Kristen, now involved with boys, had a date for a movie. Ginny had caught a cold. And Lil said she needed to shop and do laundry.

I wondered whether her weekends without me were entirely chaste. I didn't ask, and never knew how they went, unless she told me. I was sure Lil wouldn't lie, but she was sometimes silent about how she had spent the time. She'd had friends before me, and not all of them fraternal. Every man had to notice her legs. And then be led to the rest of that lovely bounty. Which, I knew,

73

was basically compliant. Beneath her ladylike skin, Lil was a sensual creature.

Dawn and I dug a new flower bed. In it we planted the peonies and day lilies we'd taken from patches that grew wild along the road. Stealing was no kind of an example, but I had explained that I'd previously asked the owner of the adjacent property who'd said they had spread before her time and were anybody's now.

Good-oh! Dawn said, with her bright quick smile.

We were companionable through supper. Then I washed the few dishes and she wiped.

At bedtime I sent her upstairs with a flashlight. *No candle* I said.

Why?

Because I promised your mother. Sleep well.

But she didn't. Lying in bed, I could hear her twisting in the sleeping bag.

Iz —

Yes, sweetie I said. *What is it?*

I don't like it up here.

It was dark. She was alone. And occasionally the house creaked. I switched on my bedside lamp. *Okay* I said. *Come down. Bring your sleeping bag.*

Then I reconsidered. There really wasn't room. She appeared in her *jammies*, which were shorts under a T-shirt. Her shapely firm legs and arms were in pleasing accord with the sound supple body, the pretty features. *Where are we going to put you?* I said. *You could curl up in the armchair in the back room* — she made a face — *or, you could have the other side of this bed.*

I'll sleep here. She quickly slipped between the sheets and lay with her back to me, her dark-haired head cupping Lil's pillow.

I had, and stifled, an impulse to lean across and kiss her brow. But I wasn't her father. Instead I drew away as far as I could without falling out. *Good night again* I said, and turned off the light.

Nighty night.

I could sense her curling up and snuggling in. Then I slept.

When I woke, some time in the night, her head was against my shoulder, her body close. In bed her mother and I were always nude. But in the seconds before Dawn came down I had drawn on pajama bottoms. They were blue, of thin smooth cotton. The top, unraveled at the seams, had long ago become a window rag. Slowly I slid my feet onto the floor.

Barefoot, with the flashlight, I went out. The dewy grass was cool and damp.

And having successfully avoided the plash and flush of the toilet, I silently regained my place in bed. She sighed and settled closer, her limbs aligned with mine. We lay like lovers. I felt an overwhelming warmth and some stirring of desire, mingled with protectiveness. And I thought *God, fate, whatever is ahead, let nothing bad happen to this healthy woman child!*

*

Next Wednesday, Lil said *You've been dallying with my daughter. Now you had part of your fantasy.* I stared at her. *To have us all in bed.*

Lil —

Oh, I know she said smiling. *Dawn was quite superior about it. Made her sisters jealous.*

Relieved, I smiled too. But the joke was darkly troubling. Because Dawn's young body in bed, which I could still feel, had been truly delicious.

75

Later, with Lil lying in my arms, I was glad of my then utter restraint. Yet never again was I alone at night with one of her daughters.

*

For several sessions the young thinkers had essentially been carping. They'd had loud complaints about capitalism, the class system, corporate greed, racial discrimination, even the Constitution. Nothing was any good.

All right, I said *we know that. What about saying how it ought to be? You're supposed to be telling us what to do.* They were silent. *Turn your beefs around and put them to work. Design your own ideal society.*

I was trying to steer them toward some tangible result. Something that could become a kind of report. Without that, I was afraid the whole thing might be a total calamity.

13

Look at this! Chip cried, handing me an open letter. I'd never seen him so excited. Cheeks flushed, eyes brilliant, hand shaking slightly. I thought perhaps it confirmed the biggest contract in Height's history. But the letter was from the Northeast Institute of Technology. It said they wished to confer on Chip an honorary PhD. And would like him to give the convocation address.

That's nice I said.

Nice! It's the greatest thing that's ever happened to me!

I could scarcely keep from smiling. *Chip, PhD usually stands for Poppa Has Dough. Every lamebrain has a doctorate.* I immediately wished I hadn't said that, because there was a sprinkling of them in the company.

They just studied a few years for it. This represents my whole life!

His passion stifled my skepticism and suppressed amusement. I began to understand. The Institute was held to be the country's finest engineering school. He felt the honor more than if it had come from anywhere else. Certainly more than from his own university in Pittsburgh.

This, he said *is the pinnacle of my career.*

I couldn't help being intrigued and moved. The man had everything, yet cared so deeply. About what I felt was a fairly empty distinction.

Iz, give it your all. It has to be the best thing you've ever written.

I told him I'd give it lots of thought. That I might take a day or two away to work on it. He nodded with such enthusiasm it became a command.

*

Being at the country house midweek, in balmy weather, had its charm. Unencumbered by pen or paper, I lay in the long grass. Slim stalks, stirred by a light breeze, were caressing my bare arms and shoulders. The sky above was an infinite blue. Gradually it came to me that I had virtually an unbounded platform. More than with any other speech, I could put myself in Chip's place, have him express my ideas. Or some of them. I'd incorporate a few of his. We'd collaborate.

The next morning I worked out the words. They began quietly:

We share a unique experience today. You — for the first time in your lives receiving engineering diplomas, as I did thirty years ago — and I, for the first time in my life, receiving this unexpected honor, so much more satisfying than anything since my convocation.

But there the similarity ends. For you are among the youth of today, while I — like everyone else who formed his values before World War II — am a pioneer struggling in the unfamiliar conditions of a new age. We immigrants from that older era still control the established institutions — the educational systems and the career ladders up which you young people must climb — we still hold the positions of power and command the forces of order — but all our social institutions are being rocked by a revolution we can no longer ignore. We thought we had reason to be proud of a technological system that uses resources more productively than ever before — but you have shown us its demanding discipline, its coldness, its human casualties, its mindless sprawling mechanization and poisoning of the environment, its lack of social justice.

It ranged over the whole of human activity, becoming a hymn to the possibility of true progress. A little naïve perhaps, but at least truly felt. And concluded with

Can we do it? Of course we can! Let me also assure you, across our common bond of engineering and of humanity, that it can be exciting, satisfying, and a lot of fun!

Whatever your own role is to be, make it count. None of us will come this way again. Experience will teach you, if it hasn't already, that there are really never any second chances,

that life has a way of holding each of us accountable for every-
thing we do. In the end you will measure yourselves by the
way you are reflected in the esteem of your few true friends,
in the contribution you have made to your society, in the qual-
ity of life you create and leave behind you. I wish you great
success.

*

Chip altered not a word. And he wanted to go there alone. Possibly because he couldn't very well take Terry. Or maybe he felt he didn't want any familiar witnesses who might cause him embarrassment, for he intended to open himself, to speak with real emotion.

However, without saying anything I sent Johnny Chappelle. I told him to stay out of sight as much as he could, but to get lots of candid shots.

*

John returned with a wonderful set of pictures. And said Chip's performance had been perfect. He'd seemed relaxed, confident and absolutely honest. And had received a wildly enthusiastic, huge standing ovation.

*

Buoyed by this, I thought of how we could build on it. And hit on the idea of printing the speech, with pictures, as a booklet, one that would fit into an ordinary business envelope. On my own, I went ahead with Height's graphic design department and together we gave it a tasteful, impressive treatment. I finessed every detail and even oversaw the printing at a plant across the river.

79

My feelings had changed. What I had begun with a certain cynicism had been succeeded by hope of my own vague visions. And a need to believe in Chip. Whatever his failings, I felt they were minor compared to what he had already achieved. And to the immense things he might yet do. An exceptionally unusual man. Modest and high minded, and so good-looking, so hand-some. It was as if he'd been cast for his role.

*

The booklet pleased him. And he was soon persuaded about how we should use it. We sent a copy to every director of Height and Favorable, to every employee, and to every associate, supplier and service person. And to Cole at the White House. Back came a letter of congratulation to Chip from the President.

Which was followed by the concluding of a large contract with the Defense Department. Height was to organize and man-age still another important military base. It meant more millions in earnings and immediately nudged up our market value. The arrangement had been in the works for months, and the signing of the contract just then was probably pure coincidence, but it magnified the mood.

*

How are they doing? Chip said. It was Friday morning and there were only the two of us in his office. Chip was leaning back in his chair, his hands behind his head, and with his eyes crinkled, as if restraining excitement. But he'd merely asked for an update on the young people. I was to his right, my chair turned to face him.

They have lots of questions I said. *Some of them even clearly thought out. But no real answers. In the end we might have a report*

80

on what they think needs to be done, but not on how to do it.

Trained enough to see problems, but not how to solve them. This was engineering rhetoric, so I let it pass. *We need training* Chip went on *that begins with analyzing social problems, and works toward solutions. Training for leadership in all fields.*

His lips were compressing, seemingly holding back a beaming smile. His entire countenance became slightly flushed with excitement. I felt myself responding to it, while still blind to its cause.

Iz, he said *you wanted to know when we were going to do that good thing. Well, this is it! We're going to build a university.*

A univers . . . What kind? I was gripped by elation. I felt, but dared not believe, that he didn't mean just engineering.

Of the humanities. All fields of course, but with the emphasis entirely on the humanities. On building a better society. In a generation or two this can be a changed country.

And then the world . . .

Yes, then the world he said, laughing. We were being absurdly grandiose, and we both knew it, but the idea was compelling. A climax to all that was happening.

Where? I said. *Have you thought about that?*

Wherever we can put together at least a thousand pleasant acres. Maybe in New Hampshire, or Vermont. Or someplace with less heating cost.

Is the Favorable money enough?

Enough to start with. Then others will come in. If I have to, I'll call on every business and foundation.

This was the old Chip — or rather the young Chip, who had boldly taken over Height. And once more he seemed young, his face shining with boyish eagerness.

Who knows about this?

Terry has heard me thinking along these lines. But so far, specifically, just you and I.

Wow!

*

The following Sunday was sunny. Since Chip's revelation, I'd anyway been lit by inner sunshine. Thinking about his plans had kept me exhilarated. This morning I was at the country house, alone, but not despondent about it. Lil had stayed in town to plan a party. Kristen had ended her school year with straight A's, which Lil felt called for a celebration.

The phone rang. *Hi kiddo* I said.

Hi. A female voice. Not Lil's.

It was Terry! *Oh, sorry* I said. *For a second I didn't know who it was.*

Just one of your many admirers.

Uh-huh.

Here she said. *Chip wants to talk to you.*

He came on and asked how the weather was.

Up here? Fine.

That's what I expected. It's awfully hot in the city. True. On Lil's street the kids would have opened the hydrant. But Terry's apartment was perfectly air conditioned. I wondered what was up. *If you don't mind,* Chip went on *we'd like to visit.*

Mystified, yet delighted, I gave directions. I had told him about buying the country house, but at the time he'd shown no special interest.

*

They arrived in the company station wagon. It normally shuttled our papers between Wall Street and the production building. But now Chip was behind the wheel. Without, of course, Howard's chauffeur's cap. Howard was a kind man who'd detour on his runs to do personal errands for people. Chip had typically ruled out a uniform, but Howard had begged for the cap. He believed it gave him distinction; perhaps it did with some cops. As a rule he took the car home with him.

I must have looked surprised, because Terry said *Howard's off for a few days. They're having a family wedding in Mississippi.* She handed me a heavy paper bag, containing a bottle of gin and one of tonic, and glanced around. *It's nice. But right now I need your washroom.*

Lil's straw bonnet, with a purple ribbon, was on a peg in the back room. Also some clothes she called *dirt dresses.* But I supposed Terry knew about us. Nobody was being fooled, despite nothing said.

I turned to Chip. *Well, Dr. Hope . . .*

He dismissed that. But something of its inference stuck. I could see he hadn't come for the air. Terry rejoined us. There were only two lawn chairs, so I brought out a blanket. We spread it in the shade of a tree and settled down with our drinks.

Chip was wearing white canvas shoes, beige slacks, dark blue socks and a polo shirt to match. His face, slightly flushed from the heat, set off sharply his curly gray hair. Terry had on a light summer silk, with shoulder straps of the same thin material. It was lined at the bosom and below the waist. She sat with legs folded, the skirt flared over them, her feet in pale sandals. She and Chip both looked lovely.

The doctorate . . . Chip began. *I never expected it. But now that it's happened, how can we use it?*

We're already using it, I thought. And why couldn't this be discussed at the office? But plainly, by coming here, he's making a personal appeal. He wants me, as a friend, to help enhance him. To help him overcome the embarrassment of wanting to blow the balloon a little larger. That mixture of desire and diffidence was in his eyes. The inflated vision and the restraint of his innate modesty.

I felt a surge of affection and pity. For a moment I wanted to kiss him.

Okay . . . let's think I said. Which made me think of Lil's party. Why not? It was a place to start. *How about . . . a celebration?*

What sort?

A big party. We haven't yet made this personal for the employees. Getting a piece of mail isn't the same as meeting you in person. It would give them a chance to participate. To share in the honor.

Chip considered that.

I thought rapidly about New York. It would mean a big ballroom. Too splashy. Philly would be no better. *Pittsburgh!* I said. Terry darkened, but I couldn't help that. *Where it all began. Your work, accomplishments — it would be the fitting place. This time of year, we could even have it in a park. Actually, it . . . it would be more appropriate at your home. But there isn't room.*

There is Chip said. *On the lawn out back.*

Is it large enough?

We have five acres around the house. Before the orchards start. They're rented, but the lawn isn't.

With snow cover, I hadn't noticed. Hadn't looked, really. Now I vaguely recalled the space behind the sunroom being clear for some distance to the trees.

We could put up a tent! I said.

Terry only listened. This again left her out.

*

Lil's party, I'd assumed, would be a small gathering in her apartment. I was surprised when she mentioned twenty to thirty people. And that her parents were coming! And I was astonished when she told me it would be held in a hotel.

Good God I said. *Which hotel?*

The Parkview.

It was large, posh, expensive. I had a sudden fear that I would have to pay a lot of money.

The room and service won't cost anything Lil added. *I'll have to provide the food. But each of the women will bring something.*

My panic lightened. But I was bewildered. *How come?*

I know the owner Lil replied. *He says it will be his pleasure.*

Best not to ask. But she anticipated.

I worked there for a while. Coat checking. Sometimes on the desk. He helped me get the job at City Hall.

Maybe for special favors. But, I reflected, hotel owners could command any number of glamorous girls. Perhaps he just liked her. People did. *Well, that's great* I said. *Then the least I can do is look after the liquor.*

*

All Height employees, everywhere, were invited to the celebration at Chip's Pittsburgh place. We scheduled it for a Saturday, so distant ones could make a weekend of it. But we weren't paying for any travel or accommodation, and realized it would be costly for out-of-towners. Few were expected from New York or

85

Jersey. More, perhaps, from Philadelphia. But it was really going to be a party for Pittsburghers. We prepared for three hundred.

*

Anne wanted nothing to do with the arrangements. They were left to Vaughan, the vice-president in charge of Pittsburgh. He met Chip and me at the plane. The sky was a cloudless, sparkling pale blue. I had been thinking of meeting Chip's mother again, and saw in the firmament the lively color of her eyes. She was being fetched by her grandson Scott, who had come from Stanford. He had taken Anne's car and was gone to get his grandmother by the time we arrived at Hope House, which had become my mental name for it.

I had envisioned tasteful decoration and was rather dismayed to see behind the sunroom a large tent, striped in garish yellow and red, like for a circus. Into it caterers were carrying trays from a white van. Alongside the driveway and around the house flower beds were bright with bloom.

Vaughan placed a polite peck on Anne's cheek and said he would return later with his wife. When Scott drove in with his grandmother the family gathered for lunch, with me as the sole outsider.

Scott was a younger version of his dad, but with Anne's dark hair. Father and son had lightly embraced. Susan had earlier hugged Chip, and had left a lipstick stain on the side of his mouth. With a tissue his wife had wiped it off. She and Chip were as casual and cool as if it were any other day. As if only familiarity had drained them of demonstrativeness. But the grandmother, sitting across from me, had shrewdly darting eyes. *Israel, pass the pickles please* she said.

86

It's Isaac, ma'am I said, handing her the dish.

Well it's not ma'am either. It's Ruth. These are excellent she said, *chewing. Best you've made, Anne.*

Yes, they got enough rain this year. Try the little onions too. I'll give you a few jars of each.

Might as well Chip's mother said. *I'm the only one in this crowd with a truly sour tooth.*

Ha, ha Susan said. We went on eating. After a moment she added *Dad, can you still get your cap on?*

Scott elbowed her ribs.

The grandmother said *When does this shindig begin?*

Three o'clock is when it's called for Chip said.

Well, the weather is perfect his mother replied. *That cool breeze is nice, after all the heat.*

God is smiling on him Susan said.

Ruth turned to Anne. *It's a pity when they get too old to spank.*

Anne smiled. *There's a mouse I'd like to spank. There were droppings on the breadboard this morning. I had to scald it.*

I'll set traps Chip said.

No, dad, I'll do it Scott said. *You'll be too busy.*

*

We were still in the house when Vaughan returned with his wife. She appeared to be a pleasant woman whose age and possible complexities were hidden behind light brown hair dye and bland makeup. Then came a car from which three young men extracted musical instruments. *Just a small band* Vaughan said.

Chip frowned.

Ruth said *That's putting honey on sugar.*

Really, Vaughan Chip said. *A band is too much. Send them back.*

Well, they're union. We'd have to pay them anyway. I thought, since it's a kind of company picnic . . .

So let them just be guests Chip said.

The players weren't at all put out. Food with no work was the opposite of what they were used to. More cars were arriving and lining up along the edge of the road.

Looks like an auction Ruth said.

The crowd was perhaps a little more than half of what we'd prepared for. I'd put copies of Chip's convocation speech booklet on a table in front of the tent, and people without hats used them to cover their heads. The sun's warmth mingled the smell of sandwiches, cakes and coffee with crushed grass and the fragrances of perfumes and Anne's flowers. Some people had brought children who were chasing each other around the tent, despite the efforts of their parents to restrain them. But conversation tapered off along with an arresting of movement when Vaughan stepped forward and waited.

He began by welcoming everyone. He said the whole of Height was honored by the president's degree. Chip sat in front with his family, on folding metal chairs. He looked tentatively happy, like he wasn't sure this should be happening.

Vaughan, uncertain of what to say next, mumbled some more pleasantries. The crowd, standing and listening, was unmoved. I felt it was all fast becoming a fiasco. On impulse I stepped forward and interrupted, asking if I could say something. Surprised, but relieved, Vaughan gladly yielded his place.

I'm fairly new to Height, and new to almost all of you I said. *And no doubt Chip's doctorate is an honor for the company. But I want you to know it's an honor for me to be working with Height, to be, in a sense, working with all of you, because I've never before, in my life*

*as a reporter, or in my life, period, known an outfit as fair and for-
ward looking. What I do is just a tiny part of the entire operation,
but I'm proud to be doing it, to be here with you today, and to know a
person like Chip. Thank you.*

It fell entirely flat. One or two people smiled politely, but most
were indifferent. Even suspicious of this relative stranger. But it
provided direction. Someone called out *Doctor, doctor* and others
took it up and began clapping. Eventually Chip was obliged to get
up and face everyone. Which was met with general and enthusiastic applause.

I took his seat next to Anne. *Sorry I made such a fool of myself*
I whispered. *And for causing you all this.*

We'll survive it she said.

I'm not a doctor Chip announced. *Don't anyone come to me
with a cut finger.* Which brought a suitable smattering of laughter. *But I'm glad of the degree, because, as Vaughan said, it's really a
recognition of all we've done together.*

He spoke well. Again, with a sincerity that evoked respect.
I didn't know whether he truly believed what he said or could
breath into it a realistic conviction. Either way it worked. Before
long his listeners were focused, following his every word, pause,
sigh. He finished with *It's wonderful to be president of such a great
collection of people. But let me tell you, there are days when I think
I would do better just picking peaches.*

Now there was wild and hearty applause. The band picked up
their instruments and broke into "For He's A Jolly Good Fellow."
People milled around Chip. Many had him sign the copies of his
speech they'd used as sun screens.

*

89

Scott was driving his grandmother home. Susan was following her father around the orchard. He'd wanted to see the state of the trees. Anne and I were sitting in the sunroom. She had lowered some of the bamboo blinds. The sun, sinking like a round red stone, was spreading pink bands across the broad planked floor.

I was a little uneasy, being alone with Anne, for I felt for her a fondness verging on affection. This had been growing throughout the day. I had admired everything about her deportment, words, and wholesome attractiveness. Yet I knew it was a minefield that was absolutely out of bounds.

We could distantly observe Chip fingering branches, examining the fruit. *Look at that* I said. *The pilots want to take off before dark, but he has time for your peach trees. He has an amazing mind. It encompasses both big and small.*

Yes.

Speaking of which, I said *when we were here for the birthday, how had he known Susan's sizes?*

Anne smiled. *I sent him a dress and shoes she wouldn't notice were missing. He had the dimensions matched.*

I wouldn't have thought of that. You know, I went on *at the end there, when Vaughan was taking the picture, and you were standing with your son and daughter and Chip and his mother, I thought you looked like a Norman Rockwell painting. The quintessential American family.*

Fiddlesticks!

I smiled. *Is that your expression?*

No, she laughed. *My mother-in-law's. But it's fitting.*

You know . . . I was using that phrase too often, but was on unsure ground. *Before I met her, I thought she'd be a kind of super-strict harridan.*

Ruth? She's a dear. You must have got that idea from Chip. It's his own ideal of what she might expect from him. His dad died when he was barely seventeen. As long as I've known him he's been trying to live up to his image of what he imagines they'd expect of him.

Well, his roots go deep. Much as he's away, I don't think he could ever separate himself from this, from you. I was feeling that if I was him, I couldn't.

Anne was silent. Then she said *He has other tastes.*

I met her gaze, which was steady. If a trifle sad.

Like that Teresa.

I didn't know what to say.

After a moment, Anne continued. *She's not the first. There were a couple of others before her.*

It suddenly echoed what Terry had told me about my status. *Didn't you object?*

Of course I did. But there were the children. And all he was doing. Working like a madman. His nerves were at breaking point. In a strange way he needed it.

Well, I said *this too will probably pass.*

No, I don't think so. He's getting too old for fresh adventures. I think this time he'll leave me.

No I said. *He couldn't!*

He will she said quietly. *He likes that girl. He likes the look of her. The feel of her. The smell of her.*

14

Kristen's party took place early in September. Her school friends were then back from holidays. And at about that time Lil's father had to be at Annapolis. From there her parents would travel to New York, where they'd stay in the party hotel.

Their rate, as a further concession, had been somewhat reduced. When they came in the room was full of teenagers, a few fathers and mothers, and some of Lil's black neighbors. A waiter in a white jacket served drinks and punch, and a waitress in black with a little white apron circulated with a tray of sandwiches and tidbits.

Kristen, Dawn and Ginny rushed their grandparents; Lil had met them earlier. Her father, tall, lean and tanned, with silver hair and an angular nose, was wearing a white shirt, a dark blue suit and a navy-colored tie with some subtle anchor design. He seemed in uniform, lacking only the gold stripes. Her mother, in maroon, was a shapely matron. She had Lil's bosom, but fuller. Her upswept white blonde hair framed a somewhat haughty face. From the hemline down, there were those famous legs.

When Lil introduced me her parents were polite, but distant. In their eyes I could see a Jew, a civilian, not socially in, some vague sort of writer, in no way striking. And without money. Certainly not a marriage prospect.

The commander soon held center floor. *I haven't come all this way, from Hawaii, just to attend a party. I've come to make a speech!* He had a strong sense of theatre. And he said all the right things. He congratulated Kristen on her splendid showing. And her younger sisters on how quickly they were growing.

I turn my back and suddenly you're all attractive young women. He regarded each with mock reproach. *Virginia,* he said to Ginny *I hope you realize there's a reason for your name.* He took all three into his gaze. *That's to be your code of conduct, until, of course, you're married.*

There were many *Ohs!* and giggles. It reminded me that they were nominally Catholic.

And I want to compliment you neighbors and others the Commander concluded *for your good sense in being friends with my little family.*

I wasn't mentioned. Which both relieved and miffed me. For self-respect I tipped the servers fifty dollars.

*

When I next went into her office, Terry was testy. She was on the phone, replying, with hardly restrained ire, to what I thought must be a rude call. With surprise and alarm I overheard that it was Chip. He was at Favorable, at a meeting running late.

I might be! Terry snapped. *Okay, good-bye.* Then with a long sigh she put down the phone and turned to me. I gave her the latest speech draft. She tossed it into a drawer. It was a few minutes to five. *I need a drink* she said.

There's booze in my cabinet.

But she didn't want to stay in the office. *Some bar* she said.

I met her, as arranged, outside the building. We walked along among the home-rushing crowd, feeling increasingly self-conscious about being together. Or perhaps it was just me. It was a Wednesday and I didn't want to be delayed. Yet I had to oblige Terry. When we reached Broadway I took her arm and steered her across to the church. The gate was open.

Let's step in here a minute I said.

She went silently. We were on the path leading to the entrance, but we soon stopped. No one was within hearing. *What's the trouble?* I said.

Oh, I'm just tired. And irritable. The last few nights I haven't slept well.

I'm sorry.

There's nothing you can do. She looked away, strongly breathing in the exhaust-filled air. Though here, in the church grounds, cut off by the surrounding low iron fence, it did seem softened.

Do you really want a drink? I said.

No. I should just go home. Maybe I'll pick up some things and surprise Chip by making dinner. Yes, that's what I'll do — she said with sudden resolve.

I saw her to the curb, where she caught a cab.

*

On the subway I thought about what might be troubling Terry. Probably being excluded from the convocation and the Pittsburgh party. Or perhaps she inwardly panicked whenever he went home there. After all, without him, what did she have? Not even, in another few years, the appeal to exact from another anything like what she was getting from Chip. I thought, we don't need this. We don't need emotional problems. There would be enough outer ones in realizing Chip's vision. I couldn't help feeling slightly annoyed with Terry.

By contrast I considered Lil. Scraping by with virtually no help. But with that understated air of class and competence. And — I felt myself smiling, which must have seemed idiotic to other passengers — with that profound innate sexuality. She saw sexual symbols in almost everything. Not just obvious things like riding a horse, the gushing of taps and fountains, trains going into tunnels. She saw it in candles, carrots, pouring tea in a cup, bending over a frozen food counter — her mind was constantly full of unspoken sexual connotations. A woman like Lil, I felt, whatever her circumstances, would never be long without a man.

The train squealed to my stop. The doors gasped open. At the top of the stairs there was still a square of fading sky. Emerging always seemed like an escape. But unless it couldn't be helped, or I was with Lil, I seldom took cabs. The mortgage payments for the country house were a big extra cost. And I was paying more for parking. Which was only fair, because almost every weekend I drove north.

*

Several Saturdays later the phone rang. I had been at the country house for only a few hours, and was sitting on the shaded side stoop. Ahead, in sunlight, trees were turning gold. I'd wished Lil was here to see it. It was the color of her hair. Otherwise I was glad to be alone. On a board across my knees were scribbled notes for two speeches. Both were needed in the next days. I had neglected them because of other demands. Cole's latest list contained the Nobel prize for literature given to Isaac Bashevis Singer. I was trying to work it in. Make it seem that a Polish-born, late-naturalized American who wrote in Yiddish symbolized the President's cultural program.

Actually, Chip liked subjects veering from business. They gave some relief from the endless clichés. He was currently under even more strain. Sandy was pushing for a Favorable expansion. These meetings were taking most of Chip's time, and becoming increasingly complex. More and more he didn't mind breaking for speeches. He was getting extremely good. Whatever lines I fed him he seemed to be able to deliver as his own. If it made sense, he no longer cared what I wrote. Well, not true — it was because he trusted me. And I did my best to make every speech meaningful. To word it freshly. It had new importance now that it was part of a desirable goal.

I went in and picked up the ringing phone.

Hi there. It sounded like Terry. But there was traffic noise and distant voices in the background. *It's me. Terry. I'm up your way.*

Where? Where are you calling from?

A phone booth. In town.

What town?

Oh, I don't know. Near you. Above Newburgh.

Her voice seemed strangely slack. Puzzled, I said *Are you coming here?*

If you'll come and get me. She sensed my confusion and said *I told the bus driver where you were and he dropped me here.*

Plainly, Chip wasn't with her. I wondered what this meant. I asked her to look around and tell me what she could see. It turned out she was near a tavern at the corner where my road met the main street of the nearest village.

Driving top speed, I was there in ten minutes.

*

In the car she smiled tightly and said *I just had to get away.*

I nodded, having nothing more to go on. My mad rush to meet her had been reckless. Stomach clenched as I topped each rise. Now I was going slowly, and keeping well to the right on the hills. My tension eased. Terry seemed comfortably cradled, her head lolling on the back of the seat, in keeping with the strange loose-ness of her speech. Her perfume faintly permeated the car. There was an undeniable erotic quality in having her beside me.

She had on a nut-brown dress buttoned to the neck, and a light creamy cardigan fastened only at the waist. The sides of it framed her bosom. Across her lap lay a dark suede jacket and a large soft gray leather bag. The color of her flat-heeled shoes matched the jacket.

*

At the house I said *Have you eaten?*

I had breakfast. And coffee at a bus stop.

It was early for me, but I decided we'd better have dinner. Terry sat at the table in a straight chair, smiling vaguely, seeming to savor the success of her escapade.

I whipped up a four-egg omelet, adding chopped green onion and a few partly-moldering mushrooms. With it we had whole-wheat bread and lettuce pieces tossed with oil and lemon juice.

What happened? I said. *Fight with Chip?*

Her pout briefly became pain and then passed into another indistinct smile. *Something like that . . .*

Whatever these expressions were covering, they were to some extent play acting. I'm not getting into this, I thought. We con-tinued with only kitchen conversation. I'd given her the larger portion of the omelet, and now, with her fork, she fed me bits of it. She had slid into a soft languor, like a lover. It was a little like she, and not Lil, was at home here.

When I was brewing coffee she took from her bag a vial of round yellow pills and with a sip of water, swallowed one. To my concerned frown she said *They're to make me relax.* From the bag also came a toothbrush and paste. She went to the washroom.

It wasn't my habit or nature to pry into others' possessions. Not since outgrowing a young boy's thrill at seeing and touching filmy feminine undergarments. Never once had I looked into Lil's purse. But this situation was bizarre. Terry's bag, left on her chair, wasn't entirely zipped. I opened it more. On top of some whitish silky fabric lay the pill vial. Its printed label read: Hope, Georginia, (100) Diazepam 5mg, Dr. Baird, William. One repeat. I quickly put it back. Baird was Chip's doctor; I'd heard him mentioned. Chip had once boasted that in his annual physicals with Baird the doctor never found anything wrong.

The patient's name was obviously a pious fraud. To fool whom? The pharmacist? And diazepam, I knew, was another name for Valium.

Terry returned. There was looseness in her limbs, in her look. Her lids were drooping.

I think you're tired I said.

Mmm . . . She half smiled, shrugging slightly. *Maybe a little sleepy.*

You'd better go to bed. Come I said, and led her to the bedroom. Fortunately, there were fresh sheets. Lil had taken last weekend's to launder. With the sun down, the room had darkened. I switched on the bedside lamp. *Here,* I said, taking some New Yorkers from the night table *if you'd like to read . . .*

She shook her head. I showed her a robe and went to shut the door behind me.

Wait she said. *Say goodnight . . .*

I turned back. She was holding out her hands. I took them and kissed her lightly on the cheek. She pressed the other against mine for a moment. Then I left.

*

The dishes done, I settled down to continue drafting the speeches. My scribbled pages were spread on the kitchen table. Some touched the wall. Backed against the other side of it was the bed's headboard. I was aware of an undercurrent I couldn't deflect, conscious that almost within my reach, through the wall, lay an attractive woman. That slight sensual excitement spurred my sentences.

I was writing rapidly when I heard a low sound. Like a muffled moan. I stopped. There were sighs, then more moans. Then what sounded like restless movements. I went to the door.

Terry? Are you all right?

No reply. If she was asleep, I didn't want sudden light to wake her. I lit a candle and switched off the overhead lamp. Then I slowly opened the bedroom door. Her eyes were wide. Seeing me, she smiled.

Are you cold? I said. The nights were becoming cool, but the room felt warm. *There are extra blankets . . .*

She moved aside and patted for me to sit. I put the candle on the bedside table and took the edge of the bed. She had pushed the covers down. She was wearing a white gown, satin or silk, shiny in the candlelight. It barely covered her round breasts. I could see the press of the nipples. Her skin was smooth. Body supple. Perfume faint, enticing. She rolled her head on the pillow.

I leaned over a little. *Terry, what's wrong?*

She held out her bare arms, exuding, like scent, all her sexuality. *I'm made of the rib of Adam . . .*

It was seducing, alluring, overwhelming. Almost. In that moment I might have set aside Lil. But there was Chip.

Terry . . . I said. *You're lovely. But if you and I ever get together, it won't be behind someone's back.* I took her hands and lowered them to her waist. Then instantly withdrew mine. *Besides, right now you're not yourself.* Or perhaps essentially herself. But I couldn't get involved.

Her smile became a prolonged pout. But she was pliant, and allowed me to draw the covers to her chin.

Sleep I said. *We'll see what tomorrow brings.*

*

Early light arrived like an unwanted guest. In the square pane, gray was giving way to blue. I knew if I looked out the little window, the tops of trees would be sunlit. I'd worked late, not slept enough, and lay there going over some of my sentences.

Suddenly, below, the phone rang.

I scrambled out of the sleeping bag, leaped down the stairs, and bounded barefoot into the kitchen. Luckily the phone was on the outer wall. I grabbed it on the third ring.

Isaac? It was a male voice. Not Chip's.

Yes.

This is Bill Baird. I'm Mr. Hope's doctor.

Yes, I know. Hello.

Is Teresa Ollinsen with you?

Chip, I thought, must be desperate. Torn between anxiety and dignity. *Yes. Yes, she is.* Standing in only my shorts, I wondered what the caller would think if he could see me.

I'd like to speak to her.

Doctor, she's sleeping. I hope the ringing didn't rouse her. She was a bit shaky when she came, so after supper I got her to go to bed. I think it's best to let her sleep.

Yes . . . he said uncertainly. *She has some Dalmane. Maybe* . . . *If she seems at all unwell, call me.* He gave me his number. *Mr. Hope is very concerned.*

Of course I said, trying for the tone of a medical assistant, or nurse. *I'll let you know immediately if there's anything troubling.*

Okay he said. *Uh* . . . *thank you.* And he hung up.

I didn't know what Dalmane was, but assumed it was for sleeping. I put my ear to the bedroom door. There was no sound.

*

It was close to three o'clock when Chip phoned. Terry was sitting out on a folding lawn chair, partly in the sun, looking at a fashion magazine one of Lil's girls had left. There had been no mention of Lil, or of the night before. At breakfast I'd told Terry about Baird's call. She said she hadn't heard it. In any case, she didn't come out of the bedroom until about an hour later. Today she seemed a bit more sober, less drugged. But I had sensed that deep down she was quite aware of what had developed, or failed to. At morning table she had seemed to be playing with me, handing me pieces of buttered toast with unhurried sensuality, as if we were lovers on some isolated island. We were close in age; both about twenty years younger than Chip. I had wondered if she was teasing me, testing her flirtation powers.

Now I said to Chip *She's fine. She's outside, reading. Do you want to speak to her?*

He said it wasn't necessary. I could hear how difficult it was for him. He wanted to know when we'd be back.

By dinner time I said. *I'm just finishing the speeches. We'll be leaving soon.*

He seemed to take my matter-of-fact manner as intended. Assurance that there had been nothing untoward. He was being, in the circumstances, extremely gracious.

*

On the way down, partly to provoke talk, I said *Something I've wondered about. Why was Chip concerned about engineers controlling the voting trust?*

Because they're children.

I looked at Terry in surprise, though it meant momentarily taking my eyes off the road.

That's what Chip says. Outside of nuts and bolts, they're not very sophisticated.

Really — I said. *I hold them in high regard.*

Oh, they're good at what they do. For a few seconds she said nothing more. Then she smiled slightly. *Don't you know the story about the doctor, the lawyer and the engineer?*

No.

It's an old one. In the French revolution, this doctor, lawyer and engineer were condemned for having served the aristocracy. They were taken to the guillotine. The doctor was to be the first to die. But he begged the captain of the guard to let him kneel with his back to the block and bend backward, because, he said, he wanted his last sight of life to be of the sky. The captain consented, and the doctor placed himself looking up. The captain gave the order, the drums rolled, the blade came down — and miraculously stopped just short of the doctor's neck. The captain ordered it to be done again, but the large watching crowd protested. Many cried that it was an act of God and that the doctor should be spared. Unwilling to anger so many citizens, the captain told the doctor to step aside. The lawyer was next, and being no fool, he too asked if he could look up. He did, and again the guillotine stopped just before his neck. So he too was spared.

I glanced at her once more, waiting for the punch line.

Then it was the engineer's turn she said. *He also asked if he could bend back and look up like the others. This was allowed, and again the order was given. But just as the drums started to roll the engineer cried Wait! Wait! I see the problem —*

Well, I said laughing *now so do I.* But the engineers I knew at Height all seemed decent fellows. Devoted to their work and respectful of Chip.

As we came to a stop in front of her building I said *Chip is under such pressure. Be nice to him.*

Terry gathered her things and her lips slid into a shrewd, sensual smile. *Oh, I will be. I know just how to be nice to him...*

15

It was Tuesday before I saw Chip. On Monday morning I had given for typing the draft of the next day's speech, for the Manhattan Chamber, to Mary Lynn, Terry's assistant. She had a little office on my side of the floor. She helped Terry with various things, took over her desk whenever Terry had to be away from it, and filled in when the regular receptionist went to lunch. Mary Lynn was a sweet-faced, amiable young woman who truly exemplified the catchphrase *always ready and willing*, whatever the task. She had recently been married, but other than the rings, in the office there was no sign of any other interest. She revered Terry and Chip, and a little of that regard extended to me. And unlike me, she typed with all her fingers.

*

Dick Chalkley, one of the VPs, came back from the Chamber of Commerce lunch and told the inner court that Chip's speech had been a great success. Terry was at her desk, taking endless phone calls. That often happened when Chip was out. He had gone straight to a Favorable meeting.

Later that afternoon, when Chip was back, I took in the typed draft of the second speech. Terry's businesslike smile was devoid of any special intimacy. Going from her into Chip's office I didn't know what to expect; I supposed I'd be under suspicion. And he was a trifle cool, but he made no mention of the previous weekend. I gathered it wasn't forgotten but was to be passed over in silence. With one hand he took my draft and with the other held out a letter. For a second I feared it was a notice of letting me go, but it was addressed to him from a small midwest college that specialized in engineering. It asked him to become Chancellor.

What do you think? he said.

They want you to raise money.

I know. Yet I'm going to accept. It's prestige for us. Part of what we're working toward. Prepare an announcement. But . . . uh . . . don't make more of it than it warrants.

Shades of Pittsburgh, I thought. *Well,* I said *will they want you to speak?*

We'll see.

When I went out into the court, Chalkley was talking to his secretary. But as I walked by he broke off and followed me into the foyer.

Iz, he said *would you like to come to dinner? How about Wednesday?*

Oh — thank you. I can't, though. Not Wednesday.

Thursday, then? Meli said either evening.

∗

Richard Chalkley was a vice-president who no longer had anything definite to do. He was in charge of some of the smaller projects, and consequently had a good deal to say about the large ones. He was listened to, and sometimes he contributed a good idea, but generally he was no longer considered very seriously. I'd heard that even as a young engineer he had been without particular brilliance, though dependable. But he had been the first to join Chip in the buy-back of Height, which had made him one of the unshakable seven.

Dick had taken me to lunch once, when I was still fairly new. He wanted to know, he had said then, how I was getting along. Which meant how close was I becoming to Chip. He was like a jealous lover who checks out all possible rivals.

∗

That evening, Lil listened carefully when I told her about Terry.

And you didn't touch her?

No. Not sexually.

Hmm. Missed your chance.

She doesn't want me I said. It sounded lame.

105

Lil, bent over the stove, basting the chicken, gave me a side-ways glance. *She wants everything.* Straightening up, she caught my eye and added, with a little smile, *We all do.*

I was ill at ease. Glad I'd been frank, before Lil found out, as women will. Guilty for having, that night, been tempted by Terry. And apprehensive about Chip's real feelings. Ready, however, to stand strong on having acted honorably.

Yet later, when I was inside Lil, wallowing in her loveliness, I had moments of wondering what it would be like to be with Terry.

*

The Chalkleys lived in Englewood, near the Pallisades. The house stood on a knoll, facing a park. I first stopped at a lookout from which could be seen a vast panorama of the blue Hudson, backed by the misty towers of Manhattan. In the early dusk, ex-cept for the movement of ships, it was like a tapestry.

Dick welcomed me warmly. In the dining room, the table was set for five. He was pouring us Dubonet when his wife, Melissa, came in from the kitchen. She struck me as pleasing, slightly plump, attractive. She must once have been quite pretty. A short sleeved brown housecoat, in lieu, I guessed, of an apron, covered most of her blue dress. *We'll eat in half an hour* she said, taking a glass from Dick. *Why don't you introduce Isaac to Stu and Kate.*

Their son and daughter, both under twenty, looked clean and wholesome.

*

Thank you, that was sumptuous I said to Melissa. That wasn't mere form. The poached Atlantic salmon, pasta and salad, with Pinot Chardonnay and apple crisp, had been very good. I assumed the meal had been earlier prepared by a maid, but Melissa had been graceful with the finishing touches. And she herself, in her blue dress and gold jewelry, had been nice to look at. Moreover, the table talk, though superficial, had been lively.

The younger pair excused themselves. Melissa said she would start the dishes. And Dick announced that he had to pay a visit to the *little boys'* room.

Left alone, I followed Melissa into the kitchen. Not surprisingly, it was resplendent. Complete with every modern appliance. A model home, a model gentile family, I thought smugly. *I suppose* I said *you people go to church?*

I do Melissa said. *Dick sometimes. The children, if I make them. In fact,* she added *I'm rather active. In committees and things. Episcopalian.*

I nodded, knowingly.

Melissa might have sensed it, for she turned to me with a wet plate in her hand and said, with a shrewd smile *It contains the wildness within.*

*

Dick and I sunk into their soft upholstery, holding our cups of coffee. *This is so peaceful,* I said *with Manhattan just across the river.*

And I can keep an eye he said with a conspiratorial wink *on the production building.*

It was actually miles away. And I wondered what needed his watching.

He neatly dropped cigarette ash into a gleaming ceramic dish. The whole place seemed spotless, except for his smoking. He was the only one in the inner court who regularly did. Chip and Terry didn't smoke. The secretaries, if they ever indulged, didn't do it in the office. Bruce Hardwick occasionally lit a pipe, but I think more for effect than enjoyment. None of the other VPs smoked. Crossing his legs, Dick said *Sandy's consulted me about an interesting idea.*

Aha! I thought. That's why I'm here.

He wants to make a Treasury offering, and then split the stock to boost sales.

Now Dick's an instant financial expert, I thought. Then aloud *What will that do?*

Well, we borrowed from merchant bankers for the Favorable buyout. Issuing new stock would give us capital to pay down the loans and interest.

And splitting? I was getting lost.

Splitting will make our stock more liquid. And he added, for my benefit *Lower the price. Splitting always causes some excitement, and combined with all the publicity Chip's getting, it will look like we're doing well.*

But we are, aren't we?

Sure. But investors have to think it. It's all psychological, the market.

He was parroting Sandy, who had cleverly gained an ally by giving my host something to feel important about. But why me? *Do you want the publicity increased?*

Yes. But not only. Chip . . . Chip is liable to be sticky.

I've no influence with him. Not on financial matters.

Well . . . you can try.

I was flabbergasted. But if these kinds of factions were forming, I knew where my loyalty lay. It made me flippant. *Why didn't you invite Chip to dinner?*

He won't come. He's never been here.

Really?

Dick sighed. *Between us,* he said *it's because Meli doesn't approve of how he's behaving. You know, with Anne . . . and . . .*

Terry?

He nodded. *She told him so.*

When?

About four years ago. Before we moved here. He came to cock-tails in our apartment, in Manhattan.

Not with Terry —

Oh no. But we've known Anne since the old days. From even before they were married. Meli feels strongly about it.

Well! So does Chip, apparently.

*

On the weekend I asked Lil how her boss felt about Chip's love life.

I don't know.

Nothing you can detect?

My boss has a wife and children she said sharply. *He's devoted to family and work.*

Her VP, John Lambert, was tall, trim, smoothly gray haired, pleasant and polite. And he was considered a good engineer and manager. He handled many of the major projects. Lil never talked about him, or what they did. I was digging at her concept of duty.

Yet the tensions in the office were affecting us both, and now our intimacy. It annoyed me that she wasn't more forthcoming. That night, a bit riled, we lay with only our backs touching. But we made up for it in the morning.

On Monday afternoon there was a Board meeting. Mary Lynn was at Terry's desk. Terry sat in on all Board meetings to take notes. From them the official company Secretary typed up the Minutes and other records. For years, until she retired, the Secretary had been the woman in Pittsburgh to whom Chip first gave the job. Since then it was someone in the office of Jamie R. Mckeown, our corporate lawyer. Jamie R. was a rosy little man, always agreeable and smiling. So he should be. J. R. Mckeown and Associates had some other clients, but it was his work for Height that had made him rich.

I was in Terry's office, trying to chat with Mary Lynn between incoming phone calls. Sandy's secretary came down with a paper he'd called for. With a nod from Mary Lynn, she knocked on Chip's door. It was opened by Sandy, who normally sat at the foot of the table. Over his shoulder I glimpsed what astonished me. Chip was wearing a houndstooth jacket.

Suits weren't mandatory in the inner sanctum. The VPs some-times dressed more casually. But Chip's attire, in the office and in public, had been impeccable. As if he'd stepped from a glossy *Fortune* or *Forbes* picture of the perfect president. And his business wardrobe, as I'd seen, wasn't limited. Deliberately wearing some-thing sportier, especially to a Board meeting, was a declaration.

*

My concern led to thinking about Lil's clothes. She carefully rotated her three or four office outfits. And varied them, as taste-fully as possible, with cut-rate accessories. For outer wear she had only a fall raincoat, into which she later buttoned a felt liner. But she was often cold.

If Lil was bought love, she came cheap. Even my part of Kristen's party, including presents for all three girls, had scarcely totaled two hundred dollars. Our arrangement was heavily to my advantage, despite her insistence that she derived equal pleasure. And that she desperately needed those brief spells of time out.

*

The next Wednesday we enjoyed a typical evening, untroubled by any talk of the office. In the morning I was staying behind, and when she kissed me good-bye, I handed her fifteen hundred dollars. It had drastically cut into my bank account, but I had determined to do it. *Provided*, I said *you spend it on yourself. Get some winter things.* She paused, surprised and with a little frown, as if she might refuse. But then she put the money in her purse.

*

On Thursday afternoons I had my regular session with the young peoples' think tank. Sometimes these conclaves were fun, but more often frustrating, even infuriating. However, I was soothed by anticipating Saturday. This time I would be going to the country alone. Lil would be shopping, and her daughters all had stronger enticements.

The think tankers had caused enough discomfort in the Broadway building to bring more complaints from the management. So I'd moved their meeting room to a rented apartment in Queens. It took up the top floor of a small squat structure, and was on a level with the raised subway tracks. There no one much minded the young peoples' noise. But, actually, there was now much less of it, because the place was also being used as a residence

111

by one of the girls. She kept it fairly neat, and the others, out of respect, had subdued their behavior.

Our meetings usually followed a set format. Each of the ten was in turn required to report on his or her activities or thoughts. Then the points made were challenged or attacked. Or passionately defended. My role was to keep order, or try. I was now much more sympathetic to the group, because of my secret knowledge of the part this experiment might have played in Chip's thinking. I looked upon it as a minor step toward what was to come.

In the sessions I was rather like a teacher with very little to say. But I really didn't have to do much steering. The young people were too intelligent to take seriously their own unfounded theories. Even the Favorable nephew was outrageous in a way that was often amusing. His reports frequently took the form of colorful abstract paintings on large sheets of paper, which he interpreted, usually to laughter. It was manifest that this group wouldn't be transforming society, not in their sponsored time. But the meetings had become agreeable, and some sort of report would result.

16

That Saturday I was at the country house, planting narcissus beside the front door. Behind me the crunch of wheels on gravel caused me to look around. A sleek automobile whose make I couldn't recognize came up and stopped behind the Jeep. It was a shiny dark red, the color of some regal velvets. But when I went to the opened car window I saw that the driver was out of keeping.

He wore a baseball cap above his weathered face, and green work clothes ending in leather boots.

G'day he said.

Can I help you?

Mister Conn'ly wants to know if you'd like t'come by this afternoon.

I'm sorry . . .

Next door. The big house.

Surprised, I said *Oh. Thank you. Uh . . . what time?*

'Bout three.

I guess I can. The car was blinding. I asked him what make.

Bentley.

Yours?

He laughed. *Naw, theirs. I work for them. I'm just takin' it t'get the oil changed.*

*

Driving there, I noticed that the Jeep needed fresh oil too. The distances from and to New York had added up.

The road past my house was new to me. I'd been too busy to explore it. On my side it was all wooded, but on the other side there were grassy patches that might once have been pasture.

Low stone gateposts, covered with climbing ivy, proclaimed the entrance to my neighbor's. The paved driveway was open. There was a lot of lawn, fancy clipped bushes, and tennis courts. The house was grand, gabled, brownish, but not new. By the garage stood a green convertible and a battered black pickup. The truck, I guessed, belonged to the man I'd met.

A maid opened the door. She had on a black dress and a frilled apron. She was middle-aged and moved with difficulty. In the

113

front parlor my host rose to greet me. *Connelly* he said, extending his hand. I had to look up at him; he was almost a head taller. Slim, with straight dark hair, possibly dyed, neatly parted near the middle. A thin graying moustache. And a perpetual, slightly-sardonic smile.

Isaac Reitman I replied.

Shall we have the ritual cup of coffee?

Sure I said.

Dora . . . !

The same maid, dragging one foot a bit, carried in a tray with two small cups of coffee, cream, sugar, silver spoons and a plate of plain biscuits. Connelly beckoned me to a chair. The polished furniture was elegant and old. This wasn't new money.

It's about your place Connelly said. *It was originally severed from this property. Or, actually, long ago, it was the other way around. Anyway, we were in France when the old couple decided to sell, or we wouldn't have missed it.*

I'd been summoned because Connelly wanted me to know he would buy it whenever I'd had enough.

What would you do with it?

The old house? Tear it down. Or maybe make it over for guests. A thin smile. *Guests we don't want here.*

I felt I was one. The interview was at an end, but out of politeness he asked what I did.

When I told him he said *Ah, the company that fellow Williams is with now.*

You know him?

We've had some dealings. He again smiled sardonically. I couldn't tell whether it was meant to be approving or damning. But when he took me to the door he said *I was involved in his little venture after he left the bank. I lost a bundle.*

*

Requests for Chip to speak usually came well in advance. But an upstate community college wrote to say that their scheduled speaker had suddenly died. With many apologies, they wouldn't normally have presumed to aspire to Mr. Hope, but because of Height's interest in young people . . . etc. *I'll do it* Chip said, sighing. *But I've got a Favorable meeting earlier that day. I don't know if I can be in two places at once.*

Then decline.

No. Write it. And in case I can't make it, you go.

I had an uneasy feeling. But I ventured *To do . . .*

Give it in my place.

There was no point in arguing. It was certain that fatigue weighed on him like stone. There was swelling under his eyes. The fine wrinkles in his forehead had deepened. His fingers shook when he took back the letter. Yet he wore a pinky-brown checked suit, a bright blue shirt, a knitted brown tie. It seemed the more burdened he became, the more absurdly he dressed. I'd no doubt his clothes were of the finest cloth, and superbly stitched, and even stylish. But for a much younger man. Someone out on the Avenue. Not in our office. Not Chip.

*

At midweek Lil brought a large suitcase and displayed her booty. All from the lower East Side, where she'd found affordable copies of uptown fashions. She had bought a stylish warm winter coat, three very decent dresses, two pairs of classic medium-heeled shoes, and a large, square, expensive lace stole. The dresses would work well for office use, and with the stole folded and draped across her back and arms, each could become an acceptable evening outfit. We never went out, but I wasn't about to squash the possibility.

Then she surprised me by handing over nearly three hundred dollars.

I'm sorry, I also got some things for the girls.

Come on! I said, and put the money into one of her shoes. *Hey, what about gloves?* Hers were worn and unlined.

She smiled ruefully. *I tried on some elegant fur-lined ones. But I had to get gloves for the girls. Kristen won't wear mittens anymore. Dawn's are past mending, and she turns up her nose at my knitted ones. And Ginny has outgrown hers, and is influenced by her sisters. I got them all new ones, with different designs on the back. Also new dresses, socks and shoes. And winter parkas. I got some really great buys, without any nasty bargaining. I'll tell the girls all this is from you.*

Don't you dare. But I wonder if Chip should know. You could be managing Favorable!

*

Despite the intense maneuvering at the top, Favorable was quietly making money. The same people who ran the day-to-day business before the takeover were still doing their job. Chip was reluctant to interfere. Sandy was all for sounding trumpets on the Street, but Chip kept any noise muffled. He had also put off the proposed expansion. And had said a flat no to the idea of a stock split. *Height has a history* he had said. *We've never been a company that plays tricks.* When it was put to a vote, none of the VPs opposed him. Especially not Dick Chalkley. Sandy was obliged to swallow it in silence.

∗

I had this from Terry, who didn't mind talking when no one else could hear. She had never mentioned the incident at the country house, but there were times when she treated me as an intimate, particularly when she wanted something. And then occasionally, out of the corner of an eye, there would be a hint of lust. As if a bit of her sexuality sometimes escaped. Or perhaps, testing her powers, she just wanted to keep me enticed.

That day she gave me a bundle of handwritten pages. Stories by Tim, which he had sent from school. She hoped I'd critique them, then later talk with him. The holidays were approaching, and with them, I supposed, the annual problem of what to do with him.

The writing was crude and overly colorful. But it was clear that Tim was a storyteller. Most of the plots had to do with being out of place, even unwanted. But some were about space travel. His reality and fantasy.

∗

The students of the upstate community college were almost violent in their boredom. They squirmed in their seats and someone had just thrown a spitball, which caused a small commotion. I was waiting for it to die down before apologizing for their having to put up with me, a poor substitute for Mr. Hope. It was apparent that this talk had been foisted on them, and that the switching to a surrogate had only made things worse. Standing at the lectern, I tried to remember what I had written. As I opened my mouth to begin, so did a door at the back of the auditorium and Chip came in. I saw he'd been rushing; effort and weariness burdened his walk. But as he came up the aisle he straightened his back and tie, and bounded onto the stage.

The dean was delighted, and taking over the mike, made appropriate remarks. Then he took his seat, which put both of us on either side of Chip. I could plainly see the speaker's profile.

Chip went at once into the theme of the speech, which was that business was a human activity and could be as creative as any art. He spoke without notes, and with surprising immediacy. As if he'd just learned the lines in the cab on the way up, which he probably had. But he was almost word perfect, and there was no sign of the fatigue he was fighting.

As he got more animated, so did his audience. His charm was potent. The kids were soon smiling. He ad-libbed a little, and several times, in response to puns, he got big laughs. It was astonishing. He seemed almost the age of the students. He ended to thunderous applause, and whistles.

*

In the car going back Chip collapsed. He let his head fall to his chest and his limbs go slack. His eyes were closed, complexion drained. Words of any kind would only have added weight, so I stayed silent. But I knew I had watched a wonderful performance.

*

Another matter, long dormant, began pressing. It was the plant to process industrial liquid waste into supposedly-pure water. The contract had been signed months before, and the Alabama partner was now pushing Height to put up its agreed share and proceed with the project. But Sandy was reluctant. He considered the whole scheme of low profit potential, and a distraction from Height's financial future. He didn't want to divert money that could be used to pay down what had been borrowed to buy Favorable. His idea was to come to a settlement with the Alabama firm that would release Height from its commitment.

Yet again, Chip opposed that. He pointed out that we had taken a public position. He said we weren't politicians, and couldn't just abandon the promise of our past ballyhoo.

But he was too burdened to become directly involved. Lately he had been delegating more and more to me, despite my lack of an official job description. He had once said, about engineering reports, thick tomes that daily cluttered his desk, that he couldn't make head or tail of most of them. *Your value, Iz,* he said to me *is that you think clearly. You can reduce complex issues to simple sentences.* He believed that ability could be applied to management problems.

We still needed state approval for the waste plant. He asked me to look into the licensing, and stir things up.

The person who from the start had been in charge of the project was Brian Holmes. He was sincere, competent and polite, with all the right background. He had started by teaching chemistry, and then had got his engineering and environmental degrees as an older student. Now in his fifties, with some fourteen years of unblemished work for Height, he had won general respect. And he had minutely studied the liquid-waste scheme, and knew more about all its aspects than anyone else in Height. But when I saw him in his office on the upper floor he seemed strangely apathetic.

His assistant, Sally Stitsky, told me privately that all the months of being blocked, of essentially doing nothing, had depressed him. Brian was not a man who took kindly to inactivity, but he had not been assigned to anything else. For weeks he had sat staring at the same plans, which he already knew inside out.

Sally was a youngish engineer, attractive and unmarried, but without the alert antenna of most single women. It was rumored, but never confirmed, that she lived with some man. On her mother's side, Sally, a Brit, was actually distantly related to the Hopes, but she hadn't mentioned that at the time of her hiring. Chip was hard on nepotism. But he didn't hold it against anyone who could do the job. Sally was knowledgeable, organized and neat. She had a bit of a palmy accent, the product of private schooling, but her father, she had advised me, was Jewish and had come from middle Europe. That she had also, professionally, kept his name, said something. I sensed from her a warmth that made me feel close. The way I still felt about Sandy, despite our differences.

*

I told Chip that in Brian's current condition we shouldn't expect any quick action.

Then you do it. I want it done.

You mean take over?

If necessary, yes.

I was torn about that. Holmes would be hurt. Not in his title or income: Height almost never demoted, and people were fired only for gross misbehavior. But however delicately I did it, Brian would know he was being bypassed. On the other hand, I began to think ambitiously. If the project got off the ground, maybe it would provide a permanent position. We'd incorporate a separate company. Chip would be president, and I could be something like executive director. It needn't interfere, I told myself, with plans for the university. There I'd be unlikely to have a direct role, and with an assured income I'd be better able to help. As for the plant, my ignorance of its technology shouldn't matter. Because Holmes, with a suitable title, would run the actual operation.

When I put it to Chip he said okay.

*

Elated, I phoned Jamie McKeown and told him to set it up. I said I was speaking for Chip. Jamie R. didn't demure. He asked, of course, what the company was to be called. I told him I had this idea of a landscaped plant with a lawn in front, where purified discharge would pass through a transparent pipe right where the public could see it. Therefore I thought we should call the company Clearwater. I said I knew there was a city in Florida called that, and other enterprises with that name, but I could think of no better one. Jamie said he would check it out, but he didn't think there would be any problem. *Sounds great!* he said.

Only one thing troubled me that day. When I had spoken to Chip he was wearing a Western shirt and a string tie.

*

Terry asked me to talk to Tim. The holidays had started and he'd been home for three days. *Come tonight* she said. *Chip will be out. The three of us will have supper.*

But it was a Wednesday. *I don't want to put you to trouble.*

Oh, come on. You know I don't cook.

I was about to make some other excuse, but then I thought of the unhappy boy. This had probably been promised. Perhaps I could put Lil off until Thursday. She always tried to be accommodating, but it might mean switching laundry times, or some similar inconvenience. And our routine had also become a fixture for her girls. They formed their own plans around it.

*

Nonetheless, two hours later I was at Terry's door. I'd phoned Lil at her desk, just before five. When we had to, we sometimes communicated that way, using stilted private code. She wasn't pleased, but had agreed I'd better go.

*

Terry was glad to greet me. She had set the kitchen table, and we sat down to pizza and beer, with tomato juice for Tim. Chip was at a party, an office dinner for directors and senior officials of Favorable. It had been Sandy's idea, Terry said. At Height, the inner court never held parties. Its members saw so much of one another that they were simply happy to leave early and go home.

Terry had dressed for the occasion. She had on flat black slippers below a dark green blanket-wool skirt. And above, a tight white sweater that set off her bosom. She must have been wearing a brassiere with wires in it, because it pushed her breasts up and forward like in some Elizabethan drama. Doting mother and chaste seductress.

After eating, Tim and I repaired to the round dining-room table. He sat with his back to the wall of those larger-than-life, idealized photo portraits. We had pushed back the standing unlit candelabra, and his handwritten stories were spread between us.

I told him their core was fine. What he had to watch out for were inflated words that didn't quite fit, and metaphors that

122

didn't match. *If,* I said *you want to say something is like . . . take both images from the same part of life. Don't compare a candle with a herring.* He laughed. Though it occurred to me that a darting, weaving fish could suggest a flickering candle. But I let it go. We rambled on around the edges of his work. Basically I felt it was good, and didn't want specific comments to discourage him. He was eager and grateful, obviously starved for someone to talk with about stories.

Writing is the only thing I really care about he said. *I do want to be a writer.*

You're already a writer. And you'll become a much better one.

His eyes shone. I liked the boy a lot.

*

Going home, I thought about contradictions. Tim and I couldn't have held that conversation if Chip had been there. And Lil's girls would be great holiday company for Tim. But like a mismatched metaphor, the two worlds couldn't be combined.

*

Kristen was attending a teenage New Year's party. It was at the home of a school friend, whose mother would be supervising. Dawn and Ginny had been invited also to a different sleepover, with the exciting prospect of being allowed to stay up until after the TV countdown.

For celebration Lil wanted to do nothing. Or as little as possible. So I brought sparkling white wine, cold cuts and deli salad to her. She had just finished a bath, and wearing only a thin slip, she sat down next to me on her iron bedstead. She had her hair down, and was still slightly damp, with a fresh clean smell of skin. On the bedside table she arranged the food and lit a single candle. We ate from paper plates, and toasted each other from paper cups.

And she listened while I talked about the new company.

I'm sure I can do it I said. *And just think about a steady executive income.* I went on, looking at the peeling paint, her crowded closet, the crude plywood dresser. I could envisage a large house, with rooms for each of the girls, and all good things.

17

Brian Holmes was a little taken aback by my advent, but he was a gentleman, and did his best to conceal any discomfort. Besides, he quickly realized that my fresh blood, as it were, and my access to Chip, promised to revive the project. There was no change in titles. As yet I had none, and I was careful to make no decisions that weren't first discussed with him. But there was a subtle shift in management, and he soon let me take the lead.

*

As quickly as I could get an appointment I went to see the Commissioner of Environmental Development. I'd pushed hard, using Height's prestige to reach the top civil servant. He politely explained the regulations, and the detailed bureaucratic process. My high slowly sank. Abiding by the rules, to obtain the needed approval it was going to take weeks, even months. *Oh,* he said genially *we have files that go back years.*

Deflated, I was leaving through the long drab hall when a woman came out of a washroom. Dark hair cut in bangs, face better looking than Lil's, breasts larger, figure nicely formed — my inevitable criteria — and the whole strangely familiar. Her surprise seemed to match mine. We both stopped, eyeing each other.

Excuse me I said. *I feel I should know you.*

You should. If you're Isaac.

I nodded, nonplussed.

She laughed. *Dorothy Laughlin. From law school.*

Dot! I cried. We had often sat next to each other at Columbia. During dull lectures we sometimes exchanged louche notes, meant to be funny. But nothing more. I wasn't her type, and knew it. Outside of classes she moved in a more moneyed, faster crowd. After getting involved with the Journal I'd drifted away.

Did you graduate? I asked.

Yep. That's why I'm here. Staff lawyer.

Congratulations.

What for? It's not much of a career.

It wasn't, for her. I remembered her as bright and well-connected.

Why did you choose it?

She dropped her voice. *There wasn't much choice. I got pregnant. I have a nine-year-old son.*

We went into her small office. She sat on the edge of her desk, I in a chair. The door was shut. In the outer room there was a secretary she shared with some others. I told her what I was doing. She'd heard of Height, and had read about Chip in the papers. But she knew nothing of the Clearwater project.

I explained my present frustration.

Her phone rang. It turned out to be a call she had to take. But she put her hand over the mouthpiece and with a slight wink, said *See Senator Reese*.

*

Reese was, in his own circles, legendary. For more than twenty years he'd been repeatedly elected. *State Senator for life*, it was said of him. He was supposed to have the ear of the Governor, and of most senior officials. All this I'd learnt after leaving Dorothy, mouthing my thanks and tiptoeing out while she talked with her caller. I felt buoyed by having met her again, and by her advice. I thought of sending her flowers, but that would be too flamboyant for her office. Even a personal note, sent to her at work, might cause embarrassment. And I couldn't find her home number in the directory.

*

Lil knew about Reese from City Hall. *He has power. Plenty. But he's honest. He lives in the same house he moved into when first elected. Doesn't take bribes, but collects debts for his favors. He can call on those debts all over the state, and manipulate them to get things done. He's certainly your man. If you can get to him.*

*

I phoned Reese's office. Said I was George Hope's assistant and acting for him. I said Mr. Hope would like to see the Senator. In the late afternoon his secretary phoned back, making an appointment for three weeks hence.

I told Chip. He wasn't excited but agreed to go. *With you* he said. *Since you're now running this show.*

126

*

There was urgent homework to be done. We'd long held an option on rural land near the Pennsylvania border. Three major highways converged close to it. And through the property ran a small stream into which we could discharge. But it was a scenic area. A state park wasn't far off, and there was a village nearby. There were bound to be local objections.

I told Bryan Holmes we'd have to call a public meeting. And that he would have to conduct it. That galvanized him. It recalled his teaching experience.

I related my running into Dorothy, and what I'd learned about Senator Reese. Bryan and I were sliding into complementary roles. He counted on me for political and PR matters, while I deferred to his technical knowledge and long familiarity with the plans.

For the public meeting . . . we'll need pictures Bryan said. *Something to show the people.*

He was right, and I at once acted on it. In the Jersey production building there was a visual workshop. There they built models and made artist's renderings of proposed projects. Sometimes the same people worked with the design studio, which had done such a fine job of Chip's convocation booklet. I asked them to drop everything else and make new, beautiful illustrations of how the liquid-waste facility would look. They assumed, I suppose, that I was speaking for Chip. Or maybe they checked with Terry, and she told them to do what I wanted. Also, I engaged a landscape architect and got him to go out and envisage the site. There was the drawing that had been used at the earlier press conference, and some tentative sketches, which Sally Stitsky had given me. But we needed something both accurate and spectacular.

The architect was excellent. After studying the ground he met with Bryan and the visual artist, and they decided the layout. The architect created a kind of rest and picnic area for people driving by. There they would see the clear pipe through which would pass the clean outflow from the plant. And beyond that a decorative pool. Which would double as another holding pond, just in case, before anything went into the stream.

I reported the expenses to Terry, who passed them on to Chip. But he didn't seem to care about what I was spending.

*

The public meeting was called for a week before the appointment with the Senator. I had put notices in the local papers. A printed announcement was distributed by the Post Office. News of the event and the date were periodically broadcast by regional radio. And I had a nearby advertising firm phone everyone in the area.

For a negligible sum, plus cleanup costs, we'd got the use of the public school. On our chosen Friday night the auditorium was packed. We had all the municipal councilors and a mixture of villagers, shopkeepers, tradesmen and small farmers. It was snowing, and there was a heavy smell of wet wool, blue jeans and overalls, boots, damp tuques and baseball caps. The people mostly knew each other and before we began there was a smattering of idle talk, laughter and sometimes dubious thoughts expressed aloud.

A projector, operated by Sally, showed the artist's renderings and the site plan on a large screen. Bryan was terrific, and spoke with true conviction. The evening had the feeling of a town hall meeting, rather than a bill of goods being sold by a big-city outfit. People were plainly impressed. But what swayed them most were our promises. We said that whenever possible local labor would be used in the construction. Steel, cement, lumber and other supplies would all be bought locally. And best of all, the plant would provide some fifty permanent jobs.

*

Senator Reese saved us a trip to Albany. His secretary phoned. On the appointed day, she said, the Senator had to be in the City. He would meet us at the same time, 11 a.m., but at City Hall. Chip merely said okay. He'd been hardly interested when I told him how well the public meeting went. He seemed relieved to be mainly left out of this matter. Most of the time now, when he wasn't at Favorable meetings, he was closeted with Sandy, Squirrel and Williams.

*

Sandy, the new sophisticate, for March break had taken his wife and a school-age niece of hers to the south of France. First, however, he told me, they'd gone to Hungary to see their home town again. They found it covered in soot from a new coal-burning generating station. Sandy was glad to escape a second time. The rudeness of the border guards reminded him that he was merely a minor traitor who'd evaded military service. Afterwards, the welcome capitalism of Cannes was as warm as its sun.

He came back sporting a classy male perfume. For days he could almost be followed by his fragrance. He also returned with a new notion. He was dissatisfied with our official accountants. They wouldn't give him the figures he wanted. He'd tried to have them bend their rules but they'd refused. They were a large international firm with many corporate clients, and much as they

129

valued our work, they weren't dependent on Height. Now Sandy proposed that we buy a smaller but respected accountancy whose three principal partners were all retiring. They were open for a cash offer, he said, because otherwise they would have to wait years to collect the full sum from their succeeding juniors. Chip refused. He said owning our auditors would be too close to a fraud.

Terry told me this. Dispensing her power of providing business secrets, she said she trusted that whatever I heard would stay between us. Implying that we had a pact that was independent of Chip, she turned this intimacy on and off. I knew I was being used in her stewing and loving war with Chip, but sometimes, it seemed, only for empathy. Sometimes she seemed genuinely to want me to understand what she too was going through. *We're both beat* she said. *Every evening he has papers to study. If I try to get him to bed he's irritable. We don't drop off until midnight or later. Then he wakes about four to go to the washroom. After that he usually can't sleep and it keeps me up.*

The high cost of being rich I thought. But that was uncharitable. I didn't really know what was occupying Chip. Also it was a self-brake on my own current ambition, which was causing an excitement that was spreading in me like smokeless fire.

*

The morning we were to meet Senator Reese I took my coat and crossed the court to collect Chip. Terry said *He's on the phone, but you can go in.* I opened the door, and was appalled. Chip was sprawled in his chair, his legs stuck out. He was wearing cowboy boots! And that Western shirt with the string tie. My stomach quaked. I had a sinking sense of disaster. Chip finished his phone call and looked at me.

It's time to go I said, wishing something would prevent it.

*

In the cab we were silent. I stared straight ahead, trying to contain my fears. It took only minutes to City Hall.

There were a few tourists at the entrance. We were directed to a room that was off to the side. It was, I gathered, where the Mayor occasionally met people he didn't care to receive in his office. There was a mahogany desk, paintings and prints on the walls, and several armchairs. While we sat and waited I evoked images of Lil. Anything to avoid seeing Chip's outfit. The gray suit he had on was itself impeccable. But the pink shirt with its scalloped pocket flaps, and that ridiculous tie, and the chiseled orange-brown boots with their pointed toes were stylistic bombast. How could Chip be so absurd? And he was acting strangely. Lounging in his seat, or folding one booted leg across the other, fingering the carved leather.

Following an aide, Reese came in. He apologized for being a few minutes late. Chip and I had stood; introductions were made, hands shaken. The aide, a thin balding man of middle age, took a chair to the side. The Senator sat his more comfortable bulk behind the desk. He was white haired and fair faced. Around his mouth played a perpetual, people-pleasing smile. But the eyes were shrewd. He exuded a sense of certitude. This was a man who had never wanted to go to Washington. Or to take a higher position. He had set his limits and within them plied his power. Governors had come and gone. Reese was everlasting.

Mr. Hope, he said *it's a pleasure to meet you in person. I've seen you, of course, in the papers.*

Likewise Chip said.

You want to discuss this industrial waste facility.

I hadn't told his secretary that. Only that we wanted an appointment.

And you seem the Senator went on *to have made a good impression on the local people.*

Here's what we showed them I said, taking copies from my briefcase.

Reese glanced at the artist's renderings and site plan, and then handed them to his aide. *Yes, I've seen those . . .*

I mentally kicked myself. I should have known that he'd be thoroughly briefed.

It will work Chip said.

Reese held up a hand. *Oh, I don't doubt your technical excellence. Your company isn't new to this state. But gentlemen, there are many things to consider. For two, there's the park and the stream. Our environmentalists have become very sensitive.*

As for the stream, I said *we could put up a testing station. At the least trace of any pollution the outflow from the plant would be automatically shut off.*

Chip slightly knotted his brows at me. This had never been mentioned. I had just thought of it.

That's interesting . . . the Senator said. *But I'm also concerned about the community. Economically it's a depressed area, so the jobs you might provide would be welcome. But you'd also create a lot of truck traffic. Heavy trucks. Passing near the park.*

Senator, I said *there's lots of truck traffic now.*

True, he replied with a small smile *but it's heading all over the state. You'd be bringing it to one spot. There's the noise, and the concentration of exhaust. Not to mention emissions from the plant.*

The plant I said *will be equipped with scrubbers. They'll take out anything objectionable that goes into the stacks.*

And what will you do Reese said *with what's been scrubbed out. With all the waste, for that matter. Where's it going?*

I was silenced. I didn't know. I'd supposed it was somewhere in the plans.

Senator Reese, Chip said suddenly *we have a reputation. We don't do harm. We try to do good.*

Reese said *Your good intentions aren't in question. But . . .*

Senator, Chip said, standing and flushing slightly *we've lighted parts of the world that were dark before. We've kept towns from being flooded. We've built roads, tunnels, bridges, airports to connect people who were cut off. Our plans . . .* he began, and I was afraid he was going to tell about the university. But he paused. *We don't always do things for profit. I think you can trust us.* Then, abruptly, he sat down.

For a few seconds none of us moved. Then Reese scratched his ear. The aide looked down at the papers in his hands. I was both stricken and saddened. Chip's surprising speech hadn't been insincere. Quite the contrary, which is what made it hard to answer. But it was beside the point. Faith was not at issue. What came through clearly was that whatever else he had on his mind, the head of Height wasn't passionately committed to what we were there for. It filled the small room with unease.

The Senator shifted, and charitably, I thought, chose to ignore Chip's outbreak. *Are you* he continued *planning to employ women?*

Oh yes I said. *Yes. Certainly.* Anything at this point.

Well then, a child-care nursery would be useful. He mentioned a few other things, but it was plain he was just making talk, though his aide was taking notes. Then, to conclude this, which evidently to him wasn't going anywhere, he said benignly *The village could also benefit from a library. There's nothing now outside the school.* He rose, and added kindly *It helps to have educated employees.*

*

Returning, Chip leaned back blankly in the cab, as languid as if he'd taken Terry's pills. I cared for him, for whatever was weighing on him, for what he was keeping to himself, but I irritably knew we had failed to make our case. I wanted to believe it was his pointless declaration, and that grotesque getup. I felt resignation seeping in and ambition draining out. By the time we'd said good-bye it was plain that the Senator wasn't about to intervene. At best he might wait and see.

*

To confirm it, a couple of days later I called Dorothy and asked if she could get me a status report. I gave her my phone numbers. *If it's absolutely necessary, is there some way I can reach you after hours?* I said.

I'll call you.

She did, that evening. *I'm afraid* she said *your file is still at the bottom. Did you see Reese?*

Yes, we screwed up. I didn't feel like assessing blame. I thanked her. But that seemed not enough. I was grateful, but also a bit intrigued. She was attractive. *Do you like Albany?* I said.

Not particularly. Professionally it's a dead end.

*

134

The next morning I phoned Jamie McKeown. As far as he knew I was still heading Clearwater. Still an important person. *Well,* he said *bright young lawyers, especially with government experience, are always in demand. I don't have an opening in my own office right now. But leave it with me. I'll see what I can do.*

A day later he called to say Dorothy should phone Coltson and Coltson. The senior Coltson would see her.

*

She was glad of it. They were a big uptown firm.

Call me after your interview I said. Before we rang off she gave me her home phone number.

*

A request had come from another community college. Terry had opened the letter and she handed it to me. *Am I supposed to draft something?* I said.

She smiled evasively. *Show it to Chip.*

When I went in he was reading a report. He shut it and looked up at once. Around his eyes there were more signs of strain. Puffy pouches below the lower lids. But this time he wasn't wearing anything odd, and he seemed youthfully confident, as if he no longer needed the outward trappings. As if something had been accomplished.

He glanced at the invitation.

No. We'll decline. I'm going fishing.

Fishing? I was astonished.

Fishing, or sun bathing or just relaxing. I'm going to Belize.

Belize! Despite my confusion I was conscious of sounding like an echo. Belize was somewhere in central America.

Terry and I will take the plane he said.

The company plane? I paused. *You can't do that.*

Why not? No one will know.

I was incredulous. *Chip, everyone will know!* There was a woman in Sandy's financial group who logged all air flights. The plane didn't move without her making a note of it. Its flying time was charged to one account or another. That the corporate president, whose time was precious, used the plane for short flights, or even long ones when there were business reasons, was understandable. But to fly right across the U.S. and Mexico for purely personal reasons . . . something had changed. I guessed it was whatever he had lately been closeted with Sandy and the financial types about. That I hadn't been privy to. I suppose I felt a bit of resentment, or at least left out, but he was Chip, and I believed in him. Yet I could imagine the murmurs that would result. *It's not right* I said quietly.

18

Nonetheless, he went. For two weeks Mary Lynn sat in Terry's chair. It was during that time Dorothy had her interview. It was a Thursday. She called and I met her at a bar on West 53rd.

How'd it go? I said.

It was a job offer! I'd sent them my resumé, and when Mr. Colt-son saw me, he seemed satisfied.

I should think so I said smiling. She looked great. Like a glowing pale blossom framed by the dark hair and black suit, set off by a single string of pearls. *Are you going to take it?*

Yes. I miss Manhattan. It'll be wonderful to be back. And the starting salary is almost twice what I get now. Thank you so much, Isaac.

You would have done it without me.

Are you kidding? An unwed mother who articled in a small-town office, with only civil service experience. Uh, uh.

You'll have a lot to do. Find a place to live, and a school . . . by the way, where's your son?

I dropped him off on the way down. In Stamford, with my parents.

They're supportive then?

They're resigned now. But not at first. They wouldn't come to my graduation. Even though the loose gown hid my swollen belly.

You didn't think about . . .

An abortion? Sure. Sure. But I thought maybe I was meant to have the child. Like it was my destiny. And I wasn't interested in marrying.

Oh I said. It was a strange mixture of courage and acceptance of fate.

Or maybe it was just apathy. Whatever I seemed like when I was young, that happens to me. Like being stuck in Albany.

I was afraid you might think I was meddling.

No, No! It was just the goose I needed. But being there served its purpose. It's quiet, and I was able to raise my son.

I asked about the father. She said he hadn't been father material. Only a hunk. And she never told him. And didn't know where he was. And didn't care. I must have looked surprised, because she said it had just been one night. Actually several nights. Even in her relatively wild stage, she sometimes fell into an apathetic pattern. That had been one. She said it was best forgotten.

Okay . . . I said slowly. *But we should be celebrating.* We'd each been sipping a glass of white wine. *Shall I order champagne?*

If we're going to do that I need some ballast. I haven't eaten since breakfast.

The bar we were in served only salted peanuts. I paid and we walked south a few blocks, looking for something more suitable. I knew there were plenty of nice places the other way, on 57th, but they were all pretty expensive. I didn't want the cost of this occasion to become excessive. I'd briefly considered charging it to expenses, but then rejected that. With my dreams of affluence dashed, I was again feeling a creeping insecurity.

Dorothy, however, seemed carefree. She almost skipped along beside me. At a crossing, when a car careened around the corner, I put out my arm to stop her. As I dropped my hand it brushed hers. Like a kid, she took hold of my little finger and swung arms with me as we walked on.

Passing a food store, I stopped and stepped back. There were oysters on ice in the window. *How about that?* I said. *Do you like them?*

A bell on the door rang when we went in.

Not only did they have fresh oysters, but crisp crusty bread, dewy butter, salad and fruit. I bought some of each, an oyster knife, paper napkins and two single packs of plastic cutlery. Half a block on there was a wine and spirits store, and we chose a chilled champagne. I wondered if we'd have to picnic on a park bench. But the sun had long set; it was suddenly getting cold and dark.

Come to my hotel Dorothy said.

I hadn't offered to take her to my place. That was Lil's, and I wasn't going to sully it. *Oh, you're staying over?*

I thought I'd go to the Met in the morning. See some art. Maybe some other places, if there's time.

Good luck! I said. *You can spend your life at the Met.*

We took a cab. Her car was in a commercial underground parking space. She had a room in a small hotel on 33rd, near Park. Its front door was thick glass, and the desk clerk looked us over before pressing a button to open it. He particularly scrutinized me, and when satisfied that I wasn't selling myself on the street, lost interest. Nor did he seem to care about our paper bags.

They're used to people bringing in food Dorothy said as we were rising in the cramped, self-operating elevator. *Half their rooms have kitchenettes.*

Hers had only a double bed, a night table, desk, lamp and radio, a television set, a dresser, and two chairs. When we put on the bathroom light some cockroaches scurried down the sink drain.

Ugh . . . Dorothy said.

It's New York I replied. *You can't help it. Like mice in the country.* They were always coming into my little house.

Dorothy closeted herself in the bathroom and took off her pearls, suit, silk blouse and shoes. She came out in a gray woolen skirt and pink sweater. I'd meanwhile covered a chair with a towel and one of our paper shopping bags split flat. There I shucked the still-cold oysters, leaving them on the half shell. The champagne we poured into tumblers from the bathroom. We ate with our fingers, tearing off chunks of the tasty bread, scooping up butter as from a dip. Dorothy was ravenous. After we'd made a pile of used napkins she lay back on the bed with a long satisfied sigh. *Oh, I'm so full* she said. *And more than a little tipsy. Tomorrow, I'm starting to diet.*

From where I sat on the bed's edge, I saw no need of that. She straightened out, pulling her skirt tight, her head at rest on the pillow.

C'mon she said. *Join me.*

I slipped off my shoes and jacket, loosened my tie, and stretched out near her. She was warm and faintly scented. Despite the food in my belly, I could still feel the sear of defeat, the collapse of my inflated dreams. Dot — she had just again become that in my mind — seemed like soothing balm. Our hands moved together. We locked fingers. Like, I remembered, I'd once done with Lil. But my head turned to Dot's. Slowly our lips met. It was sweet.

Dot sighed and nestled closer. *It's been a long time . . .*

I could feel her breath on my cheek. The sensation, the smell, was pleasant. *Aren't men always after you?*

I haven't dated. And it's not martyrdom. I felt if I was going to be a mother, I should devote myself to that. And I think I've done quite a good job.

I sighed too. I was thinking of Lil. And Kristen, Dawn, Ginny. When I had been with Lil the night before her familiar presence had seemed assurance against disaster, that everything at Height would go on as before. But now, with Dot, the fresh experience made reality inescapable. The arm I had put around her after we'd kissed must have loosened.

She gripped it. *You aren't married, are you?*

No . . .

Then who are we betraying?

I hesitated. *Well, there is someone. A woman at work.*

Oh. She shifted away slightly. *A woman. Not a girl?*

No. She has three children. Daughters. Two older, and one just a little younger than yours. Your son . . .

She single?

I nodded.

So she's what — separated? Divorced?

Yes. The latter.

She got any money?

No. None.

Hmm. Do you always prey on vulnerable women?

I separated myself and sat up. Then swung my legs off the bed. I felt — stabbed. And a little bitter. But it had some sting of truth. *What chance would I have with the other kind?* I said, somewhat annoyed. *Like you, at law school.*

She regarded me with her dark eyes. Then reached out and touched the side of my shirt. *I don't know. You didn't try very hard.*

The idea that I might have succeeded was laughable. But the thought was a lure. Moreover, now that I'd spoken of Lil, that weighed less on me.

Dot was stroking my side. The touch was at odds with her words. Soon the sanction of need filled our space. I turned toward her. Her eyes were full on me, her body bundled for taking. I lowered myself.

We can stop now she said.

For answer I kissed her again.

*

The next morning was gray. The corner of sky I could see by lifting the blind near my bed looked flat, dull, featureless. I felt as leaden.

I had left Dot sleeping. Now I was sorry, and not, that it had happened. I'd used her. Stupidly had tried to bury my disappointed ambition. By comparison her use of me had been pure.

Merely a suppressed want of closeness. Yet she'd been, like her kisses, sweet. I wondered whether to phone her, or send something. But we'd only be embarrassed if we saw each other again. Yet I had a sneaking satisfaction that my sexual prowess hadn't diminished. I hoped I hadn't made her pregnant. But she'd whispered that it wasn't her time.

19

At the office I started upstairs, to see Bryan. To say that until we had the permit there really wasn't much more for me to do. That might ease me out with what respect could be mustered.

Sandy was near the top of the stairs. He was hidden by Williams, who was leaning back against the handrail. There was a third person too: Squirrel. He was speaking.

I wasn't in the mood, as a failure, to encounter the lords of finance. They hadn't seen me, so I retreated a few steps, and around the corner of the stairs. I meant to wait until they'd moved on. Though I was hidden, I was right under them and could hear clearly what they were saying. There must have been no one around them, or with Chip away they were feeling full of themselves, because they didn't bother to lower their voices.

Squirrel was declaring *I'd like to be one of those pilots. He'll have them in the same hotel where he's staying. It's a paid vacation, first class. Christ, I hate to think what'll it all cost.*

Williams added *Well, there won't be much more of it. We'll get rid of those perks.*

Sandy said *It's not his fault that he thinks he's God. Ve let him, muddled as he is. Besides, he can't add.*

They all laughed.

I was shocked. I'd expected some disapproval, but not contempt. I'd never heard Chip referred to like that, with mockery and derision. I backed away and returned to my desk. I was shaking.

*

The next night was painful too. I felt I had to tell Lil about Dorothy. At first I meant not to say anything, but then hiding it from her seemed worse than the act itself.

Come here I said. Lil sat down, smoothing the apron across her lap. We were side by side. It was something we'd rarely done. The couch had mainly served as a cot for the kids.

There's something I must tell you.

My tone turned her to look sharply at me.

A night ago, I was . . . with another woman.

Lil's face crumpled. Tears splashed onto the hands she'd raised to her mouth. She bent away, sobbing. I suddenly felt that whatever else went on, I had violated something precious to her. Her hair was still up. I looked down at the pale stray strands on her neck. I loved them. I loved the back of her head, her shoulders, limbs, those perfect legs. I desperately wanted not to lose them.

She was still crying when I tentatively touched her temple. I thought she might thrust me away. Instead she turned and with wrathful sarcasm spit out *I know, you were carried away. You couldn't help it!*

I could. But I'm so sorry to have hurt you. It won't happen again. Never.

She didn't reply. But she was no longer weeping. I undid the strings of her apron. Then the button at the back of her skirt. Bit by bit, saying nothing, one small fastening at a time, she let me undress her. With only acquiescence on her part, we made love right there. Then she got up, gathered her clothing, went into the bedroom and shut the door. Dinner congealed in the stove. I slept where I was, on the couch.

*

Monday morning Chip was back. Terry was at her desk, looking slightly tanned. I told her it was urgent, but she blocked access to Chip. He was on the phone she said, and wasn't seeing anyone. Then he was closeted with Sandy. When I looked in again just after five, he had left. In frustration I thought of phoning, but decided not to. It had to be said in person.

The next day he was in session with Sandy, Williams and Squirrel. The three of them came and went, but I wasn't allowed in between meetings. I seethed but I had to contain my impatience. At last, just before five, I was admitted.

Chip looked the same, but less fatigued. Hardly any sign of sun. But his gaze was direct, the vagueness gone.

Chip, I said *Sandy and his people. Don't trust them. You can't trust them.*

He frowned.

I mean it. They don't respect you. Please, don't trust them.

He stared at me. *Iz, I'm doing what I have to, to realize the plan.*

The plan? You mean for the university? You're taking money from Favorable?

We can't take money from Favorable he said impatiently. *It would take forever. We need a big chunk all at once. It was arranged*

144

before I went away. The boys are just completing the details.

But you can't trust them I said.

Why? Have you any evidence?

I heard them. They were making fun of you. They don't respect you!

Well, that's your opinion.

My dismay became charged with anger. Why would he doubt me, when I — as I felt at that moment — had never doubted him. Wrenching irritation reared between us.

Please — he said. He looked at, and opened a report lying before him. And his eyes stayed there.

I'd never been dismissed like that. Dumbfounded, I retreated to Terry, who was tidying up. I said *Maybe you can help. He wouldn't listen when I told him not to trust Sandy.*

She regarded me warily. *He has to . . .*

*

The following day I was told Chip wasn't seeing anyone. No messages were left for me. There was no talk of speeches, of plans, nothing. For something to do I was reduced to going through my desk, discarding old notes, drafts, scribbled pieces of paper kept for reasons I couldn't now recall.

*

That night I asked Lil what was going on. She replied that Sandy was repeatedly in and out of the court. Beyond that she didn't know. Or wouldn't say.

She'd come at the usual time, broiled chicken in the usual way. Routine was a strong compulsion. Or perhaps she didn't want her daughters to know that anything was different.

But behind her regular activities she was guarded. Her eyes, normally a clear pale blue, were veiled with a film of pain. She stripped, came to bed and into my embrace. But without the typical warm tenderness.

Afterwards, perversely feeling deprived, I lay awake and thought about work, my thoughts seesawing. If I'd kept my mouth shut, Chip might have revealed what he was doing. That it was for the cause I was confident. And I'd had no role because I wasn't needed. No doubt the fewer who knew, the better.

Or maybe Chip didn't want to be reminded of his part in bungling the Clearwater business. Indeed I'd heard from Bryan that, seeing no progress, the Alabama firm was again threatening to pull out. There was a clause in the contract that allowed it, making Height pay a penalty. Plainly, Sandy wasn't bothered. And Chip was too taken up with a grander idea.

On the other hand, he couldn't do everything himself. He'd indicated it was a financial matter, and finances were the affair of Sandy and his cohorts. But I felt certain they weren't to be trusted. By insisting on that I'd put myself in the way.

*

On Thursday Chip was out all morning. Then once more he was too busy. I felt I had to stand by. I telephoned the girl in the Queens' apartment and told her I was canceling that day's session, and for them all to get their final reports ready. She said she'd spread the word. Late afternoon I phoned Chip from my office. Terry told me he couldn't take my call. There was no point in venturing into the court. I'd only be humiliated, because it had become evident that Chip's door was firmly closed — to me.

Without Chip, I realized, I had no status. My standing in Height had suddenly been stripped away. Personnel had no listed position for a president's assistant, let alone a freelance writer.

On Friday I didn't go in. I phoned Terry and said I would wait for a call. By four forty-five none had come. I wasn't wanted. With a deep sigh I dialed Lil's desk number. *Just listen . . .* I said. I told her I was going to the country house. I didn't know for how long.

She simply said *All right.*

20

Ed Bennet, Connelly's man, came by. It was the beginning of my second week of exile, on a dismal, dripping day. His small black truck approached up the drive.

*

After the interview with my wealthy neighbor, I'd met Ed again at the local welding shop. The pivot of my stove hob, already cracked, had broken, and I took it to be fixed. The shop was a little way outside the village, on what was otherwise a farm. Several pickups were parked outside, and I thought I recognized Ed's.

But the cavernous shop was deserted. I walked through it, past a big drum roller and a six-furrow plow being repaired. Tools littered the long workbench. Cut-off plates of steel stood against one wall. The concrete floor was swept clean, but dark from ingrained oil and grime. At the back, a corridor was lined with bins of nuts and bolts. Then a crude office, also with no one in it. But from a room beyond came voices. The door was shut, and on it a sign read: The Rusty Nail. I knocked.

Hello! someone said. Inside, slumped in worn armchairs, were Ed Bennet, another farmer-looking fellow, and in the center a big man in stained coveralls whom I took to be the welder. They were all holding paper cups of coffee, and its warm smell permeated the small room, which was decorated with posters of old cars and half-dressed women. I greeted Ed.

Put that down the proprietor said. *Take your weight off.* I sat in the single empty chair. *How d'yuh want it?* the big man said, pouring another cup from a percolator. He added a spoonful of sugar, then bottled milk taken from an old frig. And stirred the whole with a blackened, rusty, four-inch nail.

There were cursory introductions, as if they already knew who I was. I guess I'd previously been the subject of gossip. Then they went on talking about bad crops, local bureaucracy, and with sly smiles, about who was currently bedding who. I guessed this coffee time was sacred, much like a religious service. They obviously knew I was a Jew, and had probably talked about it, but face to face it didn't seem to matter. We were dressed alike, in that we all wore worn clothes, boots and baseball caps. There was a sense of comradery, even of community.

Finally the welder said *Let's see that hob.* It took him about sixty seconds to V the break, about the same to weld it, and hardly more to grind the weld smooth. The others were hanging around.

I asked how much I owed him.

Oh, buy me a coffee sometime.

But you just bought me one.

Well, I'll get yuh next time.

In that spirit I asked them all, especially Ed, to drop in whenever they liked.

*

We sat and sipped tea. Ed had slipped off his rubber galoshes at the side door. Now he had his hobnailed boots hooked on the rung of a chair. The kettle was softly singing, steaming on the stove's repaired hob. The kitchen was cozy. Outside it was warm, even for late winter, but the wet had a raw feeling.

Ed told me he lived just three miles up the road. He'd been raising turkeys when the birds became diseased. Most had died, the rest couldn't be sold. He'd been in deep debt to the feed company. It would have meant bankruptcy, losing even the land and their home, if Connelly hadn't stepped in and settled the feed bill. Since then Ed had worked for him full time. The salary was divided; some cash to live on, the balance against the loan.

Do you still farm?

Oh, keep a few head. Herefords. Enough so it's a farm fer taxes.

At Connelly's he kept the place in order, and did some carpentry. *They're always changin' something.*

And your wife? I guessed she was the maid who'd shown me in.

Dorie's there when they are. Othe'wise she goes in once a week, t' dust an' that. Her limp, he told me, was from a tractor loader that had fallen on her, leaving a break that hadn't set right. What she earned helped them get by, though she didn't like being a servant. The Connellys, he said, were away now, somewhere in Europe. Probably wouldn't be back till spring. *Anyways, they got a house in Boston.*

Where's the money from?
I dunno. Family. Banks. Like that.
They seem awfully rich.
Ed smiled. *I guess they aint hurtin'.*

*

Thursday I went down for the final think tank session. From the apartment in Queens I phoned Mary Lynn and asked her to check my desk. She reported only routine memos.

This time I hadn't bothered with a business suit. The young people were rather pleased to see me in boots and jeans, work shirt and sweater. Perhaps it made me less imposing. I'd leaned heavily on them at our last meeting, insisting that they make submissions for the summing-up report. As well as last week, telling the girl I phoned to remind them. Seven had theirs ready in typed form. Neil's was his typical series of abstract drawings, meant, he said, to represent the evils of society. Of the two who hadn't finished, one pleaded the flu. The second, jilted by his girlfriend, said he'd been too hurt to think straight. I could somewhat sympathize with that. Both promised to get their papers in soon.

Perhaps to make up for their negligence, those two were vociferous in the general discussion. However there was basic agreement. Collectively, the group had definite grievances. About the way people in America were kept from realizing its great dream, about the way the population at large was employed and governed. They truly felt much was wrong. But they lacked sensible solutions. The halfway, hodgepodge methods that were available for reform only disheartened them.

There had been talk of a wrap party, though that had died from a feeling of futility. Instead, after I'd formally ended the session and thanked them, and they thanked Height, we had beer and cookies and chatted about what each would do next. One was leaving in the morning. The others who didn't live in town would soon follow. Despite the conviviality, it was a rather sad ending to what had begun as a bold experiment.

*

The two late reports were turned in and Mary Lynn mailed them to me. They didn't essentially change what I had already written as the formal wind-up paper. I tried to make it as positive as possible, but however nicely I put it the conclusion was inescapable: the young were not much wiser than we who supported them.

The weather was mild. Most snow had melted. In sunny spots green shoots were poking up. There seemed to be a cessation of all movement, a benign stillness in which I could hear my pen scratch. I felt totally without pressure, apart from the anxiety of banishment.

*

Then Friday evening the phone rang. It was Lil! I was thrilled. But she said only *Something's going on at work.*

What?

I don't know. There are rumors. You'd better come down.

If I come tomorrow, can we get together as usual?

No, I'm sorry. You said you didn't know when you'd be back. I'm taking the girls to a Beatles concert.

Wow! Who's paying for the tickets?

Philip gave them to me.

Marcoux again. I was relieved. Though I had no right, after hurting her. It would hardly be unfair if she slept with someone else. Yet I hated the idea. The thought of alien fingers moving over that familiar skin, over those breasts, breathing that clean scent, rankled me.

It was an added unease spurring my return.

*

Before nine on Monday morning I was at the office. But a little later, when I looked into the court, all the vice-president's doors were open. A special directors' meeting was already in progress. Mary Lynn, in Terry's place, told me it had started fifteen minutes earlier. Going out through the court, I glimpsed Lil's backside as she stood at her boss's filing cabinet. That nice bottom and those lovely legs. And her tenderness, so needed. I went weak with yearning.

That instant of pathos, converted to purpose, carried me up the central stairs. I meant to see Bryan, but he wasn't there. Sally said he'd called in sick. Her face and tone were troubled, tense.

Sally, I said *what's happening. I've been away —*

You mean Sandy?

What about him? I know nothing —

Suddenly she dropped her defenses. Her words came in a burst. *He's been running around shouting that were being sold out to the Jews!*

Wha — ?

Well, not actually shouting. But that's what he's been telling everyone. I heard him with Bryan. He didn't say all that to me, but he wanted my proxy. I've a few shares too. He's been gathering proxies, here and in Jersey. And his guys went to Philly and Pittsburgh.

The voting trust! It was what Chip had been afraid of. I took Sally's hand, grateful that she was reacting in her Jewish self, or simply as an outraged, decent woman.

If I hadn't stopped for that I'd have run into Sandy at the head of the stairs. He was hurrying down, along with Squirrel and Williams. Their color was high. In his hand Sandy clutched a sheaf of papers.

If they were aware of me behind them, they didn't care. They rounded the stairs, crossed to and through the foyer, into the inner court, and before Mary Lynn could cry out, crashed into Chip's office.

Ve're taking over! Sandy cried. *Ve're buying you out!*

All eyes round the long table were on him. I had time only to see Chip's open mouthed astonishment before Williams firmly shut the door.

*

I had expected shouts, disorder, chaos. Mary Lynn and I, too surprised to speak, had stared at each other. Then at the closed door. Beyond it we heard only the murmur of voices. No one came out. Terry's phone had rung several times, and Mary Lynn had answered as if it were business as usual. She'd had no choice, but was soon choking back tears.

In the court, the girls were wide eyed. Going past them, I shrugged. Lil's glance, just flashed at me, was full of fellow feeling. I felt like taking her in my arms.

From my office I phoned Mary Lynn and asked to be told the moment the meeting broke up. Then I sat still, staring at my surroundings. The elegant little room resembled a museum piece. The objects I'd chosen with care, or lightheartedness, like the Chinese birds, were alike in seeming indifferent, unconcerned. I felt stifled, frantic and futile.

Hours later, when Mary Lynn finally called, she said they were already out. I was furious, but I guessed she'd been distracted by Terry, or whatever else had taken place. I started across, and met in the foyer, coming out of the court, Lil's boss. He had on his overcoat and was carrying a briefcase.

Paul — I said *may I speak with you?*

Always polite, he paused. The girl at the desk looked up. She was a temp. The usual receptionist had left to be with her mother, who was dying of cancer, in Cleveland.

Paul said *Well, I'm catching a train* —

I'll ride down with you.

There were others in the elevator. I had to wait till we were at the curb. The street was its usual midday turmoil. Crowds and clamor. People trying to cross. A cabbie, eyeing us, slowed. Paul hesitated, but shook his head.

I was surprised he said. *But it's not so bad. The price they're offering is fair. And we're all getting older. I'll discuss it with my wife, of course. But I think she'll be glad to have me retire.* Then he raised a finger as another cab approached.

*

When I returned, Chip's office was empty. And smelled of smoke. The long table was littered with scratch pads, pens, goblets, water glasses, coffee cups, and cigarette stubs on plates. Chip and Terry were gone. Mary Lynn didn't know where. Most of the vice-presidents too had dispersed. Bruce Hardwick's door was closed. Vaughan was at his desk, but talking on the phone.

Then I remembered, too late, that the building had a back

exit. Reached through a corridor from the lobby, it was beside the delivery dock. Howard, on his shuttle runs, went in and out that way. Cabs, when ordered, sometimes came there.

I couldn't call Terry's apartment. Chip hadn't been talking to me for over two weeks. There seemed nothing I could do. So I went home.

*

It was nearly nine o'clock when my phone rang. The TV western I'd been dully watching, without sound, was coming to an end. I switched off the set and picked up the receiver.

Iz — it was Chalkley! *Chip is here at my place.* His tone was positively gloating. With a rush I realized the extent of the disaster. *He wants to see you.*

*

When I walked into Chalkley's living room, Chip was sunk in an armchair. He had a drink in his hand. His blue eyes had paled and were glassy. Not, I guessed, from alcohol.

Kate, the daughter, had let me in. Chalkley and his wife stood on either side of Chip's chair. Guarding their prize possession. But a glance at each showed contrary feelings. Melissa was clearly upset. Chalkley was trying to be serious, but triumph kept breaking through. He held a bottle of brandy, ready to refresh Chip's drink. Also sitting there, with a glass, was Jamie McKeown, the lawyer.

Iz, Chalkley said *Chip would like you to write the press release. About the changeover. It's very sensitive stuff. We have to watch the stock price.*

155

I looked to Chip. He stared blankly at me.

Jamie will take you to Sandy and the others Chalkley said. *They'll tell you what they want it to say.* When I didn't respond he added *That's why Chip sent for you.*

If you don't mind, I said *I'd like to hear it from him.* As I regarded Chip's reduced state, I mostly felt pity. A tender, loving pity. It was the unlikeliest feeling I'd expected to have.

His pale eyes rose, but didn't quite meet mine. He just nodded.

*

I'd come by cab. McKeown had his car. For a while we drove in silence. Gleams of light from the street lamps shot through. Crossing the bridge, lights on the girders, flashing by, kept pace with the rhythmic clatter of the road plates.

Where are we going? I said.

To Williams' house.

Where'd they get the money for this?

I'm not sure. I suppose from the same people who supplied it for Favorable.

I let that sink in. Then asked *Who're you acting for?*

The new group.

I turned to him. *It didn't take you long to change sides.*

Iz, he said, looking straight ahead *there isn't another lawyer in New York who would do differently.*

*

To contain my dismay and anger, I thought about the press release. I never wrote complete fabrications — that I'd have refused. But I too had shaded facts in many ways, resulting in half lies. We were all liars, all playing roles. Like with Clearwater, when I'd seen myself as a corporate hotshot. And Chip, how could his dream of doing good have collapsed so easily? As if he'd been playing a part from which some of the script had been surprisingly snatched away.

But his performance had been motivated by truth. I believed that. And there was honesty, at least some, in my own. And maybe the play wasn't over yet. Even if these vultures we were going to were dragging down the curtain.

*

We drew up to a brownstone in the east eighties. Williams, it seemed, had the ground floor. The conspirators were crowded in the dining room around the remains of food and drink. Towering over the rest was Bruce Hardwick. Of course! They'd got him with the promise of being the new president. How long had he been boring from within? And Peter Noel, keenly eager to have his slice of pie. And his beautiful so-called assistant, looking a bit lost. What had she been promised? Or was she there only to swell Peter's share? Lyall Bishop was shuffling papers. Squirrel was smoking a cigar, while Williams irritably motioned back a strained woman peeking from the kitchen. Probably his wife. There were people I didn't know. Maybe the money men. And Sandy, who quickly took charge.

Ve have to have this tomorrow. He was flushed, his accent thicker than usual.

Okay. I suppose you want it . . .

Short. Very careful. Isaac, no flourishes. That meant no funny business. He could guess where I stood. *I tink it should say . . .*

157

Everyone started talking.

The gist of it was that by amicable agreement the Board of Height had decided to retire to make way for younger men. Continuity would be provided by Hardwick, who would stay on as the new head. It was to seem the most natural evolution.

Ve release it ven the exchange closes.

You'll have it I said.

*

Leaving them, I walked, trying to have the night air cool and clear me, but it didn't. At 5th I caught a cab. It was close to 2.00 o'clock when I entered my apartment. I knew I wouldn't sleep, so I decided to do the draft. But I felt so alone. I longed for Lil. Not now, at this hour, I told myself. Then I dialed.

The ring woke her. *No matter* she said.

I wished I was with her. Instead I related what I'd seen and heard. And about McKeown.

Apple-cheeked little bastard Lil said.

*

The next morning I was in the office just after nine. I left two sealed copies of the draft with Terry, one for Mary Lynn to take up to Sandy. I didn't want to see him. If he wasn't in he'd be looking for it soon enough. Then I sat at my desk, wondering what to do next.

Chip came to the door. He was dressed to go out. He looked downcast but otherwise recovered from last night. *Will you come with me?* he said. It was a request, rather than an order.

I got my coat and we went down and into a cab.

It sped up the west parkway. Since giving the driver directions,

Chip had said nothing. We were silent all the way past the Cloisters. I recalled my first outing with Lil and the girls. That had seemed, and was, the start of something marvelous. Now everything was surrounded by uncertainty.

I stared at Chip, but his brooding profile provided no clue. We were coming round the park. The driver had a map beside him; his eyes flitted between it and the road signs. Finally, on a spur leading to only a single property, he pulled up before high concrete pillars flanking a driveway. The huge iron gates were open.

This it?

Chip nodded, and the cab went round an inner circle and stopped at the steps of a large, vaguely-Tudor house.

The door was opened by a trim maid in black. She had on a starched white headband and a small apron. *Good morning, Mr. Hope* she said.

Chip mumbled a good morning. She took our coats and hung them in a deep hall closet, with a thick paneled door that was darkish brown. Walnut, I thought. The walls of the corridor were wainscoted in the same material. Above that they were of a light orange color and hung with scenic pictures. We were led to a conference table in a room lined with portraits. From all four sides the framed figures of men regarded us.

Who are they? I said.

The past presidents of Salustin Steel answered a stocky young man just coming in. He looked youngish, perhaps early thirties. Built like a football player. Broad, ruddy face, as if from stamina and good health. Following him was a tall leaner fellow, more scholarly looking, and obviously older. When he sat across from us I could see a small black skullcap, fastened to his dark hair by a bobby pin. The other's light red hair was bare.

The maid quietly brought in a coffee service. Then quietly left, closing the door behind her.

In a crushed voice, Chip said *How's your mother?*

She'll be okay the younger man replied. *She's upstairs, resting.*

I want her to understand Chip said, and he was pleading *that I knew nothing about this. All along I believed my people were negotiating in good faith.*

The younger man stared at him for a moment, and then said *Well, we're out of it.* He was standing, pouring the coffee. He pushed two filled cups across the table to Chip and me.

Sitting beside him, the other said *I will tell mother.* He seemed more personal, more concerned with being conciliatory.

I hope, with all my heart . . . Chip said *that none of this will reflect on your good name.*

The younger man's eyes crinkled. Almost with amusement he said *Mr. Hope, we have nearly a hundred million in cash to protect our good name. I think you should be worrying about yours.*

No one had touched their coffee.

What we don't understand, the older brother said in a kinder tone, leaning a little toward Chip *is your priorities. You stipulated so strongly that the engineering company had to be sold back to its employees. We had no objection to that, because basically we wanted only to diversify through Favorable. But now, if this turnaround, this treachery goes through, what will happen to the engineering firm? Won't it be placed in peril?*

Chip hung his head.

We're just curious the younger one said.

Chip didn't answer. He seemed incapable.

Silence hung heavy.

I hesitated. I hadn't been introduced, but my position as a

kind of companion to Chip seemed assumed. At last I said *I think Mr. Hope feels that if the world is like this, he wants no part of it.* It wasn't a satisfactory answer, but out of courtesy the brothers seemed to accept it.

They escorted us to the hall closet. The maid came to help us with our coats. The two said good-bye and turned back.

*

A local cab had somehow been called. It was waiting when we came out. Chip, still silent, sank into his seat. The blue Hudson flashed by beyond the trees.

Why are you letting this happen? I said.

Chip said despondently *What can I do?*

Fire them! You're still president. Fire Sandy and the others. All of them!

No . . . There'd be a proxy fight.

So what? You'd win it. Most of the engineers will reverse their votes. I wasn't sure they could, but the monstrosity, the injustice of the takeover was overwhelming.

He barely shook his head.

Chip! I cried. *You've done so much — And what about the university? You can still do it!*

He shut his eyes, as if to take in the entire past. Then he said earnestly *I once . . . designed a check valve. It was . . . not bad.* And with that he sank back into silence.

*

Height's bank, only blocks from the office, supplied a long boardroom. It was filled with lawyers. One or more represented each party to the transaction. None of the principals were present.

I went because I wanted to watch this calamity to the end. No one had asked me to, nor did anyone acknowledge my presence. Sitting in a corner, I was in McKeown's sight, but I might just as well have been invisible.

My thoughts were heavy. But for the stab in the back, this could have been the signing with Salustin. That family, I'd found out, had owned the steel company for decades. Their plants were in Pittsburgh. Height had built one. Chip had known the father and had attended his funeral.

The lawyers went down the list of vice-presidents. Bruce Hardwick alone was omitted. There was some disagreement, but only about the odd word. The terms had been set in advance. Most received about two and a half million dollars. Chip's compensation came to almost four million. I was surprised it wasn't more. For such a large business, the silver seven hadn't owned that much. And I was surprised to hear Mrs. Teresa Ollinsen named for a thousand shares. That gave her almost ninety grand.

*

I'm fireproof Chip said. He was packing the few personal items that had stood on a sideboard in his office. Putting them into a cardboard box. One was a picture of his children.

Well, I'm not. I was just becoming aware of what this would mean for me.

*

And indeed the next morning, when Bruce moved into Chip's chair, his first acts were to sell the airplane and cancel the lease on Chip's apartment. The next was brought to me by Sandy's assistant. Smirking slightly, Lyall said my services were no longer required.

I could submit a bill for the period ending the previous day.

Bruce's secretary had taken over Terry's desk. Mary Lynn was given the receptionist's job, and sat there in tears. I left without seeing Lil.

*

It was a Wednesday, and that night she told me Williams had settled into her boss's office. Sandy, of course, was in Bruce's. They were the only two offices, other than Chip's, with windows on the Street.

I won't work for those people Lil said.

What will you do?

She paused, then said *I'm moving to Hawaii.*

Beneath my sharp surprise was a sense of penalty, of the delayed, dire, bitter pill. I managed to muster *How come?*

My father sold his Coca-Cola shares. He started buying them when he got his first commission. He said this was a good time to cash in. With the money my parents bought another apartment, on Maui, near a beach. They meant to rent it to anyone, but in a surge of family solidarity they offered it to me.

It was a lot to absorb. *What about the girls?*

They don't want to go, to leave friends and school. But they'll soon become excited about it.

She was cool and collected. She cooked our typical dinner. We went to bed and made love. I didn't know it would be for the last time.

*

Lil finished the week at Height and left a few days later. I'd spoken to her on the phone. I wanted to help with the packing,

163

drive them to the airport, anything. She said it wasn't necessary, as they were taking only suitcases. Her furniture and household goods were all being given to neighbors. I begged for some kind of farewell, but she replied that she was too busy.

Well, my love . . . I'd never said that before. *I hope it will be good.*

Oh, it will! I'll be living by the sea.

21

With her gone, my apartment appeared shabby. Almost everything was scuffed, scratched, stained. Only the bed linen was pristine. And the suits, shirts, shoes I no longer had reason to wear. And Lil's apron, which she hadn't taken. She had brought it, that last time, freshly washed and pressed. I held it to my face, hoping for her perfume. Some scent, I thought, remained. But it was very faint.

I was lonely without Lil. Her warm company two nights a week had freed me. Now I was beset by a kind of constant brooding, fed by my having fundamentally nothing to do. I tried the novels I'd always meant to read, but my mind soon drifted. I thought about calling Dorothy, but shrank from it, mainly out of shame. But also because the circumstances of that one occasion couldn't be reproduced. Then I'd been a benefactor. Now I was merely an unemployed bum.

*

I imagined hanging around the Press Club, where I might hear of an opening on some paper. But I didn't care to hobnob, drink and trade empty stories. I'd become a loner, or more of one than ever, and for the time being I rather liked it. There was still some money in the bank. However, with the rent I paid in the city, and my parking and car expenses, and more monthly mortgage payments for the country house, I'd soon be stripped bare.

*

Of Height I knew only what I read in the papers. I'd sent my summary of the young peoples' year to Hardwick, with no response. I didn't know whether it had been released. The media had more exciting things to report.

Sandy had become president of Favorable. Then he managed to have Favorable buy Height. After that he retired both Hardwick and Peter Noel, albeit with settlements on which they could spend the rest of their lives wondering what happened. Noel's planners he simply let go. The Clearwater project was cancelled. Whole sections of Height were sold off, including the baseball team and the Pittsburgh and Philly offices. The New Jersey production staff was reduced to half and part of the building leased to a factory temporarily producing pennants and other doodads for the forthcoming November election.

Finally Sandy maneuvered the voting trust into using employee share funds to buy back what was left of Height. The senior engineer who succeeded Hardwick took over a firm reduced to a framework. They moved from Wall Street and relocated on the West Side in a much smaller space.

*

Spring became summer. With little to keep me in the city, I'd been mostly at the country house. My only nighttime companion was again the radio. The news was all about primaries and polls. The President, running for a second term, wasn't doing well. I thought of offering to write for him, but concluded that Cole wouldn't want me.

*

It was a clear crisp day. Leaves were beginning to fall, along with cones and short sharp needles from the evergreens. Occasional gusts swirled them along the ground.

I was carrying rocks, adding to a stone boundary wall I'd started building. It was pointless, really, and done only for the satisfaction of having something to occupy me, because I had only days left. There wasn't enough in my bank account to meet next month's mortgage payment. I'd already spoken to Connelly and he'd offered to cover my previous property costs, plus a thousand dollars for improvements. The Jeep I'd advertised for sale. Between the two those funds would keep me for at least a year. Long enough to settle into sensible work.

There was a boulder, too heavy to tip over, that I was inching along with a steel bar. I was taking a break to catch my breath when a call came. The voice on the phone was vague. Twice I said *Who is it, please?*

It was Chip! He asked if he could come up.

Of course! I cried. *I'd be delighted.*

*

He arrived by himself, driving a Buick. It was a late model, but already looked dusty and worn. He got out awkwardly, with slow movements. A brief flush of greeting momentarily lightened his vacant expression. When we shook hands he gazed at me with pale eyes, the pupils sort of whitish. Zombie — was my immediate, chilling impression.

How's Terry? I said.

Okay. We're married.

Married! I didn't know you'd divorced.

In Mexico. That's where we've been. His hair was whiter. The face, though more lined, was still handsome. Something like a feeble grin flitted across it. *I got a Mexican divorce. We were married there.*

I wondered whether that was legal in the U.S. But it was none of my business.

Chip helped with the big rock. He seemed glad of a manual task. With both of us pushing, we managed to roll it into place.

*

For supper I made scrambled eggs and salad. I couldn't do more, because except for a few tins, that was all I had. Chip had brought a bottle of rosé and we drank the mild pink wine during our meal. Chip sat where Terry had. If she had told him about that night I was sure she'd fudged it. In any case, it seemed unimportant now.

So what are you going to do? I said. *With all your experience . . .*

The remark was spontaneous. But prompting it was the considered prospect that he'd snap out of this slump and start some endeavor that might involve me. He was, after all, only fifty-five, with money, a great reputation and an intact good name. I was feeling some of my old regard. His coming here was certainly a sign of friendship, or at least of friendliness. Then it occurred to me that there might be no one else to whom he felt he could go.

I'm going to have surgery Chip said. *There's a prostate problem. Cancer.*

I was startled, but he added *They say it's at an early stage. Not too serious.*

When? I said. *When is this going to happen?*

Soon, I think. They're doing some more tests.

I wanted to ask if Anne knew, but set that thought aside. Despite my regard for her, as I looked at her onetime husband much of my previous respect, admiration and fondness for him came over me. Such essential goodness, I felt, must prevail. Any notion of my own benefit fled. I wanted only that he be whole and well and — yes, happy. *You'll let me know?*

He nodded.

At his car, saying good-bye, I took his proffered hand in both of mine. Then I leaned over and kissed him on the cheek.

He said *Thank you*. Ostensibly for the hospitality. But, really, I felt, for the gesture.

*

I waited a week, then another. By then my time at the country house had expired and I'd come back permanently to the city. But there had been no word from Chip. I rang Terry's apartment. If he was recuperating, I wanted to visit. To take flowers, or something like an exotic tea, or reading matter. A recorded phone company voice said the number was no longer in service.

Puzzled and alarmed, I looked up Dr. Baird in the directory. His receptionist took my name and number. Two hours later he called back.

Doctor, I used to work with Mr. Hope.

Yes, he said *I know who you are.*

Can you tell me, how is he? Has he had the operation yet?

There was a pause. *He's dead.*

What! Chip? It was incredible. *What happened? What went wrong?*

Nothing. I spoke to the surgeon. The operation was flawless. Unfortunately, Mr. Hope died the next morning.

When was that?

It was three days ago. There was a cremation.

But how is this possible? Someone must have screwed up!

Look, he said, his voice hardening slightly *any surgery is an assault on the system. To withstand that, there has to be a will to live.*

*

Staggered, I went to Chip and Terry's apartment building. I asked for Mrs. Ollinsen, or Mrs. Hope.

The concierge said *She's left.*

You mean gone away? Or moved out?

He was middle aged, and stolid. He stared at me stonily. *I'm sorry, we don't give out personal information.*

I'm not a bill collector! I said. *This isn't anything legal. I'm a close friend. I've been here many times.*

He seemed to recollect that. *I'll let you speak to the office.*

There was a connecting line from his phone. A woman answered. I repeated my relation to the Hopes, but more fervently. *Has she actually moved?*

The tenancy termination is effective the end of this month. I understand movers will be packing her things.

But where is she? Do you have an address? A phone number?

I can't tell you that.

Can't you give me a clue?

The woman hesitated. *I believe . . . she's gone to California.*

Maybe with his ashes, I thought. Certainly with his money.

*

As if in keeping with her move, the Governor of California was declared the Republican candidate. He had a team of clever writers and could memorize a script and read a teleprompter much better than the President. Money from corporate supporters poured into his coffers. I wondered how much of it had come from Sandy.

*

The little treasurer had risen to be the chairman of Favorable. And before long he effected a complicated transaction whereby he retired with well-padded pockets and a good part of the company's shares. At the same time he set up his own financial management firm, and mounted a sustained high-pressure publicity campaign. He presented himself as a magic money man, a master of mergers. As part of it he paid to have a book published, a supposed autobiography, and bought for it front-window display space in all the downtown bookstores. Splashed across the cover, in Churchillian pose, was smiling Sandy.

All this worked. It attracted money for his manipulations. He'd already moved to Manhattan and was making the society columns. At Republican fundraisers and other events he was coupled with some of the city's richest men. Unencumbered by conscience, he was proving to be a better performer than Chip had ever been.

And America had just elected an actor.

AFFAIRS

The Shakespearian sonnet is older than Shakespeare.
But he so put his stamp on it, that ever since
it has been known by his name.

1

These rhyming verses in the master's mode,
Which your delight spurred from the first one on,
Are to the huge universe he bestrode
A midge's tribute to a mighty swan.
Merely in coupled rhyme do they compare
And in freedom from puffiness and pose,
And they don't the joys of poetry impair
With narrative or fractured lyric prose.
Rhymes are word music to the inner ear
And linger like melodies in the mind,
Poets who fashionably at them sneer
Are from smug contempt being deaf and blind.
Don't you, like they, the obvious forego
Or coyly dodge what you already know.

2

These verses, rhymed and in an antique form
The racy urban wits will swiftly mock —
Let them; they ken not what does not conform
To their sly dallying and clever talk,
To the rank fright-caused sweat that underlies
The fevered revels of the fast smart set.
It might shake their willed ease to recognize
Love that needs form to contain and quiet
The wild, ardent, unending ache within.
Such love is not in fashion nowadays;
Life has grown too cynical, harried, thin
For ripened passion that all else outweighs.
But I, who must constraint endure a time
Will stay with measured syllables and rhyme.

3

I have no answers to the great questions
Of existence: where it comes from and goes,
And all the traditional suggestions
Explain less than sharpened thorns on a rose.
Yet I have seen that some coincidences
Occur uncannily in certain lives,
That something evading all our senses
Appears mysteriously, ebbs, revives.
Did you and I meet by chance or reason
To motivate blindly what befell,
And what causes all we have in common
Repeatedly our cautions to dispel?
When to this country house I came for rest
I didn't expect to become so blest.

4

If we were free to love without restraint
And could every sweet delight indulge,
And each other tenderly acquaint
With all that skin to skin can soft divulge,
And shared our secret joys and hurts and fears,
Trusting to each the plain uncovered truth,
And then, together moved, shed mingling tears
And rued the naïve mishaps of our youth,
And if we worked, spoke, mused with fond respect,
If all was thus as good as it could be,
Yet you, who can a future still select,
Would make another life apart from me.
Time, ruthless ruler, won't its laws unbend
And renders me at best an aging friend.

5

Seeing you outlined, my roused senses leapt
And followed your bending to stir the fire,
Lured by cardigan gaps where my eyes crept;
But still — suppressing all carnal desire.
Once more we spoke of baneful issues past,
Of childhood traumas and fraught teenage pain,
Of forced roles from which we'd felt outcast,
Of culture now, and pop art we disdain.
And then we freely talked of daily living,
And in our values found complete accord
Even to reasons for selfless giving . . .
Our awkward differences were ignored.
A man of any age would've been tempted,
And pictured his marriage vows exempted.

6

How precious is our rare and fleeting time
Together; it falls like tonic manna
On hungry hopes, making at once sublime
Former misery. All the arcana
Of love are then in a single sweet kiss
Contained, and the tangled world seemingly
Set straight. Yet much would it add to the bliss
Of being with you to learn your life's story
And what you do by day and dream at night,
And how you feel about all that you see
And hear; I would if I could know you right
Through; and, oh, so absorb you into me.
But as we can't our current state rebuff,
There will never, ever, be time enough.

7

Our days are doled out from the very start,
For spring's fresh dew so soon is winter's rime,
That when calamity assails the heart
It's best to live just one day at a time.
Within that day take in some pure sweet joy
Of any kind in which you find delight,
To counteract the stress your foes employ
To denigrate, gall, and undo you with fright.
And if that joy includes something of me,
Then drink it in as fully as you can,
Because it might not always present be —
No flower lasts for long, nor does a man.
Evermore, love is time's consuming beast
Devouring what at best it's granted least.

8

When you draw back your mass of auburn hair
Baring the wholesome beauty of your face,
Your rosy skin shows not much sign of care,
Nor does bane slight your robust, mature grace.
With zest and hope you've grown and wed and birthed,
Worked hard and raised your lively daughters two,
Trained mind and senses, loved, sad truths unearthed,
And all that has become this ripened you.
Autumn has long been my best liked season;
Spring is too swift, summer harsh, winter stern,
The ripe years are richer for good reason:
They mix all pleasures with informed concern.
Though fate did not you sooner me allow,
It has been kind to let me know you now.

9

You wonder at my iron-willed reserve,
Which holds back even in the throes of love,
Wonder if I your ardor quite deserve,
Or what fault, failing, I am guilty of.
Oh, if I were free of my imposed restraint
I would a flood of passion drown you in,
And leave you no conceivable complaint,
Leave you replete and peaceful in your skin.
But we can't claim we know not what we do,
Or like young bloods that we were swept away,
We'd later have to face our guilty rue
And the shame of rules we chose to disobey.
If I forsake my duty to be true
I might not then earn trust enough from you.

10

When you are filled with cuddlesome desire
And want my warmth, a hug, a fond caress,
I dare not to your lasting love aspire,
Knowing you're driven by untold distress.
At bay, beset by threats and searing blows,
A lioness defending cubs and lair,
You can't be blamed for turning from your foes
And for snatched moments breathing sweeter air.
At times of siege most norms are set aside,
Chance passions are allowed and understood —
The thrilling raptures we're now forced to hide
Condemn not more than all wise others would.
If you would avoid what could be tragic
Heed what is inwardly most pragmatic.

11

If this feeling were just inflamed desire,
Sense and distance would form a quenching flood,
But it is more a low persistent fire
That keeps you in my mind and in my blood.
Even at my job I return to this pen,
You're always present in my inner state,
I can feel your mouth, breasts, moist scented glen
Drawing me like some strange predestined fate.
Worse yet, we talk; though mute, you're never still,
I see your smile, slight frown, ironic squint,
You enter all my thoughts with airy skill,
Unbalancing me with your slightest hint.
If for you it's like this too . . . destiny
Might prove we're meant each other's slaves to be.

12

Yet love never in perfect balance stays
But is a fluid, rousing, healing force
That should go to where it's needed on days
When one is racked by grief, rage or remorse
And the other can some warm comfort lend.
Nor do we take and not at once repay,
Accepting is a gift in which both blend;
Dependable conduct can be love's mainstay.
So do not, dear, my wish to help deny,
I would much more than you from it derive,
But let's not measure, probe it, or ask why,
In this stressed time we merely must survive.
A love that serves not the beloved's need
Is less than love, is only selfish greed.

13

Kind, good, you wish no other woman ill
And say you can't stand furtiveness and lies,
You'd seem resolved, glad, if there wasn't still
That constant uneasy quandary in your eyes.
For you don't feel that what we are is right,
Nor would you have us be at all less so,
You would like us free in all the world's sight
Yet want no one who might be hurt to know.
Oh love, our love's no recipe for joy,
Nor is there any quick and sure solution,
Whether we try indulge it or destroy,
Shame or pain's the price in retribution.
Absolute love is an unlucky curse
That all attempts to blunt only make worse.

14

If passion wore love merely as a mask,
You'd see me as a tiresome player indeed,
Attempting the age-old trite acting task
Of feigning love to veil gross lust and greed.
But my thrill is real! That I can't deny,
Yet our rapture rests on warm deep goodwill,
On the complete comfort that you and I
Feel at moments we together fill.
To have a friend and hotly love that friend,
And yet have sweetness and compassion too,
And on each other be able to depend
Is in our lives the best that we can do.
Despite the forced hiding and hateful schemes,
We're lucky much beyond our wildest dreams.

15

When I behold the beauty of the Earth,
Observe the sunrise and the sparkling dew,
Scan numberless flowers of splendid worth,
Nothing is quite so beautiful as you.
Nature with matchless art bedecked it all,
Yet here and there laced dark with needless light,
Merged rough and smooth, mixed forms too squat or tall —
In you the entire blend came out just right.
Your light grays, pinks and auburns such joy
Bring to my outer and my inner eye,
That I become again an awestruck boy
Gazing in utter wonder at the sky.
For as the heavens much beyond me be,
I can't believe such beauty's meant for me.

16

From no one feature does your beauty spring;
I think it's not your wise gray eyes or smile,
Or strong shapely body sprightly moving,
Or the svelte chic clothes worn with quiet style.
It's your mind, spirit, sensitivity —
The droll glance, bright laugh, angry flash, sad rue
That when I look at you I also see
And that redoubles all I see in you.
Fret not then about faint lines and crow's feet,
Bulges, sagged breasts or stray unwanted hair,
To me these signs of mellowness are sweet,
The due changes to which all age is heir.
It's your core I love, the warmth, rage, lust and whim,
Which fell age cannot wither nor time dim.

17

Truly, I know not what love is; but kneeling,
Gazing at you, just takes away my breath,
Floods my whole being with ecstatic feeling,
Makes me feel alive! glad! unafraid of death.
Nor does any one aspect so affect,
Not alone your giving that doesn't bind,
The pleasures of your beauty and intellect,
The charm of your presence when time is kind.
It's all of that, all of you, I love so much;
Your outward form and sweetness at the core,
The aura embracing all of you as such —
A gift that's generous and I adore.
When to your house I can now and then steal
I go from waking dreams to what is real.

18

You grow more lovely under loving eyes,
Your whole body softens and gently yields,
Each new giving strengthens our inner ties
Adding promise like newly seeded fields.
Yet your daughters being home keeps us chaste,
So all sweet talk is only with our eyes,
Which often seems to me an evil waste
Allowing merely hidden hugs and sighs.
But torn from the warmth of our last embrace,
Cold beggared when you I cannot see,
I cling to the image of your easy grace,
Which I've carefully stored in memory.
Between this torment and our keen delight
I live in sunniest day and darkest night.

19

The ache of longing love that does not leave
Drags me through stricken days and sleepless nights,
Nor does the sweet recall to which I cleave
Soothe me at all; instead it more excites.
The miles between us are in minutes run,
And times when we're alone we now can find,
What torments me is not the act we shun,
But our dogmatic rules enforced in kind.
For who knows what is right and what is wrong?
The wide world, blind with loud iniquity
Would scarcely deign to hear our own faint song
Or care our tortured honesty to see.
Only these verses might us vindicate,
When one by one they do our pain relate.

20

Oh sh-h-h, quiet, let us keep love secret
Lest others deem it baleful to their weal,
Let us shut down each access we have yet
And bottle up everything that we feel,
And add to it, for an extra measure,
Your code that another woman's least hurt
Would quite rob you of all stolen pleasure
And more, cause you me sternly to desert.
So our most fulfilling and highest good
Is made to cower like a cur in chains,
And instead of shouting joy as we should
We dumbly keep apart while desire wanes.
This indeed is the classic catch–22,
Not having you, I stand to lose you too.

21

If we were but caged monkeys kept in trees,
Kept from line of sight merely by a hill,
And could our cries send only on the breeze
The social condemnation would be shrill.
But when I'm here we're free to loving be
And in minutes end our separateness,
Yet we accept others' idiocy
And like those monkeys seem trapped, powerless.
Much would be made of this, and marveled at,
If someone were us now biographing,
Baffled scholarship would our *don't* format
As *can but won't.* Why is no one laughing?
If we thus choose to make ourselves absurd
We'd best to ridicule become inured.

22

Seldom has so much fond praise been lavished
And absorbed with unmitigated glee,
But instead of letting yourself be ravished
You keep restraining and resisting me.
When you I cannot see or hear or touch
Then words of mine comfort only thinly,
And I feel these verses are much too much
Dabbling in bitter sad futility.
And then I think I'm just too old, too late,
That for me love is but buffoonery,
That your last note will only thwart, frustrate,
But desperate, I dig it out to see.
And oh, when sweet words in your hand I read
Then hopes arise and my grim doubts recede.

23

If it weren't for this sore imprisoned state,
In which I can't you see, mail to, or phone,
By degrees my obsession would abate
Into a passion less intense in tone.
Then I might behave with some discretion,
Be a man in calm tenure of his wits,
Shun self-searching and candid expression,
Become a fabler who all pain omits.
Were we living in some hatched fairy tale
Or playing at an amorous staged game,
We'd not cower before gossip, and quail
Or reel like spellbound moths around a flame.
The price of barred true love is sadly dire;
For each rare joy we pay in searing fire.

24

With my suggestion of a neutral room
You took my hand and led me up the stairs,
And there, stretched out, in its sheltered gloom
We then both indulged, drowning all our cares.
Oh, what a breathed-out dam burst that released!
And what keen joy came flooding in its wake,
And so much fleshly pleasure it increased
That we made merry with champagne and cake.
Then to your own dear room we fondly went
And left another bed in disarray,
Later still thrilling to each endearment
Relishing your daughters being away.
After so much long torturous denial
We truly deserved to celebrate awhile!

25

Looking back at that first real encounter
When each body uncoupled from its brain,
I beheld everything grow fresher
And there was a young new innocence again.
This virginal mingling of willing skin,
Of low-dashed spirits rapid to ascend,
Made me wonder what Eden we were in,
And why such happiness should ever end.
Yet as the sun its rising disk moved on,
And pale light through our nest began to creep,
The world its other face was quick to don,
Putting an end to our untroubled sleep.
But our brief glimpse of paradise will last;
I've oft relived it in the days just past.

26

Nectar's sweet and honey is delicious,
And maple syrup's tempting to the tongue,
But much more soft, smooth and moistly luscious
Is that vale of yours hitherto unsung.
Beautiful you are, eyes and touch reveal,
From your fine auburn crown to all below,
And your sighs, voice, scents have charming appeal
But that sweetness I had to taste to know.
All flesh, of course, is subject to decay,
And devouring worms are its final heirs,
But while your living systems are in play
Your body your essential sweetness shares.
You can be hurt, angered, curt, indiscreet,
But your core, love, is inherently sweet.

27

The world you touch is by my need transformed;
Your room, your bed, the crowded bureau top,
Every object is enhanced, graced, warmed,
From clothing to the merest grooming prop.
Your single pillow seems to me so sweet,
And by what code or gauge is that misread —
Is it just stuffing in a cotton sheet
And not the form that rests your lovely head?
I envy it, like all things you are near,
I too would be fingered, held, smoothed, perfumed
By your sleek scented skin, and softly hear
Your breath and sighs, in tranquil dreams subsumed.
To lie once more all night would be for me
Prolonged delight, sheer quiet ecstasy.

28

Luring, seductive lover in the night,
The full moon casts splendor on the last snow,
Draws the spring tides with overwhelming might
And soft brings forth your russet monthly flow.
It moves me much that you still fertile are,
Not that I wish for you a child by me,
But if — though wrong, unfair and singular —
These rhymes would not be love's sole legacy.
Yet this is madness — we can't time defy,
Nor depend for insight on progeny,
Fated, we'll go on living, you and I
In hearts and minds, all else is fantasy.
The one sureness we can ourselves allow
Is simply this, this very moment, now.

29

What is this lure that draws us each to each,
Why you, why me, of all whom there might be?
It's because our selves strive to mend a breach
And like all nature seek stability.
Whatever void in you that I do fill,
Or what I lack that you so well supply,
We cure by instinct just as much as will
Our healing bond to rightly verify.
The joy we feel is life's profound reward,
For those whom fate has mind and body paired,
The peace we feel comes from that fine accord
For which our former lives have us prepared.
Thus wonder not if and should and whether —
These qualms grow hollow when we're together.

30

These last few weeks like long full years have been,
A lifetime's fill of joy and pain amassed,
Already some nostalgia we can glean,
Evoking what we felt at first and last.
But partings are like death on us imposed,
Cruel delays while we must living feign,
During which nothing real can be disclosed,
Until, rejoined, we come to life again.
How long between these poles can we survive?
How long can hope o'er doom the victor be?
Against my spouse's knowing we're forced to strive
For but spasms in each other's company.
But while I breathe my love will sustain you
And after that these words will have to do.

31

Again starlight falls soft upon your face
And glows like dark rust in your flowing hair,
As I gaze raptly at your sleeping grace
And hold my breath with awed and tender care.
Of such a night I dreamt through tortured days,
While vain hope made me grind my teeth and weep,
But now this moment my fond dream obeys
When I observe your blissful carnal sleep.
To have pleasured you is my greatest joy;
To lift at times the ever-present pain,
For this I gladly all my skills employ
And count your enriched good my own best gain.
Each brief night or weekend when I return
Adds to the treasure I gratefully earn.

32

To have your love I've had to leave you free,
Keep our ties weightless and by choice alone,
And if, left every choice, you still choose me
It can't but be that all else you've outgrown.
Have I done that to you my dearest one,
Deprived you of a normal, partnered life,
Made of you a love-cursed, sequestered nun
Spurning fit swains amid innocent strife?
I didn't want for you this hapless plight,
But just the bliss with which love one adorns,
My rose given for your bosom's delight
Was never meant to pierce your heart with thorns.
I'd hoped for you to live and laugh afresh,
But have only snared you in a complex mesh.

33

Your silence is at any time your own,
Not to be encroached upon or misused,
Your confidence when given is a loan
At once withdrawn if ever once abused.
But if you show me only beauty's face
And hide the hurt that sore riles you within,
Then to our love I soon must bring disgrace
As one who failed love's needs to underpin.
So don't, my darling, spare me what you feel,
You give me most when you most open are,
Do, please, let my poor powers help you heal
Don't be a silent suffering martyr.
Your pain is mine, your good my best reward,
Let's face the worst, and we'll both be restored.

34

That you are strong I do for certain know;
Your rage towers like storm clouds set to burst,
And when held back, with mute spleen, long wreaks woe
On the spoiler who caused it all at first.
And when your needy daughters fragile are,
It's you who shelters and caresses them,
Who tries calmly to lessen any lasting scar
And spurs the stubborn strength from which they stem.
But you — who now kisses your tears away?
Holds you in loving arms till tender care
Relieves the pain that built up through the day?
I should; but perforce, I am seldom there.
In words I'm your unfailing defender,
Yet marriage makes me a shamed pretender.

35

Your charms I with great gladness feed upon,
Relishing each curve, bright tooth and shiny hair,
Yet miss what to others is so common:
A humdrum day we two could calmly share.
To wake beside you in the spreading dawn,
Breakfast at leisure and converse at ease,
Labor for us with my still lusty brawn,
And then rejoin you — oh, how that would please!
But from such simple pleasures we are barred,
Kept by veiled guilt from sharing plain events,
Our meetings in trysts are anxious, and hard,
A life lived in only stolen moments.
Yet ours I would not trade for all the rest;
With all it lacks it's still by far the best.

36

I'm pleased to learn that you have entertained,
That your house has heard happy adult talk,
That your poise as a hostess you've regained
And echoes of mirth join your daily walk.
You should resume a fully social life,
See friends, go to new concerts, films and plays,
As a lovely woman who's not a wife
Men at least will welcome you all your days.
Slowly your husband's leaving you'll forget
And restore your life with fresh energy;
I'm pleased for you, love, my sole regret
Is that there'll be no place with you for me.
Even this weekend I cannot commit,
With spouse along I'm as if in a pit.

37

A silence is descending on my soul,
If soul in me is what most yearns for you,
And writing thus can scarcely me console
For all I find that I must now subdue.
So near yet far, and soon a world away,
You're beyond what my senses can embrace,
Only in mind can I you still portray,
Where your beauty appears in dreamlike space.
Did I once really hold you in my arms,
Feel your warm living body next to mine,
Know your honest, earthy, frank, tender charms,
Endeavor our strong bonding to define?
Having lost bearings, certainty, self-trust,
I'm wondering to what I must adjust.

38

That you were real I cannot truly doubt,
I held you, kissed your warm mouth, breathed your breath,
But this departure seems an ebbing out,
A portent of some vaporous pale death.
I know not if your love for me will die,
Or whether a more subtle change begins;
Surely, my mood fate will not justify
Nor punish now for once reluctant sins.
Perhaps distance will draw you from our love,
Or some new other might intrigue you more,
Yet, now, if you could look down from above
I wonder if you'd these dour qualms deplore.
When back, I hope you will me ridicule
And prove that I've been just a frightened fool.

39

If I believed that my most fervent pleas
Could sway the course of fierce uncaring fate,
I'd beg for a fair sky and gentle breeze
Your tropic trip and stay to celebrate.
I wish I could provide some certain shield,
To keep you safe from harm of any kind,
But the defense I hope you'll always wield
Is love's strong presence in your heart and mind.
For mind needs mind in healthy living form
Each helping the loved other to survive;
I want you, in the midst of fearsome storm
To feel the utmost will to stay alive.
To insolent death this ceasing cry give:
My love needs me, and therefore I must live!

40

Warm moist air is melting the soft March snow,
And streams ape April in their headlong rush,
In your absence, walking in woods I go
As in the west I see the first pink flush.
This, your loneliest and the sun's name day,
Is when I would most like to be with you
To let my love mutely its warmth convey,
And your sense of togetherness renew.
I stop where a stricken deer died last fall,
Its corpse left for all creatures to assail,
There is no sign of its sleek grace at all,
Except, far gone, a small white tuft of tail.
We too will vanish with as little trace,
But this tale, told, time won't as soon erase.

41

Drugging clime this date's import might deflect
And increased age must now cause you unrest,
Yet this past twelvemonth, seen in retrospect
You must judge fair as both your worst and best.
You've lost much, and much hurt, rage, shame remain,
Which still cloud those years of being a wife,
But against that, see your astounding gain —
A deeper rich love, and a whole new life.
As long again, at least, as spousal span,
This time you start with means, insights, tried truths,
Knowing to take from each day all you can
Like a shrewd shopper from heaped market booths.
You've health, brains, beauty, talent now, midway,
Enough to make this your true new-birth day.

42

Though sudden sun as joy is now quite trite,
And to forced images we'd both say no,
Yet how describe a sun that shines all night
And night and day fills me with inner glow?
Such happiness is yours alone to give,
My thanks soar over all that disconcerts,
I'm thankful that your needs and will to live
Surge strongly through the present swirl of hurt.
A sea that's ceaseless in its rise and fall
Soon mixes salty waters with the sweet,
Our problems too, when we will them recall,
Might seem a mess of hope and of defeat.
Later we'll be glad that this broth we brew
Will prove the blend from which enrichment grew.

43

Except at times in vivid cryptic dreams,
When past passions tempt and torture briefly,
I can't escape the urgent sense, the themes
In which our veiled love wraps, envelops me.
One theme is fear — that you'll soon me reject,
The other joy — that you'll always be mine,
Between these poles I nil or all expect
And though you're distant still high hopes divine.
My wife does not know you are with us too
Or that in my pocket your hand I press,
Or that I mutely shout my love for you
And feel your warm, gentle, return caress.
With such masked thoughts my mind is ever rife,
The curse and splendor of our secret life.

44

How like music is your dear vibrant voice
Saying you're back in tones that swiftly rise
To woodwind trills in which I sheer rejoice,
Until speech fades and seemingly near dies.
So is it with your love, which waxes hot
When all my ardent worship inflames it
With word and deed, till like some omened plot
A mishap makes of me a chance culprit.
Being overheard made you pause, fearful
Of what might come, cautious, and rightly so,
I've no promises that match safety's pull
Nor guarantees of giving all I owe.
My wife's brooding on what she now suspects
Could lead, perhaps, to undesired effects.

45

My sweet, you tell me it's impossible
For us to withstand guilt, spite and despair,
That you wish our *mistake* reversible
For the badge of homebreaker you can't wear.
But I say love is right and true and good
And gloriously overrides all rules,
That we've found what most others never could
And are not simply dazzled erring fools.
Too, see the verses that have flowed from it
As if love alone were plying my pen,
Indeed it should be ceded all credit
For without it none would have been written.
In love as in art, whate'er we're doing,
Only the impossible's worth pursuing.

46

You tell me what I'd hoped never to hear
Or feel its truth hang heavy in the air,
That the discomforts of love now drawn near
Are a burden you can no longer bear.
From rotted matter grows the tree that gives
The wondrous juicy sweetness of its fruit,
And what gives us keen life, for us most lives
Is ever with its source in pained dispute.
Our past is part of what we wish to be
As certain as the seasoned leaves that fall,
And like them become the soil that's dowry
For a merged life that might yet us enthrall.
So do not, please, demand an either or,
We could have much, if not all, we hope for.

47

It grieves me greatly when you say *affair*,
As if what we have is passing fancy,
Infatuation clothed in verbal flair
And wanton lust grown sly, grasping, chancy.
I can't, of course, bind your future feelings,
Or more than hope that they might close match mine,
But my passion towers without ceilings
Nor will space or time likely it confine.
I prize each pore and particle of you,
Each breath, each act, each aspect and each touch,
Each short shared moment strengthens that anew
Giving me what glad life I have as such.
Of non-glib words for such love there's a dearth,
It's basic, organic, sprung from the earth.

48

My dearest, we've had our time together
And no possible future for us nears,
This heavy forbidding social weather
Will keep us severed through the coming years.
So more or less went your alarming words
That seemed to cremate all remaining hope,
Though we, like the phoenix, spirit of birds,
Could rise once more to e'en more loving scope.
But if to break free is your true intent
Then nothing I can say will bend your will,
And I must meekly wait with all ties rent
Till of bleak freedom you have had your fill.
When love can't spirit bodily enact,
It will from fantasy such scraps exact.

49

I'll always love you is a tolling bell,
A requiem for something that has died,
A gift returned, with book-pressed flower smell,
Wrapped in vague regret and my tattered pride.
For all the signs are that you love me not,
That what once enchanted you is now a bore,
That you mean never again to be caught
By love you might have reason to deplore.
Yet such fire as raged never quite goes out
But that some embers retain their warm glow,
With fit kindling, conditions turned about
A quick hot blaze can instantly regrow.
Whatever prompts your current cool intent,
Inner searching could cause you to relent.

50

If life were not so short and uncertain
Moral stances might be self-pleasing games,
As with nations that draw a false curtain
Over the lies they give high-sounding names.
But to let our lives emptily molder
Is madness, a frightening wanton waste,
Which serves nothing but to make us older
And the arid feat of remaining chaste.
The hollow chill of inner aloneness
That only human warmth can fill and cure,
Not countered, will then diffuse and impress
Till coldness develops lasting tenure.
It's for some loving warmth I hope and wait,
Trusting deliverance won't come too late.

51

In our love you always saw disaster,
Predicting in time angry skies would fall,
But calamity has come much faster
In the form of your cold abrupt withdrawal.
You can't have done it with an easy heart,
Thus some of my sad turmoil you must share,
Unless this is naïveté on my part
We must together make a woeful pair.
May it for you some worthwhile purpose serve,
For me it is extremely hard to bear,
But our love as I knew it I'll preserve
In hope that one day you will once more care.
Some things in safekeeping much richer grow,
Let it with our passion also be so.

52

That you are gone for good is crystal clear
And meant your final call to be so curt,
Especially your flip *I'm out of here,*
Which caused immediate tormenting hurt.
Is that all we were in intimacy,
External rapture and carnal accord,
To be thrown away as something dreary,
Henceforth to be virtually ignored?
I can't believe that you so little cared,
That you would dump our love as used-up trash,
My wife's guessing probably made you scared
But, darling, don't let it you so abash.
I know how distressing life now must be,
Give it time; you might yet come back to me.

53

You're done with me and seeking something new,
Expecting choice finds in a wider field,
But disappointment's destined to ensue
From hoping for much more than it can yield.
Imperfect as our present concord is,
We know at least what to us it can bring,
Joys, loathing, requiring no prognosis
And we're secured from error's sudden sting.
If I could for your unease compensate,
Bring back your sparkle and bold brilliant smile,
I would to that all measures dedicate
Meant it even continued harsh exile.
Then you might finally to me give heed
As love and tenderness you once more need.

54

Though unexpected to your house I went,
Driven by an almost unconscious will,
Held by your daughter who guessed what it meant
Until you came in, stared, and stood stock-still.
It did no good. When we parted that day,
With passion muted and our voices low,
Our fingers spoke; we'd nothing more to say
And you waved briefly as I turned to go.
The loss of love leaves a deep inner well
Of longing, and poignant pain, immense pain,
Forging in life's chaos this private hell
Of feelings that tantalizing remain.
Ours was a find too rich not to be kept,
I hope your right to it you'll yet accept.

55

Yet to sow and help grow and then not reap
Is for a lover the bitterest test,
I can no longer write with adroit sweep
Nor anymore engage in a keen quest.
Kept away for what seems like evermore
In forced ignorance, silence like a din,
I know not what goes on behind your door,
Who's caressing your form, stroking your skin.
Oh, that I've been displaced is plain enough,
By whom or what I can't at all be sure,
It's quite useless to protest this rebuff;
I've little choice but simply to endure.
Still, I will not be broken by this trial
But will my love to patience reconcile.

56

Yet that witch has my love, however maimed,
No need, for reassurance, to make it twitch,
Humiliated, flayed raw, and now quite tamed
It heels like any trained and neutered bitch.
A beggar must for a scrap be grateful,
Suddenly having her answer the phone,
Was it impulse, or was she remorseful,
Throwing me a mocking, spurious bone?
She has the feature that shows who it is,
What made her this time lift the receiver?
Was it unkind sport? Or time sneaked from his
Whoe'er he is, her latest deceiver?
If kind decency she'd deign to impart
Her body would come with her dangled heart.

57

A day-to-day frame passion just won't fit
And routine tasks can scarcely it restrain,
Household routines fast fragment under it
And mere walls such force simply can't contain.
In the dark, passion's loosed within my mind,
By pitiless day-truths quite unperturbed,
And lust and tenderness are oft combined
In fond ongoing visions seldom curbed.
But dawn such sating fancies swift dispels
Disclosing the drab and arid solitude
Of one who always spurned whores and bordels
And lovemaking for love's sole sake pursued.
Now passion cries out to the empty air,
Then dwindles to silence everywhere.

Women don't deserve the love I lavish
On them, no, nor my too-indulgent praise,
Their beauty is hardly without blemish
And their behavior quite often dismays.
Is it in their scant selves my love resides
Or in my words, which render them ideal,
Bestowing virtue, grandeur, grace besides
With fusing language making all anneal?
Is it mere image that I still revere
Reflecting my own desire, hope, regret,
Can it be that their real selves interfere
With an unfinished dream, that they upset?
But love does not in balance realness weigh
For love judged justly would most love betray.

Her light gone, now all's dark and bitter cold,
The raw wounds of rejection cased in ice,
Convention's won and made me its cuckold,
Thrust from her arms in sterile sacrifice.
Long, long before we've crumpled into dust,
And are ourselves but compost in the earth,
That for which she now reserves her trust
Will like most else have proved of little worth.
What matters to me is what's keenly felt
And that comes without much hesitation,
But I more or less draw a seemly belt
Round my still-governable imagination.
Yet while romantic dreams stir me the most
Love remains my folly and modest boast.

In love it's monstrous folly to give all,
Self-sacrifice brings only rude contempt,
Bit by bit both giving and taking gall
Till finally no factors are exempt.
Yet not to give all, when all craves giving,
Would rob me of what I care most about,
Which is to achieve grandness in living
By holding nothing back, having no doubt.
Indeed, pleasuring her gave me that thrill
But it was almost wholly in my head,
I used her, and I am using her still
Or will use someone like her till I'm dead.
My supreme need is to feel emotion
Though I know its cause is but a notion.

Enough. I used to write her, now my pen
Records events and feelings from habit,
Scribbling sonnets in order to lighten
The disappointment my mind won't omit.
I seldom leave the massed city anymore,
To go near where she is would invite scorn,
The pleasures of the country I ignore,
And my wife doesn't much care that I mourn.
My wife's too busy with her committees
Planning more well-meant charitable work,
Which costs us, with expenses and no fees;
If it wasn't for her trips it would irk.
But her leaving for weeks compensates,
It my odd adventure accommodates.

To have a longtime wife of sterling worth
Is to reflect myself doubly deplored,
An outer image of cheating from birth
And another of my true self ignored.
For a man who has always loved women
The dilemma has been plain from the start,
Marital law has been a mixed burden
To a fond and irrepressible heart.
I try to do what's right by wife and code
But am by innate nature undermined,
It causes trouble at each episode
And marks my role as cad and spouse combined.
Knowing for certain my state I'll prolong
Whatever I do will always seem wrong.

Here I should explain about my profession
And get the everyday out of the way,
I've the world-wide *belles lettres* concession
From a large firm, and I make very good pay.
We print books of the highest quality,
Literature that ranks among the best,
Ever since English in university
That's been my ambition and private test.
If 'twasn't for my other obsession
I could enjoy a calm orderly life,
But it would likely end in depression
Or worse: self-inflicted gunshot or knife.
For indifference I don't have the knack,
At which so-called friends laugh behind my back.

64

The smart set, blithely joking, casts me off,
Hiding its smiles for diplomacy's sake,
At what they truly see they're quick to scoff:
An aging romantic with a love-sick ache.
Yet the pain's as real as at seventeen
And the yearning's been as strong all the while,
Starting from the girl-struck boy I had been
And even earlier, when infantile.
My credentials throughout have been intact,
A lifelong love of women, lately crowned,
Which prudish critics would have me retract —
What in me is most basic, most profound.
I hurl that back at them, sometimes with hate —
But stop! I won't my innate self negate.

65

So I'm fallible — a human being,
Subject to yearnings, illusions, defeats,
From bodily failings vainly fleeing,
Whose faculties every day depletes.
Am I not, living yet, to know some joy?
To feel again a quickening of the blood,
My fresh thoughts, energies, wits to employ
Drunkenly drenched in an amorous flood?
This might be folly of the highest kind,
Quite doomed to disappointment and regret,
But to clear fact I'll knowingly be blind
And that special warmth thrillingly have yet.
A fool in love does with himself connive
But when all ends he's been at least alive.

66

What's being kept from me out of sly tact
By vengeful wife and chastened love agreed
Has the dark outlines of a perverse pact
Which denies everyone's basic need.
No touching, no tenderness can be had,
Fondness, like steel, is scrapped, soon to corrode,
None can be lover or even be glad
And all in the name of a rigid code.
If codes must be, then let them love include
And give to being loved what I would give,
Nor any of our partnered troths exclude —
Indeed, rejoice that all together live.
An outer war on our inner natures
Only all our true happiness abjures.

67

My wife has long considered dumping me
But I serve well the way she's organized,
Her generous forays for charity
And the many good deeds for which she's prized.
My business provides steady income
And I do helpful tasks around the house,
Mostly we're urbane, even frolicsome
And I'm always polite and chivalrous.
Nor are we usually strangers in bed,
My fond approaches are seldom denied,
And our couplings are often spirited,
Enough to keep her fully satisfied.
She could all my physical wants suffice,
If not for dreams that always me entice.

68

When much of the world with war is raging
How dare I mainly our small selves regard,
The love-torn conflicts we've oft been waging
Are ant-like scuffling in a bare backyard.
But this frail caldron our core lives contains:
Those real thoughts, loves, rash passions, gentleness,
While outwardly at most a half-truth reigns
Barely floating amid human distress.
Ladies, in life's rough surge from start to end
If tears and joys of love we can't make merge,
And to them some warm fleshy comfort lend
Then in us must fierce cold and rage converge.
Should we to such a fatal course accede
The present period will be long indeed.

69

A friend of my wife's was sent overseas,
A divorced woman, who works for a bank,
And though my wife very much wanted to please
She too went away, for which I can thank
My being stuck with the friend's apartment,
To visit it sometimes and pay the rent;
A dull chore, till it became excellent.
The manager, a widow, sensed my bent;
She took the month's check and with a shrewd scan
Asked me in to her small suite, with back view,
She'd had at half-cost, *Since the job began.*
And, very lonely, she shed a tear or two.
Then she apologized for her behavior,
And I gently broached being her savior.

70

It was a meeting of lucky good chance
And we at once understood and bonded,
A wonderful timing of circumstance,
She needed someone, and I responded.
Handsome she was in a middle-aged way
With a brown figure broad but curvaceous,
Not prepared, she said *Dinner next Sunday,*
Smiling, and fast becoming vivacious.
For the meal she dressed in pale blue chiffon
And her ample feast left me fully fed,
We grew warm as the evening went on
And at last ended in her spacious bed.
Our different colors didn't care cause,
It was Catholicism that gave her pause.

71

Caribbean, she weekly attended mass,
Yet seemed to find flesh not much of a sin,
Any aspersion would of course be too crass
But I hoped reasonableness might win.
I didn't lie, except by omission,
By the time she knew, it was far too late,
We had already granted permission
For all things that would us carnally sate.
It's a fact that I'm what is called well hung,
Long and thick and stiff as a ramrod,
I augment that with a caressing tongue
And my lovemaking is never slipshod.
Despite the uncomfortable sweat and slime
The peak moment of union is sublime.

72

It happens that our schedules nicely work out;
She's a bookkeeper and leaves work at three,
I, as my own boss, can office hours flout,
And join with this fantastic discovery.
Strangely, until now she's been quite staid,
A prim person, never showing desire,
Reliable, true, modestly arrayed,
But with me her whole being is on fire.
It's as if she'd been mentally suppressed,
Her life force held in by a feared notion,
Till loneliness made her so much distressed
That it sent her core self into motion.
Each human is a mine of many things,
Until fate unearths what from gladness springs.

73

For once I'm without silly illusions,
No romantic ideas to interfere,
And no fanciful or wrong conclusions;
It's her physical being that I cheer.
This isn't love, nor is it solely lust,
It's a kind of sensual fellowship,
Our bodies mingling in affable trust
Experiencing a prolonged pleasure trip.
Post union we join in satisfied sighs,
And still in bed have affectionate talks,
Hug and kiss warmly before we arise
And no longer panic when someone knocks.
With droll smile I hide in the dining nook,
She, robed, assumes a business-like look.

74

As folk who don't ordinarily swear,
We at no time employ profanity,
And I bring little gifts to show I care
But they're dwarfed by the huge gift she gives me.
For to lend herself is boundlessly kind,
A giving of all in the outer sphere,
She withholds private thoughts, which I don't mind,
Respecting what she might deep down revere.
Sometimes she'll forthwith cancel our session
And I'm afraid I've been left in the lurch,
Thinking this is some kind of regression —
It turns out she's just felt the need for church.
She has, I know, religious dimension,
To which I've so far paid scant attention.

75

One day there's a smell of spring in the air,
And we feel amazingly energized,
So we go at it with tremendous flair
In every way that can be realized.
Missionary, upside down, from behind,
Reveling in sheer voluptuousness,
She climaxes in waves, which all combined
Establish our essential agelessness.
The aftermath is restfully tranquil,
She's thoughtfully solemn but very sweet,
Then we each take a large vitamin pill
And laugh as if it were a special treat.
I wonder at her, outwardly so bland
But deep down such a sexual firebrand.

76

The next night, she's been to church and is tense,
Have we sinned? I joke, her mood to dispel,
But she says *Yes!* with angry penitence
Enough to fill all the coffers of Hell.
I can't go on with you, this has to end.
I go to mass, and my thinking appalls,
I attempt to prayer my mind to lend
And instead I'm lewdly climbing the walls!
I understand, her world is in chaos,
Though I plead for just one last coition,
Trying to mitigate the sudden loss,
She says *No!* causing a worse condition.
I knew not she was so much affected;
Such strong feelings I hadn't detected.

77

But I care for you I tenderly say
And she gives me a look of negation,
Haiii! she says *you're married! And anyway
You're rich, I'm poor.* There's some hesitation.
Besides, she goes on *you're white, and I'm black.*
You're not black! I say. *You're brown at the most.*
And I'm thinking of still another tack
When she says *You're a nice man. But you're toast.*
Well, I say *I wish we could this discuss.*
No, she replies. *I won't my color hide.*
I say *It made no difference to us —*
In bed! she says. *Leave me a little pride!*
I didn't mean to be patronizing,
Yet much of us made her rage keep rising.

It must have been hard to come from the islands,
Alone, mulatto, withstanding snide men,
At first likely using only her hands
And without security, now or then.
Lucky to have found that niche in housing
And work that pays enough for clothes and food,
But 'twas a life with nothing more rousing
Than indignity, and jibes, mostly rude.
Then I came, *White Knight,* big shot in the gloom,
Bringing out laughter, her deep female drives,
Diverting a friendless, childless, lorn doom
And thinking I'm enhancing both our lives.
The same's under skins of every shade,
But of attitudes we are hard to dissuade.

My erstwhile lover I often recall,
Remembering our snug sensual nights,
Her inner conflict now makes me feel small;
That didn't occur when we shut the lights.
I liked her slight accent, its lyric lilt,
Her voice rising at the end of each phrase,
A warm earthy song with an upward tilt
Which I'll still hear for the rest of my days.
About all her struggles I didn't ask
Nor once inquire into her daily grind,
Never wondered what was under the mask;
She's a metaphor for humankind.
For a time it seemed we had the same ends,
We were companions, and might have been friends.

Still I miss my West Indian paramour,
I'd like at least to stroke her comely face,
And say we achieved a kind of grandeur
Ending our closeness with no disgrace.
Being colored and poor is bad enough
When nothing worldly brings lasting relief,
Delusion's needed for a life so rough
So it's just as well she has her belief.
Maybe she belongs in a nunnery,
Except her problem does much more perplex,
Two natures, neither permitting perjury
In someone who's a blessing to her sex.
Beauty might be truth, truth beauty, but pain
She'll always inescapably contain.

Arriving on a twelve-hour early flight
My wife comes through Baggage looking quite beat,
She hasn't slept a single wink all night
Having given a child her inside seat.
She's always doing altruistic deeds,
Not for show, it's simply her good nature,
A woman who lives up to worthy creeds
And believes every weakness has a cure.
I take her bags, she carries the dress box
She acquired when coming back through Paris,
Such small vanities mark diverse epochs,
And I've prepared something special for this.
Seeing our house gives her satisfaction,
As symbol it evokes great reaction.

82

The first night she's too tired from her long trip,
Then we make up for it with warm embrace,
Joined again in doting fellowship
And I surprise her with a pearl necklace.
Yes, it seems to have the desired effect
And really, I'm glad she is safely home,
For she has charms as well as intellect
That keep me, for now, from wanting to roam.
But tedium, snail-like, takes hold of me
And it reflects in my writing as well,
These last few verses lack vitality
And on self-deceit I'm starting to dwell.
Without luring visions of some female
Essential existence begins to stale.

83

Tardy for my year's medical check-up
And not expecting any kind of a twist,
While still holding a paper coffee-cup
I come to a pretty receptionist.
Near forty, with an impersonal air,
She soon says the doctor will see me now,
Just as well, for I was tending to stare;
I wanted to get acquainted somehow.
But 'twas late in the day when I emerged,
Her desk was empty, she'd already left,
The interest that had earlier surged
Was dispelled, leaving me a bit bereft.
No telling what an encounter might bring;
To such fanciful conceits I yet cling.

But when I quit the building she was there,
Standing by a car in the parking lot,
Hello I said. *Can I take you somewhere?*
I have wheels she said, piqued at being caught,
I don't smoke in the car, or in the house.
Well, says I *if you're not going just yet —*
I'm not! she says riled. *My husband's a louse.*
Then, I hint *a drink should help you forget.*
She raises her brows. *Not with a patient!*
I say *I'm fine. I won't be back for a year.*
We go where people are often absent,
A discreet bistro that's still fairly near.
Wow — the classic casual pick-up —
And it's working! I can't believe my luck.

We've taken both cars. She wants to be free.
And I soon learn what made her willing,
A spousal fight over some triviality,
Only too common and trite, but chilling.
The husband went, tugging their son with him,
The boy's at his grandmother's and quite well,
The marriage won't end, but prospects are grim,
With each parent having on that to dwell.
She seems determined to drown it with drink
And orders more without even asking,
We're now willy-nilly nearing the brink
Of the joy in which I might be basking.
But there's a shadow of sadness on this,
Which might yet darken my expected bliss.

86

We drive to a motel, both in my car,
We'll come back to hers when the drink wears off,
I'm hoping her state won't our pleasure bar
But when I undress her she starts to cough.
I am afraid she might have to eject
But she recovers and lies back resigned
With even a slight shrug I don't expect,
Though when I mount her the clinging is kind.
Her body is as pretty as her face
And ordinarily I would both relish,
Yet feel what I'm doing is somehow base
And that in truth I can't it embellish.
I've taken advantage of loneliness
But never before of such wretchedness.

87

Afterwards, I follow her home, stopping
A block away, to make sure she's alright,
House is dark, empty; in she goes, flopping
On her bed, then flicks the lamp for good-night.
That ends that. Then to my own place I go,
Shower, and in pajamas greet my wife
Who returns from a late fundraising show,
Preoccupied with problems of that life.
I silently review the last few hours
In which my conquest was turned on its head
And used by *her* to strike with weak powers
At rage and sorrow— in a motel bed.
It's not from misery that I want my prizes;
No, at the worst of them my gorge rises.

88

Thinking of the damage I might have done
The potential havoc pleasure outweighs,
What's more it was no particular fun
And the low sense of unworthiness stays.
Sure, for minutes she was nice to look at
But she smelled of booze, smoke, and, faintly, sweat
And in dark the immersion was just that,
Little for my fantasies to abet.
Married women are bound by too many traces,
Thus mirroring my own complications,
From now on I must leave greater spaces
Between all such ill-advised temptations.
But each person's a flag never unfurled,
Blazoned with depths as complex as this world.

89

I look at that world from my point of view,
And women I don't really understand,
They have their own fears, yearnings, passions too,
Whatever for them makes their life expand.
But I have a credo: I never push
Nor even unduly nudge reluctance,
Or assume charm or try luring ambush
Or do much to enhance my appearance.
My age I find tiresome but won't disguise,
Gray hair at my temples I don't conceal,
My many years now and then I reprise,
For the reminiscences they reveal.
But by parts of my life I'm direly moved
And now wish they could be a bit improved.

My good wife and I take in an art show,
Breezing through, our being somewhat in haste,
There's still a dinner to which we must go
And we, for this sort of art, have less taste.
At the narrow front door, as we're leaving
A woman brushes past, dropping her purse,
She cries *Oh, I'm sorry!* while she's reeling
Around us, stifling an unspoken curse.
She isn't rude, but extremely upset
And my wife says nicely *What's the hurry?*
She laughs: her landlady, already owed a debt,
Who's child-minding, will be in a flurry.
Wife asks where she lives — says we go there too —
We don't, but as she has no car, we do.

En route she explains that her landlady works,
Daily serves supper to a rich old man,
Her care for the child is one of the perks
Of life there, but home by five's the strict plan.
The girl with us is an artist's model
And always leaves in the late afternoon,
Viewing the art show caused her to dawdle,
So our driving her home is a real boon.
Her house looks a narrow rundown three-storey
In a district that once was in fashion,
Her prompt to return is evocatory
Thus softly waking my latent passion.
My wife soon puts the lift out of her mind;
Typically, she's almost always kind.

92

Days later past five I go there once more
And quickly see why we were invited,
Her big front bedroom is a kind of store
Of paintings, and I'm rather delighted.
They're watercolors, quite realistic,
And I buy one to hang in the office,
She did them; since she's truly artistic
Then why does she have to resort to this?
She says no gallery has yet taken her,
Though she keeps hoping and is still very keen,
The pay for modeling is quite meager
But it keeps her closely in the art scene.
By day her landlady looks after the child;
To being poor the mother's reconciled.

93

She rents all of the small second-floor flat,
Including the kid's room, bath and kitchen,
The attic holds books for a diplomat
So seldom there he is almost alien.
That means she's alone some time after five
Except for the baby, who's only two,
There are no men here, yet the women thrive,
They bicker, but really are thick as glue.
I start dropping in for some friendly talk,
For my lady's young, only twenty-six,
At anything more I assume she would balk
So I don't engage in untoward tricks.
Who got her pregnant she doesn't mention,
But she's quite needy and likes my attention.

94

Not beautiful, though she has a nice face
And a graceful, fine, malleable figure,
Of affectation she shows not a trace
But in some ways she seems somewhat unsure.
She's very diffident about her talent
And seizes on friendships, remarkably, even mine,
Her existence clearly lacks enjoyment,
Most invitations she has to decline.
It's not much of a life, at home each night,
Tending the baby, a boy, now walking,
When I'm there she draws gauze drapes, shuts the light
And offers the child something absorbing.
This frail state could be slyly undermined;
But to sympathy I stay strictly confined.

95

One time when I go there she's plunged in grief
Over an air letter she's just received,
Saying her dear aunt found death a relief;
A loved person in whom she'd long believed.
It seems to pervade her own condition
As if all her hopes are now wholly dashed,
Then she starts to cry out of dejection;
From her tears my shoulder gets slightly splashed.
I put my arms around her, kiss her cheek
And try to console her as best I can,
She kisses me back, in a way that's meek
But I cease like a responsible man.
After all, I am more than twice her age;
I don't want complications at this stage.

96

But I ask myself why I've gone to her
And admit the visits have been pleasant,
Patently my age doesn't her deter;
Her fresh female aura I find poignant.
Is love needed, if there's companionship?
Can our fellow-feeling, warmth, intimacy
Knit a tender sexual partnership,
Or just spur more romantic fallacy?
She gives the boy a bottle, in his crib
And undresses in the front room's dimness,
Then writes a short note with an artist's nib;
Being nude causes her no bashfulness.
Otherwise timid, she's written: If you
Don't want me, I hope it won't mean we're through.

97

This is a curious situation,
With a nude woman offering herself,
Of course I'm aroused, a fated sensation
And I'm not one to sit long on the shelf.
I know she's oft used to being naked
When it's a professional occasion,
But kneeling softly on her double bed
She seems to fear I'll opt for evasion.
Gently I take her slowly in my arms
And kiss her fully, moistly on the mouth,
All is quiet, free of any troubling alarms
And faint light is fast fading from the south.
When I enter she gives a gladsome sigh
As if this does now all else nullify.

98

She likes the closeness of me inside her,
It shuts out most of the threatening world,
Long, slow and steady she seems to prefer,
Then lies in a fetal position curled.
The nice thing is she knew I was married
And never expected anything of me,
Our differences she willingly carried,
The seduction was mutual, not a spree.
We now meet for it once or twice a week,
With very little talk and minimal fuss,
I avoid any artistic critique
And to escape notice I take the bus.
Offering money I myself reject,
Strictly shunning any commercial aspect.

99

Yet it's wrong, her having all the expense,
With her tiny income and other ills,
When I suggest some help she takes offense
But lets me pay for contraceptive pills.
She maintains principles she finds fit,
Keeping integrity, raising her child,
I've past given to those who didn't need it
And been to that false bargain reconciled.
Her attitude's unusual, intriguing,
I'm assurance that things will get no worse,
She welcomes me with a sort of yearning,
And our words, though doting, are often terse.
With my holding her in a tender clasp
She'll climax with an appreciative gasp.

100

This liaison is going really well,
Afterwards we both take a quick shower,
I go to my wife with no telltale smell
And arrive home by the appointed hour.
For my artist it's an interim phase,
She must know it can't go on much longer,
Already I see her as if through a haze;
A reluctance that can only grow stronger.
It's not the act, that's enjoyable enough,
But the sense of unfitness that bothers,
I am just too old, she should me rebuff;
I don't want to be multiple fathers.
I have grown children who are on their own,
Who, if they knew, wouldn't my life condone.

101

Coupling's a psychic prop she depends on
To feel she's wanted and of innate worth,
I don't care to be into tangles drawn
But would help an emotional rebirth.
I have to escape, but don't want to hurt;
Really, none of it is in the least her fault
For in a sense I did begin to flirt
And I can't just abruptly call a halt.
She's a good person, devoted and kind,
A good mother, and inwardly honest,
Not especially to the flesh inclined
But in this adverse time a bit depressed.
Again I'm doing what is basically wrong
But this error I don't want to prolong.

102

The next time I arrive she's all elated,
Too excited for anything more than a kiss,
The bed that rightly would have me awaited
Is picture spread in joyous crisis.
A gallery showing only new painting
Has agreed to two on a trial basis,
She wants me to help pick the most tempting
For this wonderful chance she mustn't miss.
We choose them, she with boisterous heartbeats,
Keeping the toddler from smudging the glass,
The rest go where she always locks the sheets
Till washing. Then I say *I must leave, alas.*
We part tranquilly with promising smiles,
My optimism, while real, I hope beguiles.

103

Three days in I go to the gallery show;
Her works are the lowest priced on display,
One already has a red dot down below
And I buy the other without delay.
Because her paintings were the quickest sold
The gallery will henceforth represent her;
At our goodbye she needn't be consoled,
We part as friends, with nothing to alter.
The painting is in my office closet,
Later I will give it away to someone,
I employed a false name when I bought it
And withheld from the artist what I'd done.
This little chicanery has left me free
Ending this matter with some decency.

104

My wife's preparing for another trip,
This time to a locale in eastern Asia,
Ruled by a military dictatorship,
Where only tyrants enjoy ambrosia.
We're eating when wife suddenly feels faint
And then begins to black out and keel over,
She walks but would fall without my restraint
And at once, in my mind, I'm no rover.
Now she has sharp right-arm pain and nausea,
These can be symptoms of a heart attack,
She, whom I admired for her stamina;
I'm alarmingly, frightfully taken aback.
To the hospital we make a mad dash;
All my fears and hopes confusedly clash.

105

In Emergency, her heart is monitored
And various blood tests are enacted,
All prove negative; they found no discord
Except the vagus nerve, which contracted,
Probably due to virus of some sort.
In any case after sleep she feels better;
I stay home, and as nurse often report
Following instructions to the letter.
After a few sick days she recovers
And soon is back to her usual vigor,
But in the course of it I discover
Just how much her wellness is an anchor.
Her stability has let me indulge
In all the encounters I don't divulge.

106

There's a reunion of college alumni
To which my clever wife declines to go,
She says we're all just big heads getting high
While basking in our self-important glow.
Sipping drinks, I meet a Chinese lady
Who came, she tells me, with my former dean,
But that man was always a bit shady
In that he liked boys, but never came clean.
She laughs, says he's a nice amusing friend.
She's quite good-looking, with flawless English,
Learnt young, in Hong Kong, where she had to fend
For herself, when her husband proved selfish.
He's in China. Rich. Importing lumber.
Before leaving I get her phone number.

107

They've been separated for many years.
She's about forty-six, slim, elegant,
Her story is sad, but there's no hint of tears
And her phrasing is simple, eloquent.
We're having afternoon-tea in her home,
Which is small, neat, fine garden, suburban,
She has long hair, held in back by a comb,
Wears high-necked silk dresses, all very urban.
She asks not what I am, but what I feel,
My stature as man she had at a glance,
Her calm my anxieties begin to heal
And I might not need to make an advance.
Our good-bye brings her hand on my shoulder,
Her head on my chest; gently I hold her.

She knows what I want, nothing need be said,
Next time we go to her tranquil bedroom,
Where all male maneuvering I soon shed
And she gives what I could never presume.
Afterwards I lie with my head on her breast,
She strokes my hair as if I were a child,
I swear I've not had such a soothing rest
Or ever been with a partner so mild.
The physical seems secondary to her,
It's merely a complement to feeling,
New thoughts are starting within me to stir
And an inner awareness comes stealing.
She knows that facts are constantly riven,
That all men are by emotion driven.

This woman combines all I've preached about,
And I wonder if I could have her for good,
But mentioning that brings only a pout —
No she says. *I thought that was understood.*
Dear one, that world is quite another thing
Where our quiet friendship doesn't belong,
We can't to both those spheres attempt to cling,
I won't, refuse to, go back to Hong Kong.
Right, my role as husband would spoil them all,
All our serene sequestered afternoons,
I've had weeks with this astute woman-doll
And must quell any idea that impugns.
But rage 'gainst distant husband and wed state?
Beneath the calm surface there's lurking hate.

Nothing like that heard I ever again,
Our secluded happenings were resumed.
From asking about income I abstain,
That she could somehow manage I assumed.
I've since learnt she works mornings in a lab,
Wearing a white coat for their water tests,
And at work early hours are fairly drab,
A mood that my visit at once arrests.
She must have had something when she came here,
Enough to have made the house down payment,
But she seldom makes these things fully clear,
Dismissing such concerns as an ailment.
To her it's what we feel and say that counts,
Meanness, jealousy she swiftly surmounts.

For our tea she serves little home-made cakes
Shaped like leaves and roses, with subtle spice,
It's with peanut oil and wheat that she bakes
Because where she grew up they don't grow rice.
There must have been significant others
Who made her the earth-angel she is now,
I've grown jealous of those unknown lovers
And don't want them with goodness to endow.
Naturally of them she doesn't speak,
Much of her early history is blank,
I should appreciate that she's unique
And try find it in me that time to thank.
But now from her I'd like everything,
To better it, perhaps, with what I can bring.

112

One day she says in her usual way,
Soft-spoken, and without preliminaries,
Merely moving a small Buddha away
So we will have no intermediaries:
My life is a series of galleries
Of various paintings, both large and small,
When I think what I paid in salaries,
All of them I'm not eager to recall.
Some are dark, some stormy, and some just sad.
In our room, yours and mine, those are the best,
Pictures that are pleasant and make me glad.
From her tone I know this is not a jest.
It is flattering and very pleasing —
What prompted it is uneasily teasing.

113

She says *My husband, from China, is sick.*
Annoyed, I say — 'cause I have what was his
And can't attack this bugbear with a stick —
So he must fight it, wherever he is.
She says *He's old, not a Bengal lancer* —
There was almost a smile — *Not to offend,*
But it's too late for that. He has cancer.
As well, his money has come to an end.
He exaggerated his wealth. Then invested.
The scheme was dealing with goods contraband.
It went bad. He was even arrested.
She visibly wants me to understand.
It's too bad he's ill, with his faults showing,
Yet I don't like where all this is going.

114

She says further *He is here, in the city*
And staying this one night in a hotel.
I say *Well, it's certainly a pity*
But for you isn't it a kind of hell?
She says *Yes. But I have to take him in.*
My stomach comes to my mouth. I say *Why?*
She says *He has no one else. To begin* . . .
She breaks off. A tear comes into her eye.
And I've been told in the most gentle way
That we are finished, that our base is gone,
That this is the last afternoon, last day.
Not seeing her again, I must go on.
My own circumstances can only worsen,
Now that I've known a truly good person.

115

During all those weeks my wife never knew
Or, maybe, as I hoped, didn't want to,
As for my workers, they were used to me
Coming and going as I sometimes do.
So often have I fresh women pursued
While taking my wife's patience for granted,
Her qualities too I've really valued
And have never found fully supplanted.
If enchantment has now worn to fondness,
It's still almost a total commitment,
Yet exceptions make the whole groundless
Though not because of normal discontent.
But since losing my Chinese nymph I'm tense,
Distracted; my wife thinks I'm being dense.

116

She's gone for another three weeks at least,
Leaving me bored, a listless commuter,
And I'm at work, restless as a caged beast
When I scan the company computer.
There's a note asking about a book we printed
Sent by a strange name I take for a man's,
I reply, my words with thin sarcasm tinted
But the answer my saucy comment pans.
Also she corrects my false impression —
The full name is feminine, and very nice,
I apologize for my snide transgression
Then her humbly to a meeting entice.
This new female is vastly intriguing;
There's plainly intellect and good breeding.

117

She's lovely! Mid-aged, divorced, arousing,
But with details of her real self sparing,
Quiet, not much given to carousing,
Coy, not to me her inner life baring.
There's clearly more to her than meets the eye,
Past marriage, children, wary of induced joy,
None of the outer facts does she deny
But offers nothing that might them alloy.
I'm excited, yet not sure of what to do;
She won't let me probe past her exterior;
I can't conventionally her charm or woo;
Uncannily, it makes me inferior.
She is; you take her as you find her now
And I would take her if I could somehow.

118

Pondering it, I turn to honesty.
It's an approach I've never even tried,
Tell her almost the whole truth nakedly
And simply hope she finds that justified.
I describe my work, my wife, my ripe age
And something of my amorous events,
She's a little surprised but duly sage
And refrains from any moral judgments.
Whether there's sardonic inner censure,
Or if she accepts me just as I am,
From her manner I can nothing conjure,
She's blasé enough to be addressed as m'am.
But my Chinese lady I've not revealed.
She was special. That memory is sealed.

119

These are my new find's superlative years
When she needs not a thing from anyone else,
Her beauty, though faded, still moves one to tears
And she has money, brains, style that compels.
She fascinates me, but I am kept apart,
Tolerated and toyed with, but not let in,
Accepted as a superficial sweetheart,
To her Columbine I'm merely Harlequin.
If only she would let me know her thoughts
And what goes on behind her tempting mien,
In my regard those are the only blots,
Carnality I've no doubt she'd sustain.
I feel myself drawn to this puzzling source
On what might prove my final, fated course.

Living alone, grown sons too on their own
She is financially independent,
There have been suitors aplenty, some well known
And slick lovers, a few very confident.
This gave her no good reason to remarry,
Wholly owning herself was quite enough,
She didn't need a cadging adversary
And discarded each without being rough.
That she cherishes our frank dialogue
Fills me with constant euphoric wonder,
I trust it's but a brief hinting prologue
Still, I'm afraid of making a blunder.
But she doesn't yield to my constant pleas,
Trying to keep us from absurdities.

Now at an age when I spurn adventure
I am at last ready for my final love,
If the years have accounted for this cure
They've slowly pushed this culminating shove.
I'm in constant awe of her classical look
And speak with only tender reverence,
Nor, scanning her, am I ever mistook:
Her looks simply inspire my confidence.
Sometimes she'll show me some special favor,
We'll be close and she lets me hold her hand,
A good-bye kiss is something quite major
And I imagine I'm in the Promised Land.
We make progress of a checkered kind,
Crablike, two steps forward and one behind.

122

Her back she's letting me stroke, wishing it
Because her ex-husband did that long ago,
And it recalls grass on skin that's sunlit
While nude, and hearing a distant cello.
Thus, step by step, her dark secret essence
Of memories, dreams and surprising joy
Comes to light without haste or fraudulence,
Or other shams that hot suitors employ.
I must not with her make an erring move,
For fear it would lose her altogether,
Or voice a sentiment she might reprove;
Her slightest frown's an instant bellwether.
She's all things in a private, honest sense,
Beauty, charm, feeling and intelligence.

123

We meet often while my wife is still away
And are glad of the frequent occurrence,
I would like very much overnight to stay
But that, at this stage, she won't countenance.
Yet she's lured by our remarkable candor,
Our marvelous frankness with each other,
Even her former husband lacked such rapport,
As must her children toward their mother.
This kind of love I never imagined,
Or that I could be on the whole so stirred,
I can't previous romances rescind
But I think now they were somewhat absurd.
If my prior forays made me a fool
By comparison they were minuscule.

124

One night, familiarity, need and lust
Undermines her cool check of sane restraint,
She turns toward me, ready to readjust
And welcomes my fondling, without complaint.
Our thrills flow into a long-delayed sigh
As mouth seeks mouth in tender moist caress,
Oh, if we could just one and all defy —
Once more, the same wall against peacefulness.
But still she won't let me remove her clothes,
Retaining them as a kind of barrier,
She laughingly tries virtue to impose
Though it makes the problem no easier.
I can hardly my wild desire contain;
Only with will can I my poise regain.

125

Next night I ask, truth being our real tie,
Don't you want to make total love with me?
She says *No and yes, I don't want to lie.*
Then I say *Choose yes — no would untrue be.*
Her body, when uncovered, is sublime,
The marks of age are scarcely evident
Like a vision of eternal springtime,
With interaction fully competent.
Supine, I'm awed by her golden beauty,
When her wise blue eyes gaze straight into mine
Inquiring how I'll divide my duty
Or the falsehoods I think I can combine.
With wife and mistress basically opposed
Can I indeed long remain composed?

126

My wife is back, as yet blind to this murk
Though she suspects the general aspect,
I can't her anxieties entirely shirk
Or by base lies insult her intellect.
She knows too well it's someone else I want
While at the same time keeping us stable,
She much resents having it to confront
And my repeat tomfoolery to enable.
Her mute anguish, now pierced by angry jabs
I understand, and refuse to argue,
Our married life proceeds by dribs and drabs
Yet I intend my lady to pursue.
When attraction and duty are at war
The near future I can only deplore.

127

My golden belle I continue to see;
She likes me, albeit with discretion,
We can't these days be entirely carefree
But her bed is a kind of progression.
Of course we have to orchestrate our times
To circumvent any gross unpleasantries,
Our couplings grow silent like pantomimes
Despite my trying all ardor to seize.
For now she tolerates my wedded state,
And wants not to influence its outcome,
Nor to be drawn into an unplanned fate
Or to force a ruinous ultimatum.
She is wary of any final decision
Though holds my compromise in derision.

128

Yet if I cling to a double standard
I hold out an equal one for my wife,
Any jealousy I've long had to discard
Or overheated quarrels would be rife.
She has hosts of good friends, of every sex
And gives help and empathy to them all,
Her relationships are often complex,
She's had temptations, but I think no fall.
The truth is, I don't know, or want to know,
There are now conflicting issues involved,
It's not so easy to get up and go,
Too few upsetting problems would be solved.
Life would be quite simple if black and white
But even a great many grays can't make it right.

129

But one thing that's clear prevails with my flame:
To her I owe up-to-date disclosure,
If I were to venture the least false claim
It would lead to unpleasant exposure.
She asks not how my wife feels, what she knows,
But can guess at the home situation,
Discussion might just trigger untold woes
And cause everyone humiliation.
So long as my love's content to let it lie
Then I too am content that it be so,
Thus once more I don't have to clarify
And can again dodge it till tomorrow.
Tomorrow is everyone's hope and bane,
We can't know if it will bring joy or pain.

About my wife's case we remain silent,
It hangs thin, false like a theater scrim,
My thinking tries not to be violent
In this troubled uncertain interim.
Whether to leave her is still the question
To join a love I'll never meet again,
What can I offer as a suggestion
That will soften the wrench and leave us sane?
And I think too of the stale failing years
When senility and drool might me befall
And affection turns to unspoken jeers
And tolerance becomes slow hideous gall.
A spouse who is by law and custom bound
Might be more resigned to being around.

A topic avoided becomes a lie,
Yet not the same as stating an untruth;
It's not as arrant as an alibi
But yet prolonged evasion becomes proof.
The two women have never ever met,
Nor are they anything like each other,
You'd think this might neutrality beget
Or at least my anxious feelings smother.
Why can't a man have bilateral mates
Or a woman either for that matter,
A different other rejuvenates
And makes our minor resentments scatter.
We have so little healthful time to live
That arbitrary rules could stand to give.

132

Meanwhile my wife is more than suspicious,
She knows something private is going on,
Sometimes she says *Where are you?* Curious
About what's causing my new absorption.
But she too doesn't force the prime issue
Provided she's not confronted or embarrassed,
Perhaps willing to see the matter through
If she's not by it unduly harassed.
She was exceedingly hurt once before
And too often in little wanton ways,
And I can't just that bitter past ignore
Or her joyless forbearance fail to praise.
Yet a love this right I've not known ere now,
Nor will I such emotion disavow.

133

The worst thing is I don't know what to do,
Humans harbor conflicting impulses
Helped by self-serving notions we construe
That true thought discreditably repulses.
By proxy we slaughter animals and plants
While humans we just murder directly,
And this is imbued in us as infants
Who then believe they're acting correctly.
We want to embrace life, joy, everything,
Yet by our clumsiness are irked, distressed
And when we look inside we find nothing,
In a body frail, dying and depressed.
If we dare show all that we really are
We'd have to admit we haven't come far.

134

Yet when my love spreads her arms tenderly,
Her face alight, the rimmed eyes welcoming,
The lithe limbs so graceful and orderly,
My thankful heart doesn't stop pulsating.
Her breasts are smooth mounds for my eager lips,
The brown nipples erect and succulent,
Every touch I think all else outstrips
And it's always with a ravishing scent.
It is all so soft, silken, moist, fragrant
That each bit with euphoria I regale,
Swelling supreme from rubbed-on lubricant
Then entering as the conquering male.
How can I such a woman cast away?
Everything in me wants her to stay.

135

I know my love's surface is a pious fraud;
She dyes her hair, to make it solid blonde,
Then weekly it's styled and hairdresser pawed
And eyes enhanced to make others respond.
The splendid breasts, when lifted from a bra
Slowly descend with rather hanging heads;
From cream jars comes the scent of vanilla
And smart clothes hide a creeping midway spread.
Perfumed panty liners preserve her charms,
Lipstick and blush produce a pale rose shade,
The smooth-skinned legs and suave bare underarms
Are by electrolysis and waxing made.
I shut my mouth about such artfulness,
Thankful for indulgent, favored access.

Weeks follow when wife is always at home,
Her powwows seem to be on hold for now,
I'm fixing the shaft of a skylight dome
When sudden shrieks predict a ghastly row.
I run in, quite expecting the very worst,
To the kitchen at the end of our house
Where my wife's sobbing and jerky outbursts
Shrill tell me she's seen a scurrying mouse.
A mouse! I thought she had learnt my dark secret
And I had specious reasons on my tongue,
But though I was glad of the vacant threat
It left me badly, damnably unstrung.
That a wee creature can my comfort shake
Lays stark my terror of what is at stake.

At last a request comes from a sick friend
Who needs spouse to come and stay for a while,
Leaving me, *at last,* myself to attend
And my interests free to reconcile.
When my loved lady disrobes in my sight,
The vision is ravishing to behold,
A woman fully graced to give delight,
A sensual symphony in pale gold.
Nestled in the warm damp of our embrace,
Her sweet soft mouth touching mine now and then,
She says that with me gone she sought solace
In having dinner with some other men.
Though I seem at times by passion blinded,
I'm always of certain facts reminded.

138

It's for us — it's good for me to be seen
With someone else, because you're noticed here.
We don't want them thinking something obscene
Or compelling your wife to interfere.
She uses her name and I catch my breath
That my wife has been openly mentioned,
This is like a sudden yawning of death —
It's as if I've been forcibly pensioned.
Until now my wife's been a veiled despot,
I had thought to keep them completely apart,
I'm deeply disturbed but try show it not
Though can't prevent a quickening of heart.
I had wanted all this to be mature,
Had hoped at least this end would be secure.

139

Today she asks slowly, as if quite loath,
If for two women I've enough largess —
I say I sort of truly love you both
You with rapture and my wife with fondness.
She hears this out, then revels in pleasure,
Slightly moaning from my gentle caress,
Which raises the sexual temperature
And leads on to sensual wantonness.
Or so it seems. For her sly eyes stay sharp
Revealing a mind that's partly elsewhere,
On this rare disharmony I don't harp
But I can sense disquiet lurking there.
She listened with a small raising of brows,
Which is a bit more than comfort allows.

140

I've tried keeping love at a high level
Combining dignity with human need,
But the whole thing's starting to unravel
As age and decay each other succeed.
I would like to keep this golden flower
My soft splendor in the gathering night,
Slightly worn, she can still me empower
To feats of something like a youngish sprite.
I'm much envious of those other men
Who can see her without their time abridged,
Though the ambiguous life I've chosen
Is yet, I well know, highly privileged.
I'm battling years, half-truths, doubtful esteem
And it's too late now my past to redeem.

141

As flies gather round a corpse, rumors cling
And stick to me like indelible stains,
Smirking, love's char hands her my wedding ring
That was found under the bed, she explains.
The baker's leer at two tarts is slighting,
The bookish florist ignores my borne book,
The bland-faced doorman at my love's building
Now opens with a cheeky, knowing look.
Into this restlessness my wife returns,
Her friend restored; one more unsparing trip
And it isn't very long before she learns
That I'm the inferred subject of gossip.
Normally she's too proud to hear such stuff;
My safety lies in that being enough.

142

Then come calm days, which earn my gratitude,
When spouse and I might go out, have some fun,
But one night in bed, without a prelude
She asks if I'm fucking the other one.
Her voice is low, and I tensely wonder
If she has come to this sensible pass
Where they can be friends, and I grow fonder
Of both, hoping this ends everything crass.
How great would a wise society now be
In which we could express our true desire
Avoiding hurt and shame and damaged psyche;
Such freedom would countless people inspire.
To this outlook I gladly acquiesce,
And taking a long sighing breath, say Yes.

143

I think I'll call her she says in flat tone,
Gets out of bed, slips on a woolen gown
And descends to the wall hung kitchen phone,
While my pleas bring only a sullen frown.
She dials rightly, with me on tenterhooks
And my love answers on the first full ring.
Do you want him? wife says. *And get books.*
He's a good publisher. Law abiding.
Except in everything that matters most.
Still nude, hoping this can yet be allayed
I'm thinking of how or if I can coast —
Then stop — my wife's been too often betrayed.
I will have to beg them both for saneness,
But right now sheer fright keeps me numb, speechless.

144

They talk for a few minutes, tense but true,
Then conclude with a moderate ending.
Embarrassment all around, yet surely due
To all the primitive feelings churning.
Grown cool, I start for the stairs, when wife's voice
Stops me cold with a vociferous cry —
I want you out, now she says. *There's no choice* —
With rage that will be hard to pacify.
Like this? I exclaim, clearly shivering,
And bitter mirth curls her malignant lips,
While from her eyes malign wrath is glaring
Like cannon bristling from deadly warships.
I can't help loving that reproachful wit,
Though I did its barbs and stabs solicit.

145

Take clothes she says *you've forfeited the rest,*
But you can use the den couch for tonight.
She throws a folded blanket at my chest
And fast going upstairs, puts out the light.
At dawn, from phone booth, my speech curtailing
To my love I regret the disturbance.
Though woken, her commonsense prevailing
Floods me with cheering, loving assurance.
Well, it's okay, she had a right to vent
When her troubles had our mating to thank,
But just tell me, why give acknowledgment?
I own that I had to, she asked point blank.
The long moment coming is like a blow
My feelings sink to an alarming No —

Her silence is for seconds amplified,
I wait, still hoping for some compassion,
Then she says forcefully *You could have lied.*
Disheartened, yet sanguine in a fashion
I say, haltingly *When can I come round?*
Knowing she has to revive and recoup.
Oh, she says *that's history. You astound!*
God — you should know I'm no one's nincompoop!
Click. Not even goodbye. The line goes dead,
Leaving me stunned by the sudden stillness.
My large hopes having not yet contracted
I see, slowly, the extent of this mess.
But the fates can't have decreed so much loss;
To me it seems a shocking double-cross.

I left my wife everything we possessed,
As well she'll be getting half my income,
So she won't be financially distressed
Or lack any means, at a minimum.
For me, a rented room, with a shower,
Toilet, sink and for cooking a hot plate,
To which I've added a single flower
In a chipped vase on an orange crate.
Later on I'll move to something better,
But for now I'm sufficed with these basics,
From prior things I want to unfetter
And live a life pure in my own ethics.
At last I've achieved the essential me
And will henceforth behave accordingly.

My mirror reflects someone scarcely known,
Gray hair, lined skin, wan hue, shrunk nose, eyes weak,
Hanging folds under the lower lids grown,
A dark mole high on the stubbled right cheek.
This was a face once wreathed in subtle charm,
Which generally pleased and women drew,
Though that proved capable of unmeant harm
Yet I'd still sensuality pursue.
For there's nothing quite like soft naked flesh
Or the juicy sheaths of warm tender parts.
Such retentions with realism now mesh
And pierce me like a thousand painful darts.
This getting on I cannot contravene,
But within I still — feel like seventeen.

No more want I any cursed adultery
And won't pay for what has been given free,
Though there's always cost voluntarily,
Which is never without some vanity.
Self-pity's sad pleasure I won't indulge
And for my lot I'm not singing a dirge,
If my trousers should show an awkward bulge
Only fanciful hopes will drain that urge.
What's left I'll leave to my thriving children
But they will have much more from their mother,
It's what's looked for as a loving token;
They're fixed, and don't really need their father.
We aren't strangers but not truly close,
Generations are slightly bellicose.

150

My past has curled away like so much smoke,
While leaving a good scent and trace behind,
The memories of loving female folk
Who laughed, were given joy, were fed and wined.
They comprise all the ultimate moments,
All else is trivial and mostly gone,
They left an aura of magnificence,
A plenty from which current dreams are drawn.
Hurt have I my wife and the social code
Trying affection without distortion,
I regret the feelings caused to corrode
From straining to keep all in proportion.
Now I have not any thing for which to atone,
Yet I am, more than at the very start, alone.

THREE STORIES

Chaim to the Rescue

She was beautiful. Long chestnut hair almost to her waist. It fell in a shining cascade from beneath her head scarf. Chaim had only clearly glimpsed a bit of her lips and the tip of her nose before she averted her face, blushing from his astonished stare. He stood rigid, watching the back of her and two older women as they made their way across the market. Then after a moment he shut his mouth. He had seen a vision. Grace and loveliness such as he'd never imagined.

Chaim Lustig lived up to his name. He was lively. A bit of a madcap. Merry and bold, he was known around town for his outrageous pranks. Nineteen years old, tall, dark and broad shouldered, with a wide pirate moustache across his handsome cheeks, he had turned the head of more than one peasant girl. The whores laughed at his ribald propositions, knowing he had no money, but out of teasing amusement they sometimes let him touch for free. Nor was he averse to brandy, whenever he could get it, and when it came to fisticuffs, he'd shown that he could hold his own.

He had been orphaned at twelve, and lived with an aunt. A widow, she had children of her own to sustain, and could do little more than sigh at his behavior. But privately he was an honest young man, and weekly gave her all but a few pennies of his earnings.

He lost no time in inquiring about the girl. He soon learnt that she was named Gitl Ziporah, though in her family she was called Shira, song, for her loveliness gave a feeling of uplift and soft exclamation. She was the only child of Reb Motel Zaltsman, a pious comfortably-off person who lived in the better part of town.

Chaim went there. It was a solid wooden house with a stuccoed front and four steps leading to the heavy rectangular frame over the front door. The handle was polished. The jamb even had a bell. He rang. The servant said that Reb Zaltsman was not at home, and anyway would not see a stranger without an appointment.

*

Chaim canvassed his acquaintances. Many people liked him, and others were indebted for small electrical work done on the side. He was an electrician's helper. It was the beginning of the nineteen-thirties, and the town was becoming wired, like other parts of Poland. There was lots of work. In every possible way he prevailed on others to speak to Reb Motel, and finally the day came when he approached the house knowing he would be received.

He was watched. From an upstairs window, behind the edge of a lace curtain, Shira saw him cross the street. She liked his raw-boned look in the tight new suit, with his moustache trimmed back to match his mouth, and the shiny boots that tried to avoid the puddles and stretches of mud. She was fifteen, of marriageable age. But she had been pampered, and didn't relish being married to some book scholar, however nice and clever he might be. She had read, in translation into Yiddish, the novels of Sir Walter Scott, and had secret dreams about the man she might marry. She didn't know what to make of Chaim, but he excited her.

Reb Motel was waiting in the parlor. The romance, hinted at by those who had intervened, was already known to him. He greeted the young man politely, but without warmth.

Reb Motel Chaim began, breaking into a sweat. *It's about your daughter. I love her!*

Reb Motel considered that the young man didn't know her at all, except in imagination. But the father thought that the boy couldn't be far wrong, for he felt that his daughter had all the virtues.

I — I want to marry her! Chaim blurted out. He had thought of involving a *shadchen*, a matchmaker, as a go-between, but in his fervor had decided to leap that step. *If it's about money,* he said *I'm working, and I can start my own business. I can support a family.*

No, Reb Motel said. *That's not the issue.* Money was a means for Reb Motel, not an ideal. He was more than prepared to maintain a suitable son-in-law. *I'm sorry* he said. *My daughter simply can't marry a man who is not learned, who is not pious.*

Chaim had been seen in the synagogue only once a year, on the High Holidays, and then had not always stayed for the entire service. The blood rushed to his head as his hopes were dashed. *Reb Motel,* he cried *give me a chance!*

It was a cry from the heart. In the kitchen it stopped the mother from stirring the noodles; it rolled upstairs to where Shira pretended to be reading.

Reb Motel stared in silence at the distraught young man. He was not unkind. A dealer not in salt, as the name implied, but in fine fabrics, he could feel the quality of goods with his fingers. And he had taste. He bought only the finest of tightly woven smooth linens, worsteds, woolens, gabardines, some cottons, and exquisite silks. He went regularly to the mills of Lodz, and to the silk centre in the capital, and bolts of goods would follow by train, or sometimes horse and wagon. He gave his customers full measure; his cut goods always ran a few centimeters longer than ordered. Small dealers and tailors bought from him. His word really was his bond. His business was widespread and well established. He was generous with his money and gave to synagogues and yeshivas, to charity, to all the Jewish community groups, and sometimes, privately, to Zionist causes. He was in his way a man of the world. Although he did nothing illegal, he paid the police to leave him alone, regarding it as merely another cost of living a Jewish life in a hostile world. He was a man round in face and form, in beard and gold-rimmed glasses, behind which he looked with both sympathy and mild disdain at Chaim's wretched face and figure.

My child cannot marry any but a pious man Reb Motel said again, quietly. *Thank you for caring. Go in peace.*

Chaim dragged himself from the house whipped, shamed, bewildered, and possessed. Across the street he looked back at the blockish building. Somewhere in it was the treasure he craved, all the delights that life had yet denied him.

*

Like every boy in town, who started at age three or four, he had been to a *cheder*. But there he had been mostly a troublemaker, snatching off the boys' caps and scattering their books. The old teacher had been secretly relieved to see him go.

On this frail base of a little bit of Talmud Torah, Chaim built a veritable edifice of knowledge. The boys he had hung out with, the girl's he'd fooled with, saw him no more. He had neither time nor money for them. Each evening he studied with a paid *melamed*, a tutor, and on many nights he sat in the study house and pored over a page. He went every morning, before breakfast, and every evening to *shul*, and shook himself while praying with a fervency that made some people in the synagogue shudder. At *Simchas Torah*, the annual celebration of the Torah, he danced with the greatest joy, passion and wild abandon. He grew a beard, and became the disciple of a famous rabbi, attending, when he could, the rabbi's court in a nearby town. After a year of this he was accepted as a *Chasid*, into a popular sect known for its fervent and joyous piety.

*

Meanwhile Shira was plied with suitors. With all she found some fault. Her mother despaired. Even from her father there were angry words. But she begged and cried. And Reb Motel, for all that he was embarrassed by her persistent refusals, could not bring himself to hurt his only child.

In the synagogue he watched Chaim's transformation and was impressed by its zeal. He had heard that the young man had started his own electrical business, and between work and his religious duties was studying day and night. But Reb Motel was suspicious of extremes.

Shira too, in the way that women know, was well aware of Chaim's strivings. Sometimes at services, through the lattice separating the women's gallery, she caught sight of him below. The truth is, he stood out. With his stature, dark hair and beard, black caftan and spotless white socks and prayer shawl, and his energy, he was commanding. She knew that under the scholar's robe there was a practical man who worked with his hands, and felt that with his dash and intensity he could have been a character in one of Scott's tales.

*

Another year passed. The stubborn Shira was now at an age when people began to talk about her, wondering if she was going to remain a spinster. Reb Motel knew he could not let this go on much longer. He had not spoken to Chaim, except in passing. As he would with any congregant, on the eve of the Sabbath he would exchange a *Good Shabbos,* or voice similar greetings on other occasions. But he had been observing him. Outwardly the young man seemed to have become a good Jew, steadfast and pious. There was no family to be concerned with. Chaim's forebears had all been paupers, but honorable ones, whom Reb Motel, unlike most people of his station, did not despise. One Friday in winter he invited Chaim to come to dinner, for the Sabbath meal.

The two walked together, their boots making fresh crunching sounds in the snow. Reb Motel opened the door himself. *Come in, Chaim* he said. For Chaim it was like entering Eden; the house smelled of all the world's wonderful foods and spices. The Sabbath candles, which had been lit before Reb Motel left for *shul,* had burnt down into their silver gilt holders, but they stood on a snow-white tablecloth spread with sparkling cutlery and glasses, and a fresh *challah,* the braided loaf, covered with an embroidered cloth. The room was a nest of sweet warmth against the chilly air and cold world outside. After the men washed, Reb Motel introduced his family, his wife and daughter, for they and Chaim had not formally met. The servant had already left; earlier in the afternoon, after helping to prepare the meal, she had gone home to make *Shabbos* for her own husband.

Reb Motel sat at the head of the table, his wife at his left. Shira at the foot. Chaim sat facing the mother, but he was mostly turned to his host, for leadership and instruction. He tried not to look at Shira, as if he might be blinded by so much beauty. Indeed there was no need; her radiance warmed him on that side. On this occasion it had been arranged that there were just the four of them; the mother brought dishes from the kitchen and Shira served. The meal was, of course, excellent. As Shira handed out the plates, Chaim couldn't help noticing her pink fingers, the red-brown hair straying across her pretty face, and the silken bulges of her blouse. He was swept with such a sense of elegance that desire almost interfered with his rapt attention to her parents.

After tea, Reb Motel sang the songs of praise, and Chaim quietly joined in with a rich, true baritone. Then the host put to him a question of religious Law. Chaim answered it at once, and went on to expand on various versions of it. Then came a philosophical question. Chaim answered it too, and added a few, if not completely original, opinions of his own.

Reb Motel was a special man. There was little in this informal trial that was typical of the town, but then he had a daughter, his jewel, who was unlike other girls. Shira was gazing at Chaim intently, joyfully, fearfully awaiting her father's verdict, and Reb Motel felt that he could hold back nothing from her, nothing that might result in her happiness.

*

The wedding was small. This disappointed a great many people who had expected to gorge themselves. But each poor family received a portion of honey cake and a token gift of money. Shira and Chaim's present from her father was the initial payment on a small house. The bridal pair embraced with a longing whetted by two long years of waiting. And after a few days Shira found flesh no less satisfying than fantasy.

Chaim's work thrived. The only competition in town was from his old master, but there was enough demand for them both. The new young husband remained a pious Jew, and each Friday after *shul* he would accompany his father-in-law to join the women for the festive meal. It was almost invariably held in the parents' house, but there were times when Shira and Chaim, almost beside themselves with excitement, would have the older people come to them. Children were born: two blondish girls taking after Shira's mother and grandmother, and then a dark-haired boy. With each child Shira gained a bit of weight, but her beauty blossomed. She was an all-season flower.

Some of Chaim's earlier self lingered. His eyes would occasionally stray to other women. Now and then the curve of a behind, even of his own small daughters, entered his thoughts. But all such feelings were regularly buried in the willing body of his wife.

*

Then the war came, and the Germans. Reb Motel and his wife had already disappeared into the cattle cars ahead. Chaim called encouragement to Shira and the children, who were in a group not far away. He felt that they were parts of his own being. A soldier with a lunging dog told him to shut up and pushed him back among the other men.

The camp to which they were taken was being enlarged. New barracks were being built, the perimeter expanded. Wiring was often temporary. Electricians were needed, and in short supply. Chaim was given the status of special workman, excused from most other labor.

He had heard that when the camp was being set up, a few months back, a man had succeeded in escaping. And later he had also heard, from some prisoners who had been transferred from elsewhere, that Shira's parents, his own aunt and her family, had already been murdered. He grieved for them, and prayed that they would all rest in peace. But with so many deaths happening around him he could not overly long dwell on them. The important thing was his wife and children. Now there were no distractions. All his passion was focused on Shira and the little ones. He was determined to rescue them. Within himself he had almost reverted to his wild, impetuous youth.

*

But he had to keep his head, and proceed carefully. The electrical feed, for the time being, came to a box on a pole that stood up from the roof of his barracks. Several wires joined there. Chaim could see that one ran to the guard towers, and another to the barbed-wire fence. Beyond it was the women's camp, where Shira and the children were. He was wiring the barracks, so his ascending to the connection box would not rouse suspicion. In bright daylight, when there was little call for power, he quickly installed a pull-down switch that controlled the wires to the guard towers and fence. Then at another time he attached there a loose spring he had found in the maintenance shed. He reckoned that when the handle of the switch was released, shutting off the electricity, there would be fifty or sixty seconds of darkness, maybe more, until the spring slowly pushed the switch back into contact. There would be an alarm, but before they could discover the cause the lights would be on again.

*

It was a cloudy day, gray and wintry. Dusk came early, before the end of the roll call. Chaim pretended to sleep, but soon after the others were snoring he rose from his bunk and made his way to the door, as if to go to the latrine. The barracks smelled of sweat, urine, dirt, hunger and exhaustion. The Capo, used to his coming and going, merely shone a flashlight in his face, and then with a grunt shut it off. The outside cold air was hardly cleaner, with the ever-present odor of burnt flesh from the ovens just beyond the women's camp, but the shadows were dark.

Chaim swiftly gained the roof. The guards in the watchtowers were not looking his way. In a moment he had opened the switch and slid down to the other side. As he expected, the towers went dark, and in the outcry he reached the fence, slid between the horizontal rows of the now-dead wire, and only slightly tore his striped clothing on the barbs. He had just rolled over onto the icy ground when the lights went on again.

God be thanked! he thought, as he lay just outside the stream of light, listening to the guards' fading cries and mutters. *I'm in the women's camp! Now to find my own and get them out of here.* He wasn't sure how, but as he had achieved the first big step, he felt he could somehow manage the rest. He realized that an enormous load had lifted from him. And there came to him a vision of Shira, years ahead, white hair framing her radiant face, basking in their grandchildren. They were all so dear, so dear!

*

The ground was frozen, but bare. Chaim made almost no sound as he moved from dark to darker shadow. He drew towards the corner of a barracks. But someone was coming! It was a woman, tall and bony. Chaim swiftly reached out, clamping one hand over her mouth and seizing her wrist with the other. *Don't yell* he whispered in Yiddish, accenting it as German, *and I won't hurt you.* She pulled back, though Chaim dragged her into the shadow, bending her wrist painfully. She continued to struggle, but Chaim was strong and held her firmly. *Will you be quiet?* he said. *And I'll let go.* She nodded her head. Chaim glimpsed on her Capo's coat the green triangle of a German criminal.

What are you doing here? the woman hissed. *You'll be shot!*

But Chaim's hold of her wrist had tightened even more. She was afraid he might break it.

Shira Lustig he said. *And her children — two blonde girls and a small boy. Do you know them?*

The woman's angular body relaxed a little. Some of her Capo's mastery returned.

Yeah — they were in my unit.

Good! Chaim said softly. *Where are they now?*

A spiteful sardonic grin spread across the woman's face. She turned him toward the chimneys. *There* she said.

And four columns of smoke rose grayly against the dark sky.

Chavelle Tzum Geht

(Eve to the Divorce)

He was no good. He drank and gambled and made babies and, when he had any money, went to the women who were paid for it. By contrast, his wife Chavelle was gentle, patient and silently long-suffering. They had been married by arrangement. Her parents had been too poor to resist the offer. He was only six years older, and he had a job, working as a carpenter's apprentice. Her only assets had been her youth, good health, pleasant face — though she was no beauty — one extra better dress for the Sabbath, and two tin pots her mother had given her as a dowry. They started married life in a single room attached to the carpenter shop.

*

Now she lived with her five children in a wretched hovel. But it was tidy, and the children, though they wore patched clothing, were clean and well cared for. Chavelle's lot wasn't enviable, but she was liked by the women of the town. They admired her. She was careful and honest in carrying out her duties, never complained, and did her work well. It consisted of all kinds of sewing that women brought her. With the meager earnings from that work she kept her household and fed her children.

The husband hadn't contributed anything for years. Indeed he seldom came home. When he did he was usually drunk — God knows where he got it, he hadn't had a regular job for a long time — and would push her into bed, demand what money she had, and then leave. Her most acute struggle had been to maintain some dignity in front of the children. But mostly they were obedient, and sympathetic. Even the youngest, two years old, had learnt to look the other way and mentally shut her ears when the rusty bedsprings thumped.

Even after the five children, Chavelle was only in her middle thirties, and had a discernable figure. There had never been enough food for her to grow fat on. Actually, she was inherently attractive. She had a snub nose, dark blonde hair and blue eyes. In another culture, if someone had taken away the dull wig, taught her to wear her hair up and carry herself like a lady, she would have been quite a presentable person.

*

One day her husband disappeared. No one had seen him. He didn't come home for days, then weeks and months. Chavelle secretly began to hope he was dead. Her life achieved a new order. She could count on her time, save her money, and slowly better the conditions for her children and home. An elderly widower, who was relatively well off, began to take an interest in her. He would bring her fruit and sometimes flowers. On the Sabbath, when she went to *shul* with her children, scrubbed and shining, people in the synagogue would look at her approvingly, and then to the widower.

However, a tramp passing through town said that he had seen her husband in Berdichev. Chavelle's heart filled with consternation, and she hoped he was wrong. But then another traveler reported having met him in Kiev. So it went. A rumor reached her that he had been among some thieves who had narrowly escaped being caught in Odessa, and had said he was coming home. Yet he didn't come.

Years passed. Chavelle didn't know if he was alive or dead. She applied to the rabbi. He said there was no relief for her. Chavelle's eyes filled with tears. The rabbi, somewhat moved, took off his glasses and scratched his beard, but said the law was fairly strict about such a matter. Until later, when he received a private scolding from his wife. Then he had Chavelle called back and told her she would have to wait at least twelve years from the time she had last heard of her husband. After that, the rabbi said, he might hold a *Beit Din*, a formal rabbinical court, and, if he ruled in her favor, grant a divorce.

*

Much more time went by. The children grew up; three of them married and moved away. The elderly widower died. Then another man, close to Chavelle's own age, began to find occasions to meet and sometimes talk with her. His own wife, who had grown stark and shrill, had died of a bad heart a year earlier. He appreciated Chavelle's softness and gentleness. And he was more than willing to take on the remaining children. But she couldn't remarry until she had been properly divorced. And there were months yet to come. Everyone was apprehensive.

*

At last the great day arrived. Chavelle put on her best dress, the one she wore to synagogue on Saturdays, the only one without evident repairs. She brushed her hair, straightened her wig, and looked at herself in the mirror. She looked quite nice. Plain but clean. She would have liked some adornment such as other ladies wore, but her meager living had never allowed such luxuries.

*

Then a neighbor dropped in with earrings. Chavelle was elated and put them on. They made her look positively stylish. Then another woman came in with a necklace. And another with a bracelet. The word had gone around. One by one the women came, each bearing something for Chavelle to wear. Soon she was hung with jewels, real and imitation, draped with scarves and weighed down with bracelets. Almost every woman in town had contributed something, and they all insisted on accompanying her.

It was a strange and noisy procession that wound its way through the narrow streets. Chavelle was in the lead, overdressed to the eyes, followed by her children and all the other women. They were excited, laughing and gossiping. It had become both a festival and a sort of inherent protest rally, for men made all the rules, and the women, though they abided by them, were not without some resentment.

The rabbi turned pale when he saw them. Such a loud oncoming crowd usually meant a pogrom, but instead of drunken Polish peasants wielding clubs and axes he recognized colorfully clothed congregants. He recovered his demeanor and stepped to the front door. In a loud voice he rebuked the assembly, saying that they were shaming the sanctity of his court, and he would allow none of them in. But at that moment his own wife slipped past him and defiantly joined the first rank. The rabbi reconsidered. Finally he invited in only Chavelle, her children, and a few of the wives of his staunchest supporters.

When the divorce was announced, flung to the crowd from the women who had witnessed it, a tremendous jubilant cheer went up.

*

The German invasion left Chavelle's town like a tiny island in an engulfing sea. There had been no fighting nearby. The Nazis simply moved in and took over. They considered the town too small for a separate ghetto, or as a source of slave labor, so they decided to rid it of Jews by shipping them out to the already established concentration and death camps.

An order went out that on a given day all Jews, carrying no more than one suitcase or bundle, were to gather at the railroad. There soldiers formed them into two groups, separating the children from adults. They were told that they were being transported to a new home. The German officer directing the operation talked in encouraging tones, but armed soldiers, some with leashed dogs, surrounded the Jews. The man who had spoken for Chavelle was with her, but because of the war they hadn't yet married. He could only watch apprehensively as she tearfully separated from her children. She had given her whole life to their care and rearing and felt that her soul was being torn from her. Particularly in regard to the youngest, a pretty girl for whom there had already been offers, and for whom she had nurtured the highest hopes. A soldier impatiently pulled the daughter away from Chavelle's embrace, telling them to hurry, hurry. The children in front were being packed into cattle cars, with stragglers pushed up to the rear.

Chavelle couldn't bear seeing her youngest moving away from her. Crying out to her daughter, she broke from the adult group and ran after the girl, wanting one last kiss, one last caress. A soldier angrily told her to return, and when she didn't move fast enough, hit her in the side of the head with the butt of his rifle. Then he dragged her back to the adults. She stood for a moment, nursing the pain, then collapsed. When the adult crowd was driven forward, they had no choice but to leave Chavelle, with a cracked skull, lying on the wooden platform.

As the loaded train was drawing away, Chavelle expired. The officer told the soldiers to throw her body into the pit where, amid scattered lime, lay other murdered persons.

And They Lived Happily Ever After

Rivka was the pretty one. And the smartest. She not only knew Jewish law, forwards and back, but she also knew Polish and German, their literature and songs. It was unusual for a girl of eighteen to be so well educated. But her father, a learned and pious man, but with worldly interests, had early noted the quality of her mind, and in addition to tutoring her himself, had sent her to gentile schools. Whatever the subject, as a scholar she proved outstanding. Too, she helped bring up the family; her mother would have felt lost without her.

She had nearly black hair and expressive brown eyes. Many suitors had asked for her, yet the only boy she favored was one she had met in Gymnasium, the Polish high school. Like her, he was a good pupil and well read, and his character was above suspicion. But he, like his parents, was a product of the enlightenment, a Socialist and an agnostic. Rivka's father ruled absolutely that she could not marry him. No pleading was of any avail. He reminded her that she came of a family that stretched back through generations of rabbis, some of whom had been famous, and she had to marry a pious Jew, or no one at all. Her father, who could be as stern as he was beneficent, was prepared to have his eldest daughter remain a spinster, terrible as that was, rather than yield on the question of religiosity.

*

There were five other children. But the one closest in age to Rivka, less than two years younger, was virtually useless. Oh, Ruchella tried to do things, but she often made more work than she did. She had no head for learning; anything more than household Yiddish was beyond her, except for the few words of Polish she had managed to acquire. But she was clean and neat, and almost always happy. A dreamer. Her greatest pleasure was in wandering the fields around town, picking daisies and other wildflowers. In hair and complexion she was even slightly darker than Rivka.

Their father owned the court they lived in. Their large house had a passage to a store, where the mother — his second wife, the initial one had died in her first childbirth — sold pots, pans and other objects of metal. The father was usually occupied with attendance at *shul,* where synagogue services would be followed with discussion of points of religious law, or with the heavy books he was always poring over. Though not himself a confirmed rabbi, he was so well versed in scriptural law that rabbis sometimes came to him for advice. He knew almost a dozen languages and was widely known and respected. His own father had been fairly well off, and had left him a little money and the court. The other houses that comprised the rectangle were leased to relatives, sometimes for a small rent and at times, when they didn't have it, for nothing at all.

*

It was a lively household. The children, each with their own personality, were often at odds; there were tears, shouts and laughter. But for Sabbath inspection they lined up according to their ages, including Rivka. Their father went up the line seeing that hair was combed or neatly braided, face and hands, particularly fingernails, which they had to hold out, were clean, clothes pressed and shoes shined. Only when he was satisfied were they allowed to proceed to *shul.*

*

By the time the Germans began dealing seriously with small towns in conquered Poland, their policy of Jewish extermination was already under way. They went about it very methodically. The older people, those twenty-six and over, Rivka's parents among them, were led to a large excavation in the woods and machine gunned where they stood, falling one by one into the mass grave. Any bodies left above were pushed in by soldiers. The youngsters, those under fifteen, and other undesirables, were shoved into cattle cars and shipped to concentration camps where there were gas chambers and ovens. But the Germans were building many munitions factories, and needed slave labor for construction and operations. So every able-bodied person between fifteen and twenty-five was conscripted. Rivka and Ruchella were part of that selection. The males were then castrated, but the girls and women merely had their heads shaved.

*

Near a large plant that produced artillery shells was the prison camp to which Rivka and Ruchella were assigned. Electrified barbed wire and watchtowers surrounded crude barracks. Each had rows of double bunks on which thin straw-filled pallets and rough blankets served for sleeping. Rivka was able to secure a bunk for both of them; she below and Ruchella above. But they were on separate shifts in the factory, shifts that alternated day and night every other week.

In addition to daily inspections of the barracks themselves, there were roll calls morning and evening. The women assembled in rows before their barracks and each had to answer as her name was called out. There was no acceptable excuse for being absent. Sickness or weakness meant death. Slaves were dispensable: there were new ones always arriving.

These roll calls were the most dangerous times. Because in the morning anyone who looked faint or sallow was immediately taken out for annihilation. Therefore lipstick, a red pencil, crayon or anything that could be rubbed into the face to make it look rosy, was infinitely precious. In the evening it was the reverse. Rivka and Ruchella smeared on dirt to make themselves unattractive, for in the evening the guards often picked out prisoners for their nighttime pleasures. And in the morning those girls were always seen hanging by their necks from trees around the camp.

*

The two shifts each lasted twelve hours. Rivka and Ruchella both stood at their work on the assembly line, adding rings to the shell casings as they went by on a moving belt. They tried not to think of their murdered parents and siblings; only the present moment had real meaning, and its supreme dictate was to stay alive.

From the camp's starvation diet the women steadily lost weight, but it did not very markedly affect the sisters, for they had always been slim. But a frightful problem arose when Ruchella fell ill. She developed fever and diarrhea. Rivka colored her up and surreptitiously supported her during roll calls, and, during inspection, when Ruchella was in her bunk, other women connived to transfer her from one side of the barracks to the other as the inspector went by. The Capo might have suspected something, but Rivka managed to mollify her by giving her Ruchella's, and some of her own, meager food. Then after her own daytime shift, she took Ruchella's night shift.

The next day Rivka worked both shifts again. After being on her feet for almost forty hours, her head swimming from fatigue and hunger, she was observed by the factory manager. He was a middle-aged German engineer. He touched her shoulder and ordered her to follow him. She was racked with fear but too tired to dwell on what awaited her. Finally they came to the padlocked metal door of a room at the end the plant. There he turned and faced her. *How long* he said *do you think you can go on working?* Rivka stood there despairing, unable to answer. He unlocked the door. The dim space was heaped with potatoes. *Go in there* he said. *Lie down and get some rest. I'll call you near the end of the shift.*

*

Ruchella recovered. Over the next couple of weeks the manager sometimes stopped by Rivka, making remarks, ostensibly about her work. Then one day she was called to his office.

Shut the door he said. He was sitting behind his desk. *Rivka,* he said *I have been nice to you. I saved your life. I could help you in other ways. Why haven't you been nicer to me?* The sexual allusion was undisguised.

Herr engineer, she said falteringly, in good German. *I'm very grateful. I know what you have done. I wish I could reward you.*

But in our home we were taught that a girl's virtue . . . her purity . . . has to be preserved for marriage. I'm sorry. I would have to die first. Resigned, she looked up at him. *I'm prepared for that.*

He gazed at her for a long time in silence. Then he heaved a sigh. *It's a terrible war* he said.

*

Two years went by. Rivka and Ruchella were shifted to other camps. The Germans moved factories and workers as their situation changed. The tide had begun to turn. The Allies had landed in Italy and France. In the east, after they had suffered immense bloodletting, the Russians were advancing. Steadily, as they fell back, the Germans drove their slaves before them. What their strategy was, no one knew. Perhaps they hoped again to win the upper hand. Or was it pride of possession: that they couldn't let go of those they had conquered and enslaved? The ragged column of women were moved ahead of the lines. Finally they were being marched in six inches of snow. Most of the prisoners had lost whatever footwear they had clung to. Rivka and Ruchella were both barefoot, their toes frozen. Ruchella faltered but Rivka pulled her along. The German guards were in no mood to make allowances. Anyone who fell was immediately shot, the corpses left behind. Finally, in this mad march, they could hear the Russian guns.

The guards ran away. When the forward Russian scouts, on horseback, came upon the women, they could not believe what they saw. What was left of the entire column, bony, barefoot, disheveled and in tattered rags, was sitting or lying in the snow.

*

It took some time for the former slaves to be resuscitated and order restored. Meanwhile the German *Führer*, Hitler, had been trapped in his bunker by Russian soldiers besieging Berlin. He appeared to have died. The German side surrendered. Then the Americans came and set up a kind of remedial center for victims of the camps. It was, of necessity, staffed by the same German doctors and nurses who had tortured them before. Many of the former concentration camp inmates died from eating; they had become unaccustomed to ordinary food. A stomach flu swept the establishment and Rivka contracted it. As she was lying sick she told Ruchella to return home.

*

With money given her by an aid organization, Jewish and mainly from America, Ruchella took a train to her home town. The window looked out on Polish scenes seemingly unaffected by the war. Sitting in her coach seat, Ruchella pictured her beloved town, its fields and stream. When she arrived and walked through the narrow streets, she was amazed to find everything unchanged. The wooden houses were the same, the chimneys still leaned crookedly, washing hung on lines. The synagogue had been destroyed, its ruin boarded up. But her father's court was intact! The houses still stood as she had left them. A Polish woman sweeping near its entrance recognized her. She had worked for their family. She followed Ruchella's look around the court. *The houses are all filled* she said. *People moved in as soon as you'd left.*

And our house, Ruchella said *who lives in that one?* The woman mentioned the name. He had been a Polish laborer who had fixed cobblestones and done odd jobs around the yard.

He knew Ruchella at once. *What!* he cried angrily. *You're not dead yet!* And he shut the door in her face.

The woman who had been sweeping tugged at her sleeve. *Come with me* she said, for dusk was descending. *You can't stay here. They will kill you!*

Frightened, Ruchella was awake all night, crouching in the attic where she had been hidden. Once she heard screams and the breaking of glass, but she could see nothing from the tiny window.

In the early morning her hostess showed her out and cautioned her to make haste. Ruchella fled. The same day she took the train back toward the west.

When she arrived at the center, Rivka was gone. She had been moved, under Jewish direction, to Italy. But at the camp there were organizers who took charge of Ruchella and sent her south. In an Italian port, the sisters were reunited.

*

There they waited until they could board an old crowded tramp steamer. It was bound, illegally, because it had to evade the British blockade, for Palestine. The trip was made successfully, after maneuvering through the last night. Rivka and Ruchella were landed, along with hundreds of other survivors, at Haifa, in the past and future Israel.

This book is set in Minion, a typeface designed by
Robert Slimbach in 1990. Minion is inspired by classical,
old style typefaces of the late Renaissance, a period of elegant,
beautiful, and highly readable type designs. Created primarily
for text setting, Minion combines the aesthetic and functional
qualities that make text type highly readable with
the versatility of digital technology.

Printed on 55lb., 100% PCW HiBulk FSC® Natural